Best
{BRITISH}
Short Stories
2019

NICHOLAS ROYLE HAS published three collections of short fiction: *Mortality* (Serpent's Tail), short-listed for the inaugural Edge Hill Short Story Prize in 2007, *Ornithology* (Confingo Publishing), long-listed for the same prize in 2018, and *The Dummy & Other Uncanny Stories* (The Swan River Press). He is also the author of seven novels, most recently *First Novel* (Vintage), and a collaboration with artist David Gledhill, *In Camera* (Negative Press London). He has edited more than twenty anthologies, including eight earlier volumes of *Best British Short Stories*. Reader in Creative Writing at the Manchester Writing School at Manchester Metropolitan University and head judge of the Manchester Fiction Prize, he also runs Nightjar Press, which in 2019 celebrates ten years of publishing original short stories as signed, limited-edition chapbooks.

By the same author

NOVELS

Counterparts
Saxophone Dreams
The Matter of the Heart
The Director's Cut
Antwerp
Regicide
First Novel

NOVELLAS

The Appetite
The Enigma of Departure

SHORT STORIES

Mortality
In Camera (with David Gledhill)
Ornithology
The Dummy & Other Uncanny Stories

ANTHOLOGIES (as editor)

Darklands
Darklands 2
A Book of Two Halves
The Tiger Garden: A Book of Writers' Dreams
The Time Out Book of New York Short Stories
The Ex Files: New Stories About Old Flames
The Agony & the Ecstasy: New Writing for the World Cup
Neonlit: Time Out Book of New Writing
The Time Out Book of Paris Short Stories
Neonlit: Time Out Book of New Writing Volume 2
The Time Out Book of London Short Stories Volume 2
Dreams Never End
'68: New Stories From Children of the Revolution
The Best British Short Stories 2011
Murmurations: An Anthology of Uncanny Stories About Birds
The Best British Short Stories 2012
The Best British Short Stories 2013
The Best British Short Stories 2014
Best British Short Stories 2015
Best British Short Stories 2016
Best British Short Stories 2017
Best British Short Stories 2018

Best
{ BRITISH }
Short Stories
2019

SERIES EDITOR **NICHOLAS ROYLE**

SALT

CROMER

PUBLISHED BY SALT PUBLISHING 2019

2 4 6 8 10 9 7 5 3 1

Selection and introduction © Nicholas Royle, 2019
Individual contributions © the contributors, 2019

Nicholas Royle has asserted his right under the Copyright, Designs and Patents Act
1988 to be identified as the editor of this work.

First published in Great Britain in 2019 by
Salt Publishing Ltd
12 Norwich Road, Cromer, Norfolk NR27 0AX United Kingdom

www.saltpublishing.com

Salt Publishing Limited Reg. No. 5293401

A CIP catalogue record for this book is available from the British Library

ISBN 978 1 78463 185 7 (Paperback edition)
ISBN 978 1 78463 186 4 (Electronic edition)

Typeset in Neacademia by Salt Publishing

Printed and bound in Great Britain by Clays Ltd, Elcograf S.p.A

In memory of Dennis Etchison (1943–2019)

CONTENTS

NICHOLAS ROYLE
Introduction   xi

MELISSA WAN
The Husband and the Wife Go to the Seaside   1

STEPHEN SHARP
Cuts   21

SALLY JUBB
The Arrangement   28

SAM THOMPSON
The Heights of Sleep   37

ANN QUIN
Nude and Seascape   52

NIGEL HUMPHREYS
Beyond Dead   58

ADAM WELCH
Toxic   66

VESNA MAIN
A Hair Clasp   76

JOHN LANCHESTER
Reality   78

VICKY GRUT
  On the Way to the Church   101

NAOMI BOOTH
  Cluster   110

JULIA ARMFIELD
  Smack   124

ROBERT MASON
  Curtilage   141

ELIZABETH BAINES
  Kiss   151

LUCIE MCKNIGHT HARDY
  Badgerface   157

RUBY COWLING
  On Day 21   170

REN WATSON
  Optics   180

PAUL MCQUADE
  A Gift of Tongues   188

KIERAN DEVANEY
  Sitcom   209

SOPHIE MACKINTOSH
  New Dawn Fades   219

  Contributors' Biographies   229
  Acknowledgements   235

INTRODUCTION

IF I HAD a pound for every time over the last year someone has remarked to me that the short story is enjoying a notable renaissance, I'd have enough money to submit numerous stories to *Ambit* and the Fiction Desk. But more on that later.

First, the *New Statesman*. I like the *New Statesman* – I subscribe to it and look forward to its arrival in my letterbox every Friday – but I wish it would do more for the short story. Among US newsstand magazines, *Harper's Magazine* and the *New Yorker* regularly publish short stories. (Indeed, the *New Yorker* published a very good story, 'Cecilia Awakened', by Tessa Hadley, in Sepember 2018.) The *New Statesman* does, too, but regularly only in the sense of two or three times a year. The 2017-18 Christmas special featured an extract from a forthcoming new collection by Rose Tremain and the 2018 summer special extracted a story from Helen Dunmore's final collection, *Girl, Balancing & Other Stories* (Hutchinson). The 2018-19 Christmas special giftwrapped us a new story by Kate Atkinson. How about a new story every week instead of just in the summer and at Christmas (and sometimes in spring)? That way we would get to enjoy not only more stories, but more new stories, rather than mostly extracts from forthcoming collections (rather a lazy way to publish short stories).

Short story competition anthologies have clearly become a bit of a thing. The *Bristol Short Story Prize Anthology* has reached volume 11; the *Bath Short Story Award Anthology* has been going since 2013 (in print form since 2014). The *City of Stories* anthology is on its second incarnation; it has a tag line – 'Celebrating London's writers, readers and libraries'. Spread the Word are responsible for it and this edition features over 60 London-based writers who took part in creative writing workshops in June 2018 in libraries across the city. A competition for 500-word stories was judged by four writers-in-residence – Gary Budden, Meena Kandasamy, Olumide Popoola and Leone Ross – who have all contributed pieces that appear alongside the winning stories.

May You: The Walter Swan Prize Anthology, edited by S. J. Bradley, is published by Scarborough's Valley Press in association with the Northern Short Story Festival, Leeds Big Bookend Festival and the Walter Swan Trust. Bradley presents nineteen of the best from a field of more than 300 entries, including a short-list of six and three winners. The judges, Anna Chilvers and Angela Readman, awarded first and second prizes to Sarah Brooks and Andrea Brittan respectively, and they're very good stories, but I would have been tempted to give top spot to P. V. Wolseley just for the description of a hamster – 'He was golden-brown and sagged like a beanbag' – in her story 'All Things Bright and Beautiful'. Megan Taylor's 'Touched', short-listed, was also among my favourites.

Megan Taylor also appeared among last year's chapbooks from TSS Publishing, with 'Waiting For the Rat', a worthy addition to an always-enjoyable sub-genre, holiday-let horror stories. It was the fifth in TSS's series and it was followed by Christopher M. Drew's very powerful 'Remnants', which reminded me of Cormac McCarthy, in a good way. I was delighted to see Rough Trade get in on the chapbook boom with Rough Trade Editions. Mostly non-fiction, the series has included one short story, 'The Faithful Look Away', by poet Melissa Lee-Houghton; I hope it goes on to feature more stories.

In yet more chapbook news, Word Factory and Guillemot Press formed a collaboration, the Guillemot Factory, to publish, in the first instance, four new stories in chapbook format. Lavishly illustrated, the four titles, by Jessie Greengrass, Carys Davies, Adam Marek and David Constantine, were received with great enthusiasm. In Constantine's 'What We Are Now', my favourite of the four, an unhappily married woman bumps into an old flame. Nightjar Press, meanwhile, if I may mention my own baby, although now ten years old, published four more chapbooks, two in the spring and two in the autumn.

From single stories to single-author collections. Vicky Grut's *Live Show, Drink Included* (Holland Park Press) is a selection of her published stories from the past twenty-five years. There are a couple of previously unpublished stories and two that appeared for the first time in other publications during 2018. My favourite of these was 'On the Way to the Church'. I would have chosen it for this volume even if it hadn't featured my favourite track on my favourite album by my favourite solo artist.

Other interesting collections included Sean O'Brien's *Quartier Perdu* (Comma Press), Vesna Main's *Temptation: A User's Guide* (Salt) and the publishing phenomenon that was Ann Quin's *The Unmapped Country* (And Other Stories).

To say that the latter was 'edited and introduced' by Jennifer Hodgson, as is recorded on the title page, I'm sure gives very little idea of the amount of love, dedication and sheer hard work that must have gone into creating this book of 'stories and fragments' by the great British writer who died in 1973 at the age of 37. Hats off to Hodgson and to her publisher.

Is it a book? Is it a magazine? From issue ten of *The Lonely Crowd* the answer was on the cover: 'the magazine of new fiction and poetry'. It still looks like a book, like quite a chunky anthology, and it's still publishing tons of really good stories. In issue nine I particularly liked Courttia Newland's 'A Gift For Abidah' and James Clarke's 'Waddington', while stories by Kate Hamer, Jane Fraser, Lucie McKnight Hardy and Neil Campbell were the highlights, for me, in issue ten.

Newsprint is not dead: two new publications launched last year. Firstly, the *Brixton Review of Books*, an excellent and very welcome free literary quarterly created by Michael Caines, whose day job is at the *TLS*. Well, free if you happen to be wandering around south London when a new issue hits the streets (it's given away outside tube stations, I believe, and I've seen it in the Herne Hill Oxfam Bookshop), or you can pay £10 for a subscription (check the web site). It features reviews, articles and columns, and, in issue three there was a notable story of 'formless dread', 'Down the Line' by Richard Lea. What's not to like about formless dread? More, please. Secondly, at the Dublin Ghost Story Festival in June last year I picked up a copy of *Infra-Noir*, edited by Jonathan Wood and Alcebiades Diniz and published by Jonas Ploeger's specialist press Zagava. The first issue contains stories by Brian Howell, previously featured in this series, and poet Nigel

Humphreys, whose first-published short story 'Beyond Dead' is reprinted in the current volume.

Staying with literary magazines, the most interesting things in *Hotel* issue four – and they were very interesting – were either not short stories or not by British authors. In *Structo* issue 18, I was struck by Paul McQuade's 'The Wound in the Air' and was similarly drawn to his not-unrelated story, 'A Gift of Tongues', in *Confingo* issue ten, which also included notable stories by a number of writers including Simon Kinch and Giselle Leeb. Jumping back to spring 2018, *Confingo* issue nine was packed with good stories. Stand-outs: Charles Wilkinson's 'Berkmann's Anti-novel', one of those stories about oddball school friends and how they turn out, which are always interesting, especially when they're this well written; Elizabeth Baines' 'The Next Stop Will Be Didsbury Village', which is best read on a Manchester Metrolink tram leaving either East Didsbury or Burton Road in the direction of Didsbury Village; David Gaffney's 'The Dog', which, like Baines' story, was written to be performed in the Didsbury Arts Festival. 'Performed' in this context may strike you as an overstatement, when such performance generally takes the form of reading the story to an audience, but Baines and Gaffney (if that doesn't sound like a new ITV cop show partnership, I don't know what does) always read well.

Lighthouse continues to illuminate the darkness with excellent writing. 'One Art', by C. D. Rose, in issue 16, was very good, but 'Smack' by Julia Armfield in the same issue was outstanding, probably the best story to appear in the journal during 2018. I don't know what the jellyfish represent, but I don't care. And yet I do care about the story.

The same dimensions and format as both *Lighthouse* and

Confingo, Doppelgänger was a new publication edited by James Hodgson. Its web site states that it aimed to publish twice a year, with six stories in each issue, three realist stories and three magical realist stories. As far as I can tell, there has been no follow-up to the first issue, dated winter/spring 2018 and featuring work by Dan Powell, Andrew Hook, Cath Barton and others. Max Dunbar takes a risk with his story, 'The Bad Writing School'. If you're going to satirise the teaching of creative writing, you've got to be pretty sure of your ability.

If I had to pick a favourite story out of all those published in horror magazine *Black Static* during 2018, it would be Giselle Leeb's 'Everybody Knows That Place', set on a camp site, which immediately makes it pretty horrifying for me. Some people find taxidermy horrifying, whereas I'm drawn to it, and that's one reason why I liked Sally Jubb's 'The Arrangement' so much. It appears in issue 42 of *Brittle Star* alongside other stories, Ren Watson's 'Sky-sions' (reprinted in the current volume, under another title) and Josie Turner's 'The Guide', that emerged as winners in the *Brittle Star* short fiction competition.

A friend alerted me to the fact that *Ambit*, the great avant-garde arts magazine founded by novelist and consultant paediatrician Martin Bax in 1959, had recently started charging for submissions. To submit a short story used to cost nothing, unless you counted the cost of photocopying, stationery and postage (not forgetting the stamped addressed envelope); now it costs £2.50, which *Ambit* says is to pay for the cost of using Submittable, a service that charges *Ambit* a monthly fee. There are advantages to *Ambit* in using Submittable, editor Briony Bax tells me: it enables their editors to work wherever they are; they can respond to submissions in a timely manner; it creates a virtual office for their eight editorial readers for whom an actual office would be prohibitively expensive etc. All reasonable arguments, of course, and Bax emphasises that there is a student/unwaged category with no proof required of such status, or people may still submit by post for free.

I don't much like this development, even as *Ambit* celebrates its sixtieth birthday, but I haven't let it stop me selecting two stories from last year's issues of the magazine: Stephen Sharp's 'Cuts' from *Ambit* 231 (in the same issue I also liked John Saul's 'Tracks') and Adam Welch's 'Toxic' from *Ambit* 232.

Ambit is not alone. Magazines such as *Ploughshares* and *Glimmer Train* in the US have been doing it for years, and, as Rory Kinnear says as Stephen Lyons in Russell T. Davies's post-Brexit drama *Years and Years*, 'We are American. Our business is American, our culture is American. We're certainly not European, are we?'

Also doing it is the Fiction Desk, whose £3 fee can be avoided if instead you buy one of their anthologies, the latest of which, their twelfth, is *And Nothing Remains*. I may not like submission charges, but that's not contributor Alex Clark's fault and so I will say I enjoyed her story 'Briar Rose', as I did her story 'The Thief' in *Stroud Short Stories Volume 2* (Stroud Short Stories) edited by John Holland. This second volume in the series features stories read by their Gloucester-based authors at Stroud Short Stories events between 2015 and 2018. In particular I enjoyed Joanna Campbell's 'The Journey to Everywhere', its exuberance of language and character reminding me of the great William Sansom.

There was no shortage of anthologies published last year, among them *Unthology 10* (Unthank Books) edited by Ashley

Stokes and Robin Jones – congratulations to them on reaching that milestone. The blurb on the back of *Tales From the Shadow Booth Vol 2* edited by Dan Coxon describes the *Shadow Booth* as a 'journal of weird and eerie fiction', taking its inspiration from Thomas Ligotti and Robert Aickman, but nothing in it reminded me of either writer. It feels more reminiscent of *The Pan Book of Horror Stories*, and, speaking as someone whose first short story sale was to that long-running series, I'm not saying that's a bad thing. Mark Morris, a contributor to the *Shadow Booth*, is the editor of *New Fears 2* (Titan Books). In his introduction he acknowledges the lasting influence of un-themed horror anthologies, such as the Pan series and others. He goes on: 'My aim with *New Fears*, therefore, is to bring back the un-themed horror anthology – and not as a one-off, but as an annual publication, with each volume acting as a showcase for the very best and most innovative fiction that this exhilarating genre has to offer.' What a shame, then, that publishers Titan pulled the plug after this second volume, in which a highlight for me was Stephen Volk's stomach-churning 'The Airport Gorilla', which may be narrated by a soft toy, but is extremely hard hitting.

Jez Noond's 'Zolitude' drew my eye in *The Cinnamon Review of Short Fiction* (Cinnamon Press) edited by Adam Craig. I liked it, even if I didn't really understand it. I sense strongly that the lack is within me and not the story. I always enjoy Courttia Newland's stories; 'Link', in *Everyday People – The Color of Life* (Atria Books) edited by Jennifer Baker, was no exception. Ramsey Campbell led from the front in *The Alchemy Press Book of Horrors* (The Alchemy Press) edited by Peter Coleborn and Jan Edwards; Campbell's 'Some Kind of a Laugh' is followed by a further 24 stories by a roll-call of horror writers. Standing out among the stories in *Dark Lane Anthology Volume 7* (Dark Lane Books) edited by Tim Jeffreys is 'Your Neighbour's Packages' by Megan Taylor, which you read with a dynamic response of mingled horror and delight, as the neighbour's packages mount up in the protagonist's home. You hope the packages remain unopened while the story delivers on its promise. You're not disappointed. It's followed by Charles Wilkinson's 'Time Out in December', which could hae been called 'Hotel Lazarus' and could have been written by Franz Kafka.

Running a small press is a draining business in lots of ways, not least financially. Manchester's Dostoyevsky Wannabe don't charge a submission fee, but nor do they supply their writers with contributors' copies. This didn't put off the writers contributing to *Manchester* edited by Thom Cuell, among them Sarah-Clare Conlon and Anthony Trevelyan, whose stories, 'Flight Path' and 'Repossession', respectively, were my favourites. While I can't help feeling that, if you're not paying your writers, providing them with a free copy of their work is the very least you can do (co-founder Richard Brammer puts forward a case for it being more punk operation than big corporation), I love the look of Dostoyevsky Wannabe's rapidly growing list of publications, for which credit must go to art director Victoria Brown.

Let's stick with the north for two more anthologies published last year. Firstly, Bluemoose Books published *Seaside Special: Postcards From the Edge* edited by Jenn Ashworth, whose prompt for stories inspired by the coast of the north-west of England, produced a fascinating anthology with some outstanding stories. Melissa Wan's 'The Husband and the

Wife Go to the Seaside' is remarkable, mainly for its style and its embracing of doubt and uncertainty. Pete Kalu's historical piece on the subject of slavery is impressive, partly for the unflinching examination of its subject matter and partly for its original approach, the story taking the form of a will being dictated. Also notable were Andrew Michael Hurley's 'Katy', a missing-child story with a difference, and Carys Bray's haunting tale about the song of the Birkdale Nightingale, or Natterjack toad.

Secondly, and finally, there was *We Were Strangers: Stories Inspired by Unknown Pleasures* (Confingo Publishing) edited by Richard V Hirst. It so happened that my favourite story in this anthology of stories inspired by Joy Division's first album was Sophie Mackintosh's 'New Dawn Fades', which also happens to be my favourite track off the album. Other highlights, for me, included David Gaffney's 'Insight', Zoe Lambert's 'She's Lost Control' and Jessie Greengrass's 'Candidate'.

There were more stories in more magazines, anthologies and collections, as well as on web sites and broadcast on radio. I can't claim to have read them all, but I have read as widely as I can and selected what I think are the best. Next year's volume will be my tenth – and last – as editor of this series.

NICHOLAS ROYLE
Manchester
May 2019

Best
{ BRITISH }
Short Stories
2019

MELISSA WAN

THE HUSBAND AND THE WIFE GO TO THE SEASIDE

THE HUSBAND AND the wife arrived at their cottage on the coast one moonless night. Both were ready for a change and told themselves this time away was the beginning. From a distance they saw that their cottage, mid-terraced in a row of holiday homes, was the only one with its lights still on, shining into the dark. The wife said it looked exactly like the pictures and when the husband stepped from the car to unlock the gate, she smiled at him as he turned back, before realising he wouldn't see her in the glare of headlights.

Approaching a house with all the lights on made the wife feel like an intruder, but the husband turned the key and edged her in with his hand on the small of her back. Everything awaiting them seemed exactly as they expected.

'Nice of them to leave the heating on,' said the husband, peering into the dining room. The wife walked upstairs, half expecting to come upon another couple in their bed, but instead the towels and blankets were neatly folded, not a crease in sight. Downstairs, the husband had left a trail into the sitting room, his brogues kicked off, suitcases abandoned in the hallway. He was flopped into an armchair – the best one, she noticed – and tapping into his phone.

'After this we're turning them off,' he said, 'and I'll find a place to hide them.'

'Do we have to?' asked the wife. 'What if I need to get in touch with you?'

The husband looked up with raised eyebrows. 'You said we needed some time away, so that's what we're doing. It's two weeks.'

The wife nodded and turned into the kitchen. She found a gift basket on the counter with a handwritten card reading *Welcome to Arnside.*

'We can always eat these,' she said, holding up a tin of spaghetti hoops.

'What an odd thing to leave in a hamper,' said the husband.

'They're nostalgic. We used to have the alphabet ones. I'd eat them from my bowl which had the alphabet around the side.'

'That's cute,' said the husband.

The wife told him she could heat them up.

'No thank you.' He fished out a packet of shortbread and sat down at the dining table. 'We never ate anything tinned.'

The wife put the hoops back into the basket and sat across the table from the husband. She kept mistaking the tap of a twig on their kitchen window for a knock at the door and every time she'd snap up her head. She could hear the husband chew above the thin vibration of the fridge.

'It's so quiet here,' she said.

'That,' said the husband, 'is the sound of having left it all behind.'

2

The wife turned on the television, glad for the false laughter of a studio audience, and asked if they could go to the chip shop tomorrow. The husband said she could do what she wanted.

'It's what I've been dreaming about,' said the wife. 'The drip of all that chip fat.'

The husband unfolded his paper and raised it to hide his face. On the cover, the wife read the headline: *Body Found in River Bela*. The photograph was of the river, static in black-and-white, and didn't show the corpse. They'd crossed the river on their drive through Milnthorpe, had stopped to walk over the footbridge, and the wife's eyes widened at the thought of a corpse drifting cold and stiff below their feet.

'What's that noise?' she asked, looking up at the black window.

'What noise, darling?'

'It sounds like breathing.'

The husband told her not to let her imagination run away with her, and turning up the volume, the wife stared blankly at the screen as the husband turned the page.

When the wife got into bed, she left her light on for longer than usual. Her eyes would lose their place in her book, find it again and read the same sentence over. She wore her new satin nightclothes spotted with pink roses and slipped herself between the sheets. When the husband came in wearing his flannels, he kissed her on the head, switched off his light and turned away onto his side.

'"It was times like these,"' the wife read, '"when I thought my father, who hated guns and had never been to any wars, was the bravest man who ever lived."' She turned to look at the back of the husband's head; she could detect where his hair was beginning to thin. She closed her paperback, sipped at her water and turned off her reading lamp.

'Goodnight,' she said.

The husband made a noise with his throat.

'It'll be nice to be here, won't it?' she said. 'To refresh.'

The wife adjusted her pyjamas until an audible sigh came from the husband's side and she was still. There was a skylight in the ceiling through which, on her back, she watched the drift of cloud.

In the morning the husband and the wife were woken by the sound of drills. A team of builders were busy on scaffolding around the front of the house next door.

The husband retrieved his phone to email the cottage owner, who wrote back to tell them it had been on the website. Indeed, he found the small print: 'From mid August until January there will be building work next door. Some noise and disruption may be experienced.'

'You mean it's going to be this loud the whole time?' asked the wife.

The husband said they would be out most days anyway, and told her not to look when he put the phone away.

In daylight the house looked tired, its walls and surfaces more grey than white. On the website the sitting room had been described as historic, but the bookcase was stuffed with second-hand romance novels and the wife knew the throws were bought in Ikea.

'It could do with a lick of paint,' she said, to which the husband replied that this was what they called shabby chic, that it was a style.

The wife boiled the kettle and took her cup of tea upstairs. Since the husband had claimed the armchair, she contented herself either with the sofa in the sitting room or this chair with the view. She sat by the window and looked down onto the street beyond their front garden, from where she could see the labourers moving back and forth. She watched, trying to ignore the noise, and when the bronzed arms of a worker caught her eye her cup stopped before her lips. His muscles shifted as he hoisted a plank onto his shoulder and he walked with extraordinary confidence for somebody so high up. When he lifted the board, she glimpsed the dark growth of hair beneath his arms.

After breakfast, through which the drills whined and the wife overcooked the eggs, she left the house arm in arm with the husband. The promenade was a few hundred metres away, a mixture of express supermarkets, small-town cafes and upscale boutiques; to walk from the pub on one end to the chip shop on the other took about five minutes. This morning the sky was turned white by a layer of cloud, and as they passed groups of elderly ramblers in fleeces and walking boots, the husband greeted them as though he knew them, shaking their hands because it was a small town, and as he said, things are done differently in small towns. The wife smiled but kept her eyes squinted on the mudflats, her legs trembling as gusts of wind blew up her skirt. Luckily she'd packed a jumper but eventually she had to ask the husband if she could buy a pair of trousers from the shop.

'I did tell you,' he said, handing her their credit card.

The husband waited in the pub, sitting down with a pint as the wife closed the changing room door. It was a shop for ramblers and the wife looked so ridiculous in the waterproof pants and sandals that she reluctantly bought a pair of their cheapest walking boots and asked to wear both immediately.

She read on the handwritten labels that the fleeces were made from a flock of rare Woodland sheep, farmed only a few metres away. This and the antiquated tin of Werther's Originals on the counter made the wife think it might all be staged, as though if she opened a wrapper she would find a piece of folded card inside.

'You know there are rambling groups here,' said the shopkeeper. 'And Cedric does cross-bay walks. They're very popular.'

The wife took her receipt, saying thank you but she wasn't a big walker.

Arriving at the pub – hoping to have lessened the effect of the mismatch by taking down her hair – the wife found the husband talking to a crowd of older women at a table outside. Their trekking poles were stacked against the wall behind them, their faces browned with sun and their silver hair sporting the occasional well-placed streak of dark hair. The wife thought this crowd made the husband look even more distinguished, and she had the notion of him as a stage actor well known for performing Shakespeare. His jeans and jacket of cornflower blue were the precise balance of casual and chic, his hair peppered just enough to make the wife in her present state feel humiliated.

She went inside to order half a pint, hoping the women might have left by the time she came back, but when she did, they'd surrounded the husband and were all energetically laughing together. The wife approached the group from the side and handed the husband their card, excusing her appearance by gesturing to her trousers and explaining the shop was too small to have any options. The ramblers cackled and stuck their legs into the air, telling her she was one of them now.

'You'll have to come on our next walk,' said one.

'We have a pole you can borrow,' said another.

'And a spare coat that should fit.'

'Oh no,' said the wife, blushing, as she looked at her husband. 'This was just for the cold.'

The ramblers shook their heads, the sunglasses on their headbands like rows of additional eyes.

'She says that now,' said one.

'Just wait 'til you've been in them pants a few days,' said another.

'You won't be able to get her out of them!'

They all screamed with laughter. The husband told the wife that one of the women had a partner who'd also gone to Cambridge.

'They were different years of course,' said the woman, 'But I'm sure they'll have lots to gossip about.'

'Isn't that a coincidence?' said the wife. 'I'm sure if I met anyone from my old poly we wouldn't have anything to say.'

The women chuckled and the husband said his wife had a wicked sense of humour, at which she smiled and supped her porter.

'How did the two of you meet?' asked one.

'We both teach at the same school,' said the husband.

The wife said, 'He's history and I'm English.'

'Luckily we're all English here,' said one.

'Although we are getting a lot of Poles,' whispered another.

'And not the right kind!' They lifted their sticks and roared.

The wife stayed quiet as they moved on to talking about property and how dead the market was. Conversation then turned to their partners; their other halves went fishing whilst the women walked and enjoyed their freedom, and in the evenings the two groups came together to watch the sunset.

'Turner said Margate had the best skies in Europe, but he'd probably never been to Arnside,' said one.

'Nigel has the perfect viewing spot. Always comes with Prosecco,' said another.

'He'd be happy to pull out a couple of chairs.'

'It will have to be next time,' the wife said, explaining they needed to catch the next episode of a show they were addicted to.

Luckily the siren sounded and the group was up, downing their pints to catch the bore, saying that next time they wouldn't take no for an answer.

'You'll want to meet Nigel,' said one to the husband.

'He'll take you canoeing,' said another.

'Amongst other things.' And they laughed for a final time.

When they left, the husband finished the wife's porter and said he was going to see the bore from the pier. The wife had no choice but to follow, the sound of the women's laughter still ringing in her ears.

'They seem to have their routine worked out,' she said. 'Too much activity for us though, don't you think?'

Although sunbathing in this weather was nonsensical, a young girl lay on the jetty in two pieces of red string, magazines heaped beneath her towel. Passers-by looked at her and laughed, shaking their heads and zipping their parkas up against the wind. The siren sounded again and the girl tucked in her breasts, flipping onto her front. The wife went to comment, but the husband had walked on.

She came up by his side and asked when the tide was coming in.

'That was it,' said the husband.

The wife looked down at the water: it wasn't more than a couple of centimetres high and the same dirty grey as the sky.

'Oh,' she said.

'You know this is one of the only places it happens on the whole planet?'

By the time she turned around, the husband had walked on again. She saw him on the promenade, tufts of hair blowing in the breeze, shoulders lifted in a shrug to the question they were both asking.

The wife quickly learned to occupy herself as she saw fit, and by the end of the first week both were spending much of their time apart. The wife decided she didn't have to cook if she didn't want to, she'd eaten at the chip shop twice and tried hard to leave mess she could then avoid clearing up: a sock in the kitchen, hardened crusts on her plate, a used toothpick on the doily. It wasn't long before the husband was out every day, fishing with the Nigel mentioned at the pub. The husband was asked to bring bait in exchange for borrowing Nigel's equipment, and in the morning the wife chopped pieces of chicken into food bags, wincing at the raw flesh between her fingers. She kissed the husband goodbye and shut the door behind him.

The wife began to frequent the gift shop at the end of the promenade which sold artisanal ice cream, and this was the furthest she would walk. Most mornings she darkened her lips, did her hair in a French twist, and looked only at the top half of her body in the mirror. Now she walked alone, she often drew the gazes of men, and today a crowd in shooting jackets tipped their hats her way.

Passing the pier the wife could never find the husband amid the anglers, who were all old and portly, flat-caps pulled over their thinning hair. She continued her walk until the gift shop with its gaudy blue paint, tacky postcards and baskets with multi-coloured hats. When she ordered her rum and raisin, the shop assistant asked if she was staying at Highbank. Initially the wife forgot this was the name of their house, but when she remembered she shook her head and said no, she was staying with relatives in Milnthorpe.

'I was sure it was you,' said the woman, wetting her scoop and rolling a perfect globe. 'Marda said she'd bumped into you and your husband last week at the Albion.'

The wife smiled but stayed quiet. The woman rolled another and asked, 'Doesn't your husband go fishing with Nige?'

At last the wife said that yes, he did.

'Oh, he'll have him in a canoe soon,' said the woman, licking the end of her finger. 'Nigel has an adventurous nature.' She smiled and pushed a plastic spoon into the ice cream. 'You're not as talkative as your husband, are you?'

The wife thanked her and told her to keep the change.

'You want to be careful on that sand,' the woman called after her. 'It's not like other beaches. Some people have sunk up to their waists.'

The wife walked back down the prom and stopped at a bench facing the sands. Sometimes big crowds crossed the flats, but today it was empty. She sat and licked at her ice cream and watched the train roll in across the viaduct. It was quiet and when she bit into her cone, the noise made her conscious of being a woman alone. When a crowd of seagulls flocked down to the bench, she was sent to her feet in surprise and dropped her ice cream. They struck at the mess with their polished yellow beaks and she rushed away, followed by their shrieks until she turned the corner.

When the wife got home, the husband was in his armchair. He had fallen asleep with his phone on his knee and when he stirred she asked him what he was doing. He sat up and rubbed his eyes, saying he took it out to quickly use the map.

'Well then I'd quickly like to use mine,' she said.

He looked at the wife's trousers. 'You've not been walking around in them all day?'

The wife ignored him and said she wanted her phone so she could talk to her sister. 'And I want to meet this Nigel. I'm not sure why I haven't been introduced already as everyone else seems to think he's really something.'

The husband sat up. 'You'd honestly have nothing to talk about.'

'Because I didn't go to Cambridge?'

'He's not Cambridge,' the husband said, then mouthed *Oxford*.

'God knows you lot think you're a breed apart,' she said.

'I was joking,' he said. 'If you want to know the truth, he did want us for dinner but I fibbed and told him you get migraines.'

'You told him I get migraines?'

'It rolled off my tongue.'

'Your tongue again,' said the wife. 'It's always going places you didn't intend.'

The husband told the wife there was no need to be spiteful. He walked into the kitchen and said she could do what she wanted but that they were a bunch of bores when they got together.

'And how do you know that?'

'I can imagine.'

'I suppose you go on imaginary fishing trips too? I never see you down at the promenade.'

The husband poured himself a glass of wine and told her everybody knew you had to go to the river to catch the real fish. 'And it's terribly boring when you play the suspicious wife.'

'That's one way to shift the blame.'

'Why do you always need somebody to blame?'

'It's just that nothing seems to matter. It doesn't make a difference what time we go to bed, or what I wear . . . none of this,' she motioned at the room, 'seems to make any difference. You always say it's because we're busy or because you're stressed—'

'Well it doesn't help, does it?'

The husband walked upstairs, leaving the wife to listen to the clock, ticking in time with the thump of her heart.

The following day the wife was up and out soon after the sun had risen. The night had been restless and full of dreams in which she'd driven home early, letting the husband take the train. In the morning she tried to find the key to the cupboard where her phone was locked but gave up when she realised she didn't have a clue as to where he might hide it.

One of the cafes on the prom was open and the wife sat there into the early afternoon, drinking cups of tea and staring out of the window. Her paperback sat untouched in her lap and she watched people drift in and out, dotting the tables around her. A couple arrived and sat by the window, on the same side as each other. They shared a black forest gateau and the boy refilled the girl's teacup whenever it was empty. He let her have the cherry. The wife realised she wanted a drink. Young couples in love, she thought as she paid the bill, have no regard for the rest of us.

The wife spent the rest of the afternoon moving between one pub and the other. Once or twice the crowds inside recognised her and said hello, but she feigned deafness as best she could and they soon left her alone. She buried her face between the pages of her book, never reading a word. As the afternoon drew on, she watched as ramblers returned from their walks, skin ruddy with cold, mouths lifted at the corners. She ordered another beer. These were wonderfully cloudy, golden beers and she soon lost count of what number she was on. The wife always ordered porter around the husband as for some unknown reason it was the only beer he approved of her drinking. At first she'd tried to work out if he was joking – and she suspected he was – but in the end it felt easier to grow to like it than mention it again.

'Everything okay for you, miss?' The wife looked up at the waiter through hazy eyes and said yes thank you everything was just fine. The potted shrimp smelled delightful but, thanks, she'd just finish her beer.

'You want to set off home soon,' he said, taking her empty glass. 'Looks like the weather's going to turn. One minute it's clear, and then . . .'

When she stood and drained the last of her bitter, the wife felt glad for her thick walking boots. Approaching the cottage, she heard the workmen packing up, shutting the doors to their vans. The lad she'd seen last week with his shirt off now stood on the kerb, smoking. He was young enough to remind the wife of some of the older boys she taught.

She stopped as she walked by. 'Couldn't spare one, could you?'

He fished into the pocket of his tracksuit bottoms and pulled out a pack, flicking open the top. She took one and asked him for a light. He had on his poker face, keeping his mouth shut to feign indifference around the men, all of whom had fallen still. The wife took a drag, feeling the warmth work its way down her throat. She looked at him, couldn't say if he was good looking; he was just young.

'It's going to rain,' she said at last. 'Don't want to get wet.'

As she opened her gate, she heard the conversations start up again. She bent to untie the laces of her boots on the doorstop, cigarette in mouth, and didn't turn back when they drove by.

The wife knew the house was empty before she put her key in the lock. She supposed an evening alone would be welcome. Kicking off her boots, she walked through the house to turn on all the lights and in the sitting room she stood and looked at the husband's armchair: pristine white, unruffled. The wife lowered herself into it and put her feet on the table, smoking until she got to the stub. She'd missed that wave of calm, watching the smoke drift and curl in the air. She turned on the television to murmur in the background and decided to eat the tin of spaghetti hoops. As she was alone, she slurped and tried to make noise when she burped, letting the thick arms of the chair hug her into a stupor.

Before she fell asleep – with the heat and beer, stomach full – she watched the TV through narrowed eyes. The show was about single mothers and on screen was a young woman, her mascara smudged, crying into her tissue. The wife felt her own eyes water, but then she was asleep, and afterwards she wouldn't remember whether or not she'd dreamt this.

It was dark and raining by the time the wife woke. Something loose rattled on the roof and the rain had left dirty streaks on the windows. The tide was in, glossy black with gulls hovering low over its surface.

The wife called out for the husband but no reply. The clock read quarter to midnight but she checked the grandfather clock in the hallway to make sure it was right. She couldn't help but think of the headline on the paper the day of their arrival, imagined the husband washed away in a river flood, being sucked into the sand and buried alive. The wife believed in premonitions. She forever told of how out of sorts she felt the day before Princess Diana's death, of how there were hints everywhere: a burned-out car on the motorway, her niece's plastic crown snapped in two. *It's like something was telling me*, she told her sister. *I could feel it.* She'd had the same intuition of fear when they first approached the village, its streetlights blinking from afar, the only sound the low murmur of their car.

She walked into the kitchen to pick up the newspaper by the bin, but there was no longer any headline about the body in the river. Instead the picture was of a woman crying, her inky lashes running into the white of a tissue. It felt familiar but the wife was sure it hadn't been there before. She checked the date and it was the same *Westmorland Gazette* of the day they'd arrived. Flicking through its pages, she found no reference to the death she was certain she'd read about.

'Where is he?' she breathed and the thunder answered in a

long, ominous roll. The wife walked up the stairs. Accidents happened, she knew, the line between life and death thin as a hairline crack. All it took was a step in the wrong direction.

In the bedroom, rain hammered on the skylight like hail. She was glad she'd turned on all the lights. The air was icy and she noticed the draught was coming in through an open window. She pulled it shut and noticed, for the first time, a framed photograph of a river beside the bed. Leaning in closer, she knew the name she'd find before she read it. Typed in silver, glinting as she approached, she read 'the River Bela'.

A gurgling erupted from the bathroom. The wife walked into the corridor and put her hand to the door, pushing it open so it slammed against the wall. The toilet was belching, throwing up sludge from below the surface, and despite herself she slammed the door shut and rushed into the bedroom, closing the door behind her. She pulled the husband's jumpers from his suitcase and buried herself beneath them on the carpet. A flash of lightning illuminated the white sheets on their bed and her thoughts shifted between possibilities. For a moment she wondered if the husband wasn't playing a joke. He could be somewhere in the house, maybe even with Nigel. Perhaps they came back when she was asleep and, knowing her fears, had cracked open the window and conspired to have a laugh at her expense. She wouldn't have put it past him. She tried to convince herself the husband had stayed with Nigel and those laughing crones. Perhaps he'd found something there he liked. She wouldn't have put that past him either.

Eventually the storm quietened and all other noise stopped with it. The wife was stiff when she stood. In the bathroom she excavated the cabinet for her husband's sleeping pills – the floor was wet and it looked like someone had hurled mud into the bowl of the toilet - swallowing two to send her out cold for the rest of the night. To stop me worrying, she thought, though she knew you didn't need to worry after the fact.

The wife crawled fully dressed between the covers of their bed and swaddled her head in the duvet.

The next day the sky had cleared and the wife was relieved to hear the workmen. She called out, knowing already the husband wasn't home. His jumper was limp on the floor and she felt momentarily embarrassed by last night's conduct.

She walked down the stairs and peered out of the front window; the potted plants were green and swollen with rain. The boy from yesterday was smoking by her gate and he looked over when she opened the door. The wife gestured at him to come through. He threw his cigarette to the floor, hitched up his jogging bottoms and opened the latch. She told him there was a problem with their bathroom and the toilet had kept her up with its noise.

'Couldn't have a look, could you?' She watched his eyes move over her face, to her lips and back when she spoke. 'Quickly,' she said, letting him in and closing the door. She told him it was upstairs and watched him climb the stairs, never looking back to see if she was following. He rattled around, flushing the toilet a few times before shouting down that this kind of thing was normal in a storm. He spoke with an accent, as the wife had expected. She looked at her reflection in the hallway mirror, at her knotted hair and crumpled clothes, and told herself she was something fuckable. There was a long pause in which she waited with her ears pricked up, before she realised she could hear him taking a piss. The sound travelled down the stairs, full of intent, more direct than that of the husband.

When the wife appeared in the doorway, the boy turned to look at her. He shook it out and put it back into his trousers.

'You're alone?' he said.

She nodded and he walked up to her, the smell of sweat.

'I've seen your man. He likes his tight jackets.'

She told him the husband was no longer around.

'Where is he?'

The wife looked at his arms, darkened by days working in the sun.

'I'm a widow,' she said, running her fingers along the tiles as though trying to feel the effect of that word through the stone. 'You know I played with Polish boys when I was a girl. For a while I pretended I was one.'

He told her she couldn't be from Poland.

'They don't know that,' she said. 'It's harder for them to recognise your class if you pretend you're foreign.'

He turned away from her and stuck his hands under the tap, splashing water onto his face and running his fingers through his hair. The wife didn't move until he looked at her in the mirror and said, 'So you're a widow. What do you want me to do about it?'

The husband came home that afternoon. As though the wife had known, she'd sprayed the hallway and bedroom with air freshener. She was curled into his armchair and heard the door when he came in.

The wife thought he looked exactly as he had before he'd died.

'What are you doing in my chair?' he said.

'I was waiting for you.'

'You've got other chairs to do that in.'

The wife stood. She noticed a smear of mascara on one of the cushions and turned it around.

The husband walked up the stairs and the wife prepared lunch. She wondered what he might say about the state of the bedroom, the sheets tangled and his clothes on the floor. She knew he wouldn't say anything.

The wife hardboiled two eggs and flattened them into mayonnaise, spreading it onto the stale bread she'd bought yesterday, or was it the day before? She sliced the sandwiches in half and slid them into food bags, then sat by the window to wait. Although she couldn't see them from down here, she could hear the workmen: an occasional call, a tool being dropped.

The wife and the husband walked along the promenade until they reached the pier. The husband ignored everyone who greeted them and the wife answered with a meek hello. Without discussion, they took the steps hewn into the side of the pier down to the sand. The tide was out and the wife perched on a large boulder while the husband continued to stand. He didn't touch his food and after a bite the wife realised she didn't want hers either.

'Where did you fish yesterday?' she asked.

'The river,' he said. 'We went canoeing.'

The wife had known that. On the River Bela. She watched the husband walk across the wet sand, his footprints fading as he moved.

'Did you catch anything?' she said, and the husband shook his head.

'Probably just a cold.'

He smiled and the wife's face crumpled. She remembered the girl in her bikini and thought about how she too had just wanted a real beach. You could hardly call it one when you couldn't slide your toes between the grains, or make castles that washed away with the waves. The wife said she hated rambling and that she never wanted to come here in the first place, feeling she could say that now.

'Everything here is grey,' she said. 'And this place was supposed to make us better.'

The wife stood and grasped a pebble between her fingers, mottled and brown. When she threw, the stone landed with a wet thud a few feet behind him.

'You don't think we're better?' asked the husband.

She turned away to look into the white of the sky and the point at which it met the bay. There was a thin, horizontal line between one world and the other.

'What, now?' the wife said.

She heard a stone sail past her ear. It skimmed the surface of a channel in the sand, touching the water four, five, six times before it disappeared. She stopped still and watched as another danced across the shallows. They seemed to skip on for ever.

When she turned to look at the husband, he had his eyes fixed on the line of the horizon, squinting at the light. There was a look on his face she'd never seen before. The wife watched the elegant flick of his wrist and the stones as they flew through the air.

The stones, each time, became weightless.

CUTS

ONCE OVER 65 you need five hours' kip a night. Princess Diana said in a letter, her 1981 honeymoon was an opportunity to catch up on sleep. Alastair Campbell used to drift off when Harriet Harman spoke. I changed my anti-psychotic because it was making me drowsy. The psychiatrist said the new drug would leave me more awake. It would not cause sexual dysfunction. She was correct. I got erections and woke at 2.00 a.m. The auditory hallucinations got louder. They kept repeating 'Go on do it now'. The voices did not specify what the 'it' was. I could not put the radio on without waking my brother. So I read Alastair Campbell's *Diary*. He punctuated the first four volumes badly, but in the fifth he seemed to have learned what he was doing. The *Diary* must be as long as Proust. Campbell started several sentences with E.g. Alastair had arguments with his partner Fiona about the amount of time he spent working for Tony Blair. He had a breakdown . . . Nurses are more likely to commit suicide than other women. One in five people in the UK cannot name one author. Anthony Burgess reviewed one of his own novels. The radio made a fuss about his 100th birthday. He created slang for *A Clockwork Orange* that would not date. It was partly based on Russian.

An online shopping supermarket substituted tampons

for baby food in a delivery. Kitchen knives are used in 60% of UK homicides. Kubrick said description was the most boring thing in a novel. He would hurl tedious books against the wall. There was a red-handled sharp knife in the cutlery drawer. I didn't like handling it. I feared I would stab my brother with it while his back was turned. Norman Mailer stabbed his wife. The alternative to succumbing was going to a mental hospital again. I didn't want that. I was worried that I would be searched when entering the hospital and my pen confiscated as a potential weapon, with which I could kill myself. I have to write every day. Paul Theroux said you should not keep a diary but rely on memory. I don't agree with him. Enderby wrote literature while sitting on the lavatory. Turkey expelled 40 Dutch cows. It is a country in which you cannot flush toilet paper. Ian Fleming publications endorsed denture polish and hair removal cream. Ring notebooks were not allowed in hospital. Burgess said anyone can write a first a novel, after that you cannot rely on memory and must use your imagination. Old tea bags were displayed as art at the Serpentine Gallery. I can only drink decaffeinated tea. They don't have it in the hospital. The voices told me to do it now. I loved my brother. He was the only person I lived with. He gulped his tea loudly and took an hour to drink a mug. Every man kills the thing he loves. I did not want to kill him. But the voices seemed to emanate from him and the only way to achieve silence was to shut him up. A Japanese company hired out fake friends to pose in your photographs. I was almost 60. 59% of women think about their ex during sex. The mentally ill die prematurely by about 20 years. So I probably did not have long to go. But I could not bear another day of it. The shrink changed me back onto my old tablets. But this did not silence the voices. They told me to do it now. I instructed my brother to shut up. He denied saying anything and suggested we stagger our meal times. The schizophrenic who raped and killed women on God's orders went blind in prison. Many mentally ill people hear God. Burgess said we had never had a Catholic PM. Tony Blair converted shortly after leaving office. My brother went to see Blair at the local town hall in 1990. Oliver Sacks didn't know who Michael Jackson was. Sacks went without sex for 35 years. Burgess was Sexist Pig of the Year in 1980. He said the female orgasm played no part in the sexual process, that women were better equipped to be novelists and that Tolstoy the genius was inseparable from the man who abused his wife. Michael Jackson was born after me and yet he died years ago.

The television sent me messages. I watched the news channels because they were live and people on live television could read my mind. The psychiatrists call this Thought Broadcasting. My thoughts were broadcast to the world and the newsreaders could pick them up. It was like telepathy only it was done scientifically. The female on the news used code words such as 'border' to say everything was all right. Border meant ER was bored. She didn't seem to think I was heading for Broadmoor as a murderer. Fay Weldon said feminism had reduced the male wage so it could no longer support a family on its own. Women who fake orgasms are more likely to be unfaithful. A Christian priest said women who wear jeans should be drowned. The presenter said, 'A man spent £40,000 on having his genitals removed.' A Polish MEP asserted women were less intelligent. A man was arrested for having sex with a fence. Girls were missing school because they could not afford tampons. The auditory hallucinations said I could have any woman. The BBC cut LGBT lyrics from a talent show song.

When it came to dinner time. My brother got out the red knife to open his plastic packet of salmon fillets. I moved away from him. I watched the TV. The female presenter said it was fine, everything was OK. I wanted to eat my food. Campbell felt Mo Mowlam belched too much. For a soccer tournament in Russia you need certification of your BMI to get an extra-big seat for being obese. After training, a WWE wrestler ate 12 eggs and six rashers of bacon. Each time my brother swallowed I felt angry, the noise annoyed me.

If I was to go into the hospital my benefits would be suspended and this I could not afford. We would still have to pay our council tax. They might put me on injections. I would have to lower my trousers for the jab. The food would be inedible in hospital. They don't give you five fruit and veg a day. If they said 'Clozapine worked for you before' then that crap would give me constipation. It can cause sudden death. But this is not guaranteed.

MPs say suicide methods should not be depicted in TV dramas. I could always throw myself in front of a train. That would be more efficient than an overdose. With an overdose you have a chance for second thoughts. But a train is final. There was a railway station with fast nonstop trains going through near the post office where I used to work. It would be better to kill myself than my brother. 'Go on do it now,' the voices said. My brother's voice and the news presenter's voice. But always almost the same message. Adam Faith spied on Fidel Castro for MI6. I hummed the 'Summer of '69'. 'Those were the best days of my life' before the voices began. It was the summer I left primary school. In Scandinavia child sex dolls for paedophiles might reduce abuse. 69 was the last time I was happy. I tried to recall who was in the Wimbledon final. Was it John Newcombe? A 60-year-old was given a map of places to avoid so he would not meet the schizophrenic who stabbed him. Mick Jagger was originally to have starred in *A Clockwork Orange*. Burgess criticised A. N. Wilson for mentioning Terry Wogan (Irish DJ) in his fiction. Such references were parochial. I dreamed my brother reprimanded me for thinking Burgess a sloppy writer.

The psychiatrist was on holiday. The police sirens began to wail. This meant the Americans were angry. It was the American style of siren. The British one was phased out as my illness began in the 1980s. I could hear the president's voice as I watched him on TV. 'Come on do it now.' The incessant mantra louder and louder. Campbell told George W. Bush his breakdown was the best thing that happened to him. I took the knife and began to cut my arms. This was evidence of self-harm. Brain activity continues for ten minutes after the heart stops. B.F. Skinner said if he could press a button to get Nixon out of the White House then he would. The German Chancellor read the US President's interview in *Playboy*. Jack Kennedy thought Hitler was one of the most significant figures in history. Nigeria's President said he needed more time off. My brother asked why I was not saying much. He could not see the wounds. I didn't feel like speaking. One in four young men under 24 self-harm. I went for a walk. Saira Khan had sexual fantasies about a dog which she told *Loose Women* about (Campbell explained in brackets who Princess Diana and the Archbishop of Canterbury were but not who Jeremy Beadle was). Tories feared Diana would become a Labour MP. Robin Cook wanted to protect the

Coronation from satellite TV. The dog owners I met seemed to urge me to do something. Their voices were increasingly irritating. I wanted to euthanise them. I thought one man was suggesting I was gay. Then I saw KV on a car number plate. The initials of Keith Vaz, an MP who was supposedly straight but actually gay. Cardiff University wanted to ban the word homosexual. A cinema in the US would not allow a Disney film to be shown because it had a gay character. During an out-of-body experience a woman met Walt Disney. I was almost 60 and unmarried. I blamed other people for this. Christopher Marlowe said Christ was gay. Campbell and Peter Mandelson were accused of spreading the rumour Gordon Brown was gay. People in their big cars with two or three children when I did not have any kids. I used to think it didn't matter because I had an immortal soul. But now I wished I had reproduced my genes. Left something behind. Susan Hill left her husband for a woman. Big diesel cars pouring out poison that killed people like me who walked. It was Gordon Brown's fault for encouraging people to stop using petrol. The drivers didn't deserve to live. I wanted to kick a couple of teenagers in the head. They were laughing at me. Sick laughter. Teenagers think about sex 600 times an hour. I'd show them. Kick their teeth out. Bill Clinton had size 13 feet. Caffeine reduces the level of a protein which causes dementia. Cherie wanted to stop Tony Blair drinking tea and coffee. People think schizophrenics are all murderers. They want to lock us up. I'd like to lock them up. 59% of *Express* readers believe in alien abductions. I think Skinner explained how it is possible to read another person's thoughts. We think in our throats without vocalising the words. A microphone was inserted in my throat on the instructions of

President Reagan. He listened to what went through my mind when I masturbated. A *Guardian* reader who masturbated was unable to reach a climax with his partner. Jane Austen falsified a marriage register to give the impression she had wedded. The chief offered me anal sex with the most beautiful women on the planet. 'Go on all you have to do is ask. That is all you have to do.' Well I asked and asked. But it never did any good. It got me locked up as a loony. Mind and Rethink wanted an end to face-down restraint of mental patients. The needle with the anti-psychotic was inserted in my buttocks. I felt calmer. Some dogs are on Valium. The people in the hospital were not that bad. The food was awful. Aunt Bessie's are bringing out parsnip and carrot chips. Being on anti-psychotic medication makes you gain weight. A nail salon in Memphis charged overweight customers more. Smoking was banned and that drove some inmates up the wall. Campbell says Jean-Claude Juncker reeked of fags. The doctor thought I had not been taking my tablets. A scientist blamed Parkinson's medication for his tendency to download obscene images. Netflix are to film alternative plots to give the viewers a choice of endings. A CNN presenter ate a human brain. The rooms in the hospital came with WCs. In Beijing toilet paper is stolen from public loos. Human faeces were found in a Coca Cola can at a Northern Ireland factory. It was a millionaire who slashed a Gainsborough at the National Gallery. Dick Cavett told Burgess he had to urinate before hosting his chat show. Anthony said Turkish squat toilets were better for your health. A psychotic art dealer killed his friend because he was a green alien. Burgess said the state in his novel was wrong to remove the capacity for free choice.

THE ARRANGEMENT

IT STARTED WITH the owl.

'Feathers repel me,' said Erin, twisting her mouth. 'I prefer living things. Can we change the subject?'

At the table, Matthew hunched over his laptop, his back to her.

'Aha, Falco Rusticolus,' he said, softly. 'Now we're talking. Eat your baby for breakfast.'

'What?'

She turned back to the stove, her faded mane twisted into a thick knot at the nape of her neck, her denim skirt skimming her knees. Her legs were long, still honey freckled from the summer.

'The Gyr,' he said.

At one time she might have said, you're my Gyr, pressed herself against him, and he would have chased her up the stairs, flapping those great Gyr wings.

'You're beginning to sound like some weird catalogue,' she said.

He'd gone quiet, lips parted.

She trickled saffron between her fingertips, trance-like, watching the strands bleed into the stock. Silence. Just the rhythm of the wooden spoon scraping the base of the pot. The liquid began to turn yellow.

When they first met, he'd made noises about cooking (he'd called it *cuisine*, which she'd adored), but over the years he'd let her take over.

'I can't believe what you said a minute ago.'

'I'm sorry,' he said, turning round. 'I wasn't thinking—'

'Not that,' she said. 'About Fleur.'

It had been dark since three. On the patio, glistening trails marked the comings and goings of slugs. Further down the garden, pockets of seed heads were being scattered by hedgehogs.

They'd met on an art history course. For Erin, a New Yorker, there'd been something fetching about the ripped cuff of his tweed jacket, the hand-rolled cigarettes, and that faraway look was a challenge. Childless at thirty-eight, she could hardly believe her luck when he'd proposed.

'Even as a joke' she said, adding tofu.

Neither of them had touched meat for several years, and they'd recently agreed, again at her suggestion, to omit animal products.

'You obviously don't really love her,' she said.

He looked up. Were her eyes somehow smaller these days? He turned back to the screen.

'To be honest I don't know if I can trust you with her,' she said.

'You're obsessed with that fucking cat.'

She'd always admired the fact he rarely swore; for her, it demonstrated a degree of reticence, of self control. She stared at the back of his head, the spoon dribbling juice onto the white tiled floor.

'It was a joke.' He'd lowered his voice again.

'But you actually went as far as getting the price.'

They'd bought the cat – a thin pedigree with distinctive markings – a year after the stillbirth.

'Perhaps I love her more than you,' he said, turning. 'Perhaps I hate the idea that I'll never be able to look at her again.'

He noticed a tiny cluster of purple veins down the back of her left calf.

'Look,' he said. 'I was merely surprised that badgers, much bigger animals, were cheaper to do. You once suggested having her turned into a muff.'

'We both knew that was a joke.'

'Sorry, Erin,' he said. 'It was a jape.'

She looked at him blankly.

'A jest?' he said.

He returned to the screen, trying to remember where he'd put the dope. In the dash? Or behind the work-bench?

'Oh, by the way,' he said, casually, after a minute. 'I notice your swans are back at the lake.'

It was dusk as they'd driven back from the antiques fair the week before. He'd suddenly swerved onto the hard shoulder, braked, banging her knee hard with the gearstick.

'For God's sake,' said Erin. 'It was a dead pigeon.'

'Wasn't.'

He'd already unhooked his seatbelt.

'Please – this is dangerous,' she said.

The car door slammed shut.

She nursed her knee, watching him through the rear-view mirror pace down the hard shoulder. A stream of trucks buffeted the van from side to side. He eventually returned, holding the bird slightly away from his body, like some sort of offering. It was larger than she'd expected.

'I hope it hasn't got fleas,' she said.

He placed it gently on the seat between them, inside his coat. They drove the rest of the way in silence.

It lay on a tea-towel on the dining-room table, a pinkish trace of blood on its downy chest.

'Have you ever seen white this pure?' he said.

Bird beside him, he was already on the laptop.

'Do we have cling-film? he said. 'Apparently it needs wrapping carefully—'

She scrabbled half-heartedly through kitchen drawers.

'I don't like it on that table,' she said. 'It could disturb the cat.'

He was scribbling notes . . . *make sure no fluids leak from item* . . .

'No cling-film, sorry,' she said.

. . . *having skinned up to the neck, detach the head* . . .

'I think I might go up soon.' She lingered in the doorway. 'Coming?'

'In a bit—'

'Can you put it in the shed?' She was speaking to his back.

'Yep.'

'Say it?'

. . . *without having to skin the head* . . . 'Love you.'

He heard the bedroom door close.

When she came downstairs early next morning, he'd already gone.

Pulling off the motorway, he took the sharp fork to the right and followed the long lane with stubble fields either side, as instructed. The house, more like a series of low barns, was set back from the road behind tall trees.

The man was somewhere in his sixties, short, with a firm gaze; a bunch of keys dangled from his thick leather belt. Matthew noticed the size of his fingers. When they shook hands, the softness of his touch took him by surprise.

The man led the way through long, low-ceilinged rooms. The walls were crammed with alligators, exotic birds, weasels, bear skins, sambars, gazelles. A black monkey with mournful eyes stretched forth one arm.

'A doleful fellow,' said Matthew, trying to sound casual.

'Black Bearded Saki,' the man said. 'Chiropotes Satanus. Nothing doleful there.'

Behind, a massive stallion reared, its eyes rolled back inside its sockets. In front, a hideous fish stared out from a long glass case; beneath, a brass plaque with ornate scroll: 'Monster of The Deep'.

'The Arapaima. Nine foot six,' said the man. 'Amazon river.'

'My grandfather used to catch these,' said Matthew, nodding at a pike, relieved to have found a point of reference.

'Dark creature,' said the man. 'Eat your kiddie. If you let him.'

A fair young woman brought tea in delicate cups on a silver tray. Matthew noticed the whiteness of her skin; her long, flawless neck. She approached softly, leaving the faintest trace of perfume behind her. The scent was unusual, not quite sweet.

He looked to the man, as if to acknowledge her, but the man was looking at him.

'I've never actually seen one of those.' Matthew pointed to a kingfisher quickly. 'Alive, I mean.'

'Touch it,' said the man.

Matthew raised a finger to the tiny outstretched wing. It quivered.

'With a cargo of ivory and apes, peacocks, sandalwood and sweet white wine. That's poetry,' said the man. 'My wife's French, you know.'

'Very nice,' Matthew said. 'I'm sorry, I didn't mean—'

'Likes to be quiet does Seraphina.'

Matthew searched for an appropriate expression.

'Unlike my third wife. She was fiery, as they say,' said the man, touching his keys. 'You got a lady?'

'We've got a shop,' Matthew said.

'Very beautiful is she, your wife?'

'She's not actually my wife,' Matthew said.

By four o'clock the lane back to the motorway was shrouded in mist. A thin moon hung over the fields. With the lights on full beam he kept the van at a crawl. Ignoring the mist, he picked up speed, rounding a blind corner, not caring, half daring catastrophe, when he felt the thud beneath him.

He climbed out. A pheasant started up from the hedgerow. Glancing round again, he moved to get back inside the van when he heard it.

The fox lay in a ditch. Blood bubbled from its nostrils, glistening in the moonlight. He squatted beside it, letting his palm rest on its side, feeling it breathe. When the breathing stopped he lifted his hand, feeling the warm, sticky texture between his fingertips. He turned the van around.

The man seemed unsurprised to see him. Matthew held the creature in both arms.

Behind, down a long corridor, the woman was lit by a dim bulb. Matthew saw that she had changed into a pale evening dress and white satin shoes.

'An accident?' The man smiled.

He looked into Matthew's eyes and called to the woman. She came forward, the slow rhythmic click of her heels echoing through the silence around them.

'I can't do her before Christmas mind,' the man said.

'How do you know it's female?' said Matthew.

'Scent.'

The man caught the glitter in Matthew's eye.

'No good without scent,' the man said.

'Do we need to discuss the price, positioning, and so on?'

'Perhaps we can come to some arrangement,' said the man.

Only then did Matthew notice that the fox's eyes were open.

He didn't mention the fox, only that the man was more than happy to do the owl. Erin had never understood that expression. How could you be more than happy? At first it had seemed charming. He might use it on customers when he was trying to close a sale. He'd be more than happy to deliver the armoire for no extra charge. He'd never used it on her.

'I thought I'd do the antiques fair tomorrow. We need stock.'

'But we always go together.' She sounded hurt.

'It's the run up to Christmas, Toots,' he said. 'We can't afford to be closed.'

The week dragged. In the shop, Erin wrapped herself in woollen layers, but the cold seemed to penetrate her skin.

She shuffled the greeting cards and re-arranged the display cabinets.

She found the owl, the following week, in the centre of the mantelpiece. It was in a domed case, perched on a grassy base, its enormous eyes like two watery marrons glacé. The Meissen figures that her mother had left her, which were usually either side of the mantelpiece, had vanished; the Meissen figures, she'd thought, both she and Matthew adored.

She closed the door on the bird, leaving it to gaze through the milky afternoon light. She sat in the car, looking up at the window.

That evening, he explained he'd merely been fooling around; the Meissen figures, he promised, would be reinstated. They made love for the first time in weeks. He left the lights on, exploring every inch of her, which excited her. Afterwards, in the dark, she rolled over, letting him brush his fingers across her stomach, the way she liked it. Suddenly he stopped.

'Hey, sleepy,' said Erin.

While driving home that afternoon, when the sky was almost vermilion, he'd seen the pair of swans crossing at the beck.

'Say it,' she whispered.

Rather than slowing to let them pass, he'd put his foot hard onto the accelerator.

'Matthew?'

He remembered a sort of popping sound.

'Do you know something?' he said.

She nestled against him, her hot toes tickling his.

'You still have the body of a teenager.'

She curled in closer, quietly grateful, remembering her teenage face covered with acne.

As she dozed, she became aware of a delicate scent, the faintest trace of musk. She inhaled more deeply, unsure whether it was coming from her, from Matthew, or the room itself. Was it the pillow? The down inside? She thought of her mother's favourite French quilt, silk edged. After a moment, she sensed something soft fall onto her cheek – snow soft, but warm, like ash – and imagined Matthew holding her, her eyes shut, her mouth crammed with feathers. She listened to the rhythmic pounding of his heart, lifted her fingers lightly from his chest, and, inching herself away, lay there, incredibly still.

THE HEIGHTS OF SLEEP

THE NOVELIST J. S. Gaunt gets described as a writer's writer, but for me, he's more than that. I sometimes think he's the writer that made me what I am.

When I met him, fifteen years after I started reading his work, I told him so. This was one of the many ways I embarrassed myself during those ninety minutes of conversation in a Soho coffee shop. In person, Gaunt was gentle-mannered, accommodating, sometimes lost for words – the man was unlike the writing in all these respects – but even so, I spent the encounter disoriented, saying foolish things. Some books come to feel as if they belong to you alone. And then you find yourself face to face with the person who made them, and what are you supposed to do?

I was seventeen years old when I discovered Gaunt. I knew I was going to do English Lit at university – in those days a fairly modest ambition – but alongside my curricular reading, I had a taste for the more disreputable stuff. I thought I had a radical streak because I liked horror and space opera and dungeonpunk fantasy in just the same way I liked Austen, Dickens and Woolf. I was a rebel in my own head because I refused to make a distinction.

I kept coming across Gaunt's name in magazine interviews

with genre writers I admired. When asked about their influ-
ences, they all said the same thing: J. S. Gaunt was a stylist
and a visionary, and it was a crime his work was not more
widely known. I needed no further encouragement to make
a day trip to Charing Cross Road. Tucked away on the top
floor in Foyles, I found a copy of the old omnibus edition of
the Masquador novels, with its ugly cover and its selection of
cryptic critical praise on the back. 'Perturbing fables, twisted
and occasionally perverse'; '*The Man Who Was Thursday* as
rewritten by Ballard'; '*The Alexandria Quartet* meets
Lovecraft via Djuna Barnes'; 'These hallucinations would
crumble if they were not sustained by prose of such unfalter-
ing precision'; 'From its pulp-fiction roots the Masquador
cycle blooms as a strange new flower of evil'.

It was an ideal introduction to Gaunt. I tore through the
three novels. In *The Silver Curtain*, the story of supernatural intrigue was largely conventional, but *A Conspiracy of
Wasps* twisted the same scenario into baffling surrealism. And
then came *Among The Masquadors*: I had never finished a
book with such a strong intuition that it contained a hidden
pattern, some secret I needed to understand. The omnibus
concluded with the handful of short stories usually known
as *The Masquador Dances*: really they were no more than
sketches for the mythos, but I combed each of them for clues
to what it all meant.

While I was a student, I read all the Gaunt I could find.
I tracked down his first two novels, *The Remnants* and *The
Foal*, in the library stacks. They were set in 1970s Manchester
and dealt with the adventures of bohemian young men who
were mystified by women and angry with the world. There
was a lot of cynical sex and hippie philosophy, broken up

by moments of unexplained violence, betrayal and magic. They weren't great, but I read them studiously. There was a thrill in recognising Gaunt's way with a sentence, his daredevil adverbs and ruthless commas, highly characteristic and already there in his earliest stuff. From the beginning, he was using some of his favourite motifs: iridescent green beetles, bereaved women, poker, strange buried machinery, one-eyed cats, a pair of clasped hands that suddenly takes on the appearance of a face. These images, and certain key phrases relating to them, recurred through all the Gaunt I had read, as if they were a tarot that he dealt and re-dealt, finding new meanings each time.

I read the books he had published in the twenty-odd years since the Masquador sequence. It took me a long time to get through *The Ablation Colony*, *The Heart's Retreat* and *Crocodile Fires*, though all three of those novels are so short. For a while, I was defeated by their density and their refusal to belong to any obvious category, and even when I had finished them, I had an odd feeling I shouldn't move on. It was as if I had glimpsed something lurking in the edges of the fictions, as if getting the three books into alignment would reveal a figure that had nothing to do with what the stories seemed to be about.

When I tried introducing friends to Gaunt, I always ended up regretting it, always feeling they hadn't quite seen what I was getting at. It gives me the same shiver that I get when I remember stupid things I did at that age: blurting out private matters to people I had just met, getting infatuated with girls I didn't like, making obnoxious remarks because I didn't know what I believed. That urge to share Gaunt's work was no different.

Once I ran into another fan. I was in the union canteen, reading my new hardback of his novel *Form*, and she came over. We enthused for a while over the sheer fact that he had written another; I told her I was only up to page seventy-nine but so far it was astonishing, that you could see how it grew out of what he had been doing in short stories like 'Caffè Atrocità' and 'Dancing in the Disaster', but it went so much further. She begged me not to say more because she was going to read it the first chance she got. It flashed across my mind that maybe we would start a relationship, an affair. Maybe this was how it was done – we'd be thrown into it by shared passionate intimacy with Gaunt's work. Instead, we found we had nothing else to say.

Form was the longest book Gaunt had written. The reviews said it was his most ambitious but also his most accessible. I wasn't sure about that, but it was a major feat, big and picaresque, with five protagonists on odysseys through the past, the present, the future and several parallel universes. The satirical edge was sharper than ever, and the ending was as bleak and enigmatic as anything he had written. Obviously, it was going to be understood as a comedy of despair at contemporary culture, and its inventive vigour would be seen as redeeming its nihilism. But as I read, I found myself dwelling on smaller details. When Lulu Zhong finds her daughter, why is the nail bar where they meet called 'Rainbow Foam' – the same name Gaunt gave to a bioengineered psychedelic virus in a story he published in a New Wave magazine more than thirty years earlier? Why is Rossi quite so frightened when he mistakes Lamb's face for his own in the mirror? What's with all the molecular chemistry stuff? Why does Dorian Scurf, who first appeared as the proprietor of the junk shop in *The*

Silver Curtain and turned up again in *The Heart's Retreat* to usher the protagonist to his doom, now feature as an occult card-shark? And what's actually at stake in the last game? I had dozens of questions along these lines.

A year or so after *Form* was published, I had an argument with a young woman. I was about to travel two hundred miles by National Express to a provincial book festival where Gaunt was making an appearance, and the young woman, to whom I would later get married, ribbed me for being so into a writer no one else had heard of. I responded so humourlessly that I still cringe to think of it, getting indignant and asking if she had even read him. She said she had tried one of his books but found its attitude so singularly male that she lost interest. I fumed for the whole coach journey and decided she and I had no future. As for the author talk, I didn't remember much of it afterwards. Gaunt was a slight, trim man in jeans and a hooded top, who kept his feet flat on the floor and had a way of pressing his palms together between his knees. The slate-grey hair was cropped close to the small, handsome head, and the steel-rimmed spectacles flashed when they caught the lights. At one point the chair quoted Henry James: 'We work in the dark – we do what we can – we give what we have,' and so on. I thought Gaunt was going to skewer the man's pomposity, but instead, he said that for him writing was like sleep. It takes you to the same place you go when you fall asleep, he said, but the gravity is reversed. Up becomes down, so you can't get there by falling. You have to climb. When the chair invited questions from the audience I did not raise my hand.

⚜

Gaunt followed up *Form* with a novel called *Harm*, ostensibly a sequel although it bore little resemblance. It was a quarter of the length, and instead of a rambling epic, it was a tight three-hand psychodrama set in a single location. *Harm's* nameless characters don't appear in *Form*, but the sharp-eyed reader recognises that the isolated, decaying manse where the woman, the man and the daughter play out their catastrophe is the same house where the Nyberg children go missing in the earlier book. I reviewed *Harm* for the *Times Literary Supplement*. I had got into book-reviewing the year I graduated when I sent the *TLS* a clipping of something I had written in a student paper and they sent me back a copy of some novel and a deadline for 600 words. Since then I had been doing a piece every few months and had not ceased to be amazed at what a painful process it was to review a book. Less harrowing than my attempts at fiction, for sure, but its own special kind of misery. In a review, there are so many ways to be lazy, dishonest, timid, ignorant, bullying, spurious, inexact, ungenerous or unjust, and so few ways to be true. Reviewing Gaunt was ten times worse than usual. I re-read everything he had published, then spent most of a week on my opening paragraph, trying to encapsulate his career, his style, his preoccupations and his significance to date in eighty words. I scribbled all over my review copy. I wrote nine different plot-summaries and rejected them all as too reductive. I realised the apparently straightforward action of the book was in fact irreducibly ambiguous. I kept leafing through Gaunt's collected short fiction and finding clues in stories he had written over four decades. Stories like 'Little Quadratics', 'Spider Dimension', 'Singularity Blues', 'Disco Lazarus': all bore vitally on this new phase of work, and, what was more, the post-apocalypse sections of *Crocodile Fires* now had to be seen in a completely different light. I couldn't imagine how it was possible for a life's writing all to map together like a great fractal falling into itself forever on every scale at once. What it was or what it meant, what figure might show itself at last, I had no idea.

A couple of months later I went along to the TLS summer party, out of some impulse to drink warm white wine with several hundred people who would all prefer to be at home. To my surprise, Gaunt was there among the moleskin jackets and balding heads. He sometimes wrote for the paper, but he didn't seem the sort to come to drinks parties. He was in motorcycle leathers, not holding a drink, listening closely to a woman in a purple shawl. I felt I should speak to him – perhaps I would always regret it if I didn't – but I couldn't think of a single thing to say. I hovered for a while and then, murmuring *Hey I'm no one you know but I've read all your books and what do you think about that,* I left.

I wrote a book of my own. I thought that publishing a novel would answer some question I had not fully articulated. I wasn't so naive as to imagine life would change in any practical way, but I had a notion that when I saw the thing in print I would know why it had been worth doing: why I had spent four years of evenings and weekends shut in my room, instead of giving that time to the young woman who found Gaunt's work excessively male, and to our daughter. I expected that once published, the book would feel different from all the failed fragments, terrible stories and unworkable novels I had been writing and discarding for as long as I could remember. But when I picked up the first proof copy I found that each page was a mass of flaws and vulnerabilities. The book's whole purpose, it appeared, was to expose the limitations of its author. The debt to Gaunt was painfully obvious. I had known he was one of my touchstones, but now I saw I had produced nothing but a thin imitation. Even my title seemed shamefully Gauntian, and for a while, I cast around for an alternative that would at least throw readers off the scent. But nothing else fit, and I had to accept that the book was called *The Heights of Sleep*.

I had slept poorly in the last weeks of the final draft, lying half-awake for hours with structural problems flailing in my head. Then I would slip into a dream in which the world was a single infinite house in whose grey rooms and gardens I kept accosting family and strangers, trying to convince them of a peril that had been revealed to me alone. Every time I dreamt it there was the same shock as I grasped that they knew the abominable truth already: they had been living with it all along. I had never had a recurring dream before, and I grew concerned it might not go away. But once the book was signed off I stopped remembering my dreams.

My editor asked for a list of writers to send advance reading copies, the idea being that if they liked the book they might give us a quote for promotional purposes. I hesitated before including Gaunt's name. He would see at once that I had written a knock-off of his early stuff; he'd be furious, or he'd pity me, or sue me for plagiarism. In the end, though, I decided to send him a copy. If not now, I told myself, then when? He probably wouldn't read it anyway. And in the days that followed, I felt lightened, as if I had been freed from a compulsion.

A few weeks later my editor forwarded me a message from

J. S. Gaunt. He was grateful for the copy of *The Heights of Sleep*. He never gave publicity endorsements, but he had enjoyed the book. He looked forward to my next one, and in the meantime, I should get in touch if I ever wanted to meet up.

A bright, cramped, Italian coffee bar: grubby Formica, Soho crowding past the window, light echoing off steel surfaces, the espresso machine's snarl. I got there early and was immediately mired in logistics. Which table? Should I order now? Would I recognise him? How should I make myself known? I was rearranging my coat on the back of my seat when I saw him standing in the entrance, blinking as if the scene were a surprise. Close-cropped hair no longer grey but white. Leather jacket, hoodie, worn jeans, biker boots, messenger backpack. My pulse beat in my temples as I stood up. I wanted this to be over already, and at the same time, I wanted us to hit it off so well that before we knew it we'd be falling out of a late bar in the small hours of tomorrow morning.

He ordered a double espresso, and I asked for the same. My copy of *Form*, which I was planning to ask him to sign, lay on the table between us. He did and did not look as I had expected. He looked like a man of his age, with liver-spots at his hairline, grey hairs in his nostrils and a trace of milk in his pale blue eyes. I had taken up poker as a result of reading his accounts of the game. He saw it as a practice in which you could discover your illusions about the world: not as a metaphor for anything, but poker as a way of actually confronting yourself. I wanted to tell him how this idea had beguiled me, but it seemed a weird thing to bring up, and besides, I was hardly in a position to swap poker stories with a veteran of

45

the card table. I had played a few nights with friends and then let it slide.

I emptied two sachets of sugar into my coffee. Gaunt sipped his straight. I told him that one of my most vivid memories was of lying in a park in hot July sun, smelling the chlorine from an outdoor pool and reading the whole of *Among the Masquadors* in an afternoon. I told him I was extremely interested in the way he had taken his stories 'Taboo Parade' and 'The Insufferablist' and crossbred them to produce his novella *Persephone Potts*. I told him I was all too conscious that my review of *Harm* hadn't even scratched the surface of what was really going on in that book. I told him I had a theory that whatever the daughter sees in the upstairs bathroom is linked with the crooked murder investigation in the central section of *Form*. I told him I had read on the internet that he had finished the third book in the sequence and I couldn't wait to see how the pattern was going to unfold. He asked me what I was working on now.

I was dumbfounded less by the question than by the fact I hadn't thought to have an answer ready. I stumbled through a couple of half-formed ideas. Then, confused, I told him how nervous I had been about sending him *The Heights of Sleep*, given the book's debt to his work.

Gaunt looked puzzled.

'I hadn't noticed a resemblance,' he said.

At that, we both seemed to lose the thread of the conversation. Gaunt looked at the ceiling and I swallowed the sludge at the bottom of my cup.

He began to talk about Cynthia Cleaver. She had been kind to him when he was starting out, he said. There had been one night, around the time of his second book, when she had asked him round for dinner. I leaned forward, excited, because – it now seemed obvious – this must be the reason distinguished writers met with tyros: to pass on this kind of story.

Cynthia Cleaver was an important name to me, not that this was unusual on my part. She was the kind of writer I could only have admired more if she had been a little less well-known. I had first come to her when I did *The Fox's Tower* as an A-level text, but it took me years to realise what a figure she actually was. Cynthia Cleaver: prolific experimental novelist in genres from kitchen-sink gothic to surreal satirical SF to postmodernist Victorian pastiche, leftist campaigner, feminist provocateur, folklorist, writer of stage plays, screenplays and radio plays, translator of *Beowulf* and the *Arabian Nights*, travel writer, pioneer of long-form first-person cultural criticism, tireless polemicist, reviewer of everything from literary fiction to sixties fashion to punk rock to pornography to political rallies. She had died in middle age, eleven years after I was born. I had a shelf of her books.

Gaunt was explaining that in the late seventies Cleaver liked to invite young writers for dinner, two or three at a time, at her house beside Hampstead Heath. She would roast a joint and serve it in her little basement kitchen, then pour the wine and hold court. Along with Gaunt, Cleaver had served dinner that night to Will Stagg and Charlotte Borden, both of whom at that time were trendy youngsters who had done a few things. Stagg was as much of a dick then as now, Gaunt said, and Borden was going through a troubled period. As for the young Gaunt himself, he was callow, arrogant and rude. He was convinced that they were laughing up their sleeves at him and that they thought he should be mopping floors for a living. He shook his head.

'I must have talked some rubbish that night.'

But Cleaver, he said, had been equal to his shortcomings as a dinner guest. Briskly, discreetly, with a glint of irony – and doing the same for the other two idiots at the table – she had coaxed him into loosening his grip on his own ego. She conducted an acerbic conversation, demanding hard thought and quick wits from her guests. She didn't let you off on any particular point, but she drew you up to her level. The atmosphere in Cynthia Cleaver's kitchen told you that writing was too serious a matter for writers to be allowed to get in its way.

'I saw things differently after that,' Gaunt said.

We ordered more coffees. Out of sheer discomfiture, I picked up the copy of *Form* and opened it at random. It was the passage where Vincent gets kidnapped. I told Gaunt – chuckling at how unlikely it sounded now I came to say it out loud – that I had always had this notion of something hidden in his work, something with its own separate existence. He looked blank. I began to speak faster and less coherently as I tried to get across what I meant. Not a point or an idea, I said, not a pattern or a design, but something big, something else, something you've been getting at all this time. A kind of fractal shape, so we have to know how to calculate it before it can appear. I wasn't explaining well, I said. I heard a pleading note in my voice. At that moment, I felt that I was not asking Gaunt to confirm the existence of the secret figure, but to deny it.

He did not reply. He wasn't surprised by what I had said; only embarrassed by the jumbled emotional demand I seemed all of a sudden to be making. Twenty minutes later we parted at a bus stop.

❧

That day, seven years ago, was the last time I saw Gaunt. Life has changed since then, but I've been working on my next book the whole time. I still have a way to go. It's an ambitious one, I suppose.

Encouragement is important, and I often look at my copy of Gaunt's novel *Germ*, which arrived in the post a month after we met in the coffee shop. It has an inscription from the author. The date, my name, his name, and one other word: *Upward*. When I first saw that, the meaning was clear. Now it seems less so. I emailed Gaunt to thank him for the book, but there was no reply.

For a long time, I blamed myself for not having struck up a friendship. Now and then I felt I had defeated the whole purpose of writing *The Heights of Sleep*. The regret was useful, though, because it drove me on in the early stages of this new book. I liked to imagine that when it was finished it would redeem that failure. It would show beyond a doubt that I understood.

Gaunt dropped out of sight after *Germ* was published. He wasn't reviewing. Nothing fresh came up when I searched for his name. My editor, in one of the conversations we still occasionally had, told me she had heard he was working on a new project. I imagined him in a late surge, setting out on a new inward journey at an age when most would be content to rest on an honourable career. Then one day I saw an arts-and-culture item which said that the cult author J. S. Gaunt had died at the age of seventy-six after a short illness.

I could hardly claim to have known the man, but it did have an impact. We would never have another book. We would never have another inimitably Gauntian sentence. Whatever happened on this planet from now on would happen without him. For a while I stopped writing, the first shock turning into gloomy months in which I couldn't see the point. The woman with whom I had once argued over a literary festival was sympathetic, but I knew she thought it wouldn't be such a bad thing if this was the end of my attempt at a second book. It might be good news for us all. It's a pity she felt like that, and a pity I didn't try harder to change her mind.

But setting a project aside can produce new insights, and soon I was seeing things I hadn't noticed before. Unfinished as it was, the work in progress showed traces of a pattern or a shape that had yet to be revealed. I hadn't planned it, but there it was, lurking in the edges. One night I dreamed that the world was one infinite house, and woke up convinced that if I could finish my work I would grasp the secret that was hidden there. A form would resolve itself into existence, the figure that had been implied all along although it had nothing to do with what the story appeared to be about.

Since then, I carry on. Some days progress is good, others not. I've learned not to force it. When the work won't come, I walk around the city, not thinking about where I'm going. Not long ago I walked all day, and at the end of the afternoon found myself standing on an enclosed pedestrian bridge between a shopping centre and a multi-storey car park, watching the people in the street below. I stood for several minutes with my forehead close to the bronze-tinted glass, and then I saw my wife and daughter. They came out of an overground station and waited at the lights, hand in hand. They crossed the road and began to walk along the pavement, passing underneath me. I moved to the other side of the bridge to keep them in sight.

I watched them for as long as I could. I didn't know why I was so afraid of losing them in the crowd, or why I was filled with this unexpected joy, this certainty that everything had been worthwhile. My daughter was wearing a plastic rain-coat I hadn't seen before. My wife looked young. They were nowhere near home.

ANN QUIN

NUDE AND SEASCAPE

HER HEAD GREW out from the surrounding rocks, part of the grey pock-marked structure of the shore, that was probably why he felt no surprise. The body, admittedly, might not be in harmony or in tone, a little too pink, still it could be considered a good contrast. Hair mingling with seaweed floated in a pool of pus-like water. Dark hair crawled up the wrist, stiff fingers stretched out, as though in a last attempt to grasp an insect, flatten some sea-creature, or just to cover a small area of sand for reassurance. He noted the absence of a ring.

He lit a cigarette and glanced at the cliffs, austere white knights, ready to advance. Inhaling he quickly looked down. If he moved round, his back to the sea, then his shadow fell directly upon the body, and from a certain angle it looked almost beautiful. Definitely the pink fleshiness spoilt everything. He took his coat off, and gently covered the body up. Even then the head emerging from the grey gabardine was far from satisfactory. He struggled into the coat, the lining was damp, the cigarette went out, he had no more matches. He threw the cigarette away, watching it float, drift between the strands of hair, finally, like a boat, it bobbed up and down in the same place. He picked it up and threw it towards the incoming tide. A few gulls circled above, cat-calling, one swooped and tried to peck the woman's hair, he waved the bird off, it scornfully screeched into the wind. It began raining. He brought his hat well down, and pulled his collar up, looking round for a flat piece of dry rock to sit on. He felt distracted by the body that was such a separate thing from the fine formation of the head, and he could no longer look to his shadow for assistance in the matter of improvement. He would move the body further up.

He caught hold of the woman's shoulder, cold but how soft! He dragged her across the pebbles and rocks, soon he would have her in the right position, he looked round for a suitable place. Driftwood, pieces of iron, newspaper, saturated orange peel, broken bottles, this would never do for a background. If he could only have smoked, he would have solved the problem in no time. He stared at the body, it had become patterned by pebbles, the hip-bone jutted out, that also was covered with sand and small stones; at least the crude pink had been relieved. But he would have to find an entirely different setting.

Perhaps round the cliff there would be a clear expanse of sand, clean polished pebbles, a desert compared to the jungle he was now in. He curled his fingers into the armpits, feeling the razored hair, and recalled how he had never touched anyone there. About half way he rested, sliding his hands away from the body, so that the head lolled to one side. In such a position the body alone took on a certain eye-catching quality, fish-like in the way it curved, but it was unfinished.

The cliffs from a closer quarter looked less menacing, he could see a line of damp clay at the top, an ink stain that spread, or blood, even a hair line, anything, it didn't really matter, it was there in its reality, entirety, whatever he chose to identify it with. This time he would carry the body. The rain felt like pellets of earth on his back where the body did not cover him. He heard the waves, but did not feel the spray, he tasted salt in his dry mouth, and noticed his hands were speckled with blood. As he approached the cliff that was like a piece of cake cut out against the darkening sky, the weight on his back became heavier. He stepped over the rocks, and at one time slipped, the water splashed his trousers, sliding down, though he hardly noticed.

This side was clear, except in one place where there had been a landslide. However there was plenty of sand, and the pebbles were noticeable for their scarcity. As he lowered the body he was aware of the darkness that had enveloped everything. He sank down, everything, it seemed, had been wasted. Was it really too late? He glanced round, but the rain swept over the beach, even the cliffs could not be seen. He felt for the body as a blind person would, and wiped away the sand, pebbles and seaweed; smooth flesh, though still wet, under his groping hands. He would find shelter for the night, there must be a cave somewhere. Soon he came up against the cliff, and only then realised that he had left the body behind. He was filled with overwhelming sadness, as though separated from a loved one, his mistress, wife, mother, women he had loved, or never loved. He stumbled forward and fell. He crawled the rest of the way down, feeling the sand, like insects, creep into his shoes.

The tide was nearly in, he could hear the waves lashing the rocks nearby. Where was the body, perhaps already carried out? He came to the water's edge, turned right, feeling sure he must be near it by now. In his haste, he practically tripped over the body; clasping the head he could have cried out in relief. He dragged the body across the sand, running backwards, until he felt the cliff again, here he propped the body, and began searching for shelter. At last he found a place, not exactly a cave, but adequate enough for a night. He went back quickly, the rain spat on his face, the wind swept his hat off; his hands were cold, but his head was bathed in sweat. Catching hold of the woman's hair he pulled her into a corner between a breakwater and the cliff.

The morning light so dazzled him that he had to shield his eyes before he could see anything. The tide had receded, probably now on the turn, which indicated it was well past midday. How had he overslept at such a time as this? However it wouldn't take long to accomplish what he had set himself. He looked the body over critically, already with the objectivity of familiarity; it wasn't all that pink, not even fleshy, apart from a slightly swollen belly, not nearly as bad as he had thought at first.

He looked across the beach, taking in, or dismissing a space here, a slight angle there, where the shadow of the cliffs fell. Several times he scoured the beach, until finally he decided to move the body about a hundred yards up, where the sand was whiter, and there were no pebbles at all. He was about to pick the body up when he heard voices nearby. Automatically he fell on top of the woman, and pressed her face close. The voices came nearer, he held his breath, pulling himself completely over the body, and felt the cold brittle lips against his own. The voices died away, only when he could no longer hear them did he roll off, lying for a time panting beside the body, his head to one side. Rubbing his lips he struggled up. A few flies settled on his neck, one crawled into the corner of his eye; he picked the body up, and marched on, it was not far to go now.

He placed the body in a horizontal position, so that the head faced the sea, then he tried it at a right-angle. In fact every position he could think of; what was wrong, the place, the body, or merely himself? He looked round the beach once more, perhaps nearer where the rocks and stones had fallen.

This time he caught hold of the woman's legs, already feeling tired, he walked slowly. Against the landslide he found the body alone spoilt the effect, it was really only the head that was needed. He searched for his pocket-knife, it was a little rusty, which meant it would take some time. He caught the woman's hair and holding the head between his legs, he started to hack. He began, after a while, to feel slightly dizzy from bending his head too low, he let go, watching the woman's head fall back upon the sand. The sun was already half way across the sky, a bright burning hole. He went on, looking almost dispassionately at his unfinished work, think-ing that with the head half off the body already looked better. He wiped the knife's blade on his sleeve, and started cutting into the sinews of the neck, until the head was segregated. Triumphantly he held it up, laughing, and raised it towards the sun, as though that alone was the witness to his success. He carried the head, by the hair, into the middle of the beach, a golden patch of sand, and here he gently put it down, as he might a child, face upwards. But it refused to stay in this position, and began rolling away, until he stopped it with his foot. He picked it up, and then made a deep hole in the sand, for it to rest in. For the first time he noticed the eyes, green like sea-stones. He stepped back, it seemed too perfect, far too beautiful. The joy he had anticipated was rapidly replaced by disappointment. He began making a deeper hole, then he threw the head in, and pushed the heap of sand quickly over.

He walked back until he became aware of the headless body, the mouth slightly open, as though laughing. Now in a certain light and shade, in the corner, where he had left it, forgotten, the body looked better than it ever had before. As he approached he heard the voices again, this time much nearer. He looked at his clothes, his hands, they were covered with blood. He waded into the sea.

BEYOND DEAD

I AM BEYOND dead, far from life, having quit the safe-keeping of bones. I have no mass. I am no longer relevant, like a moment's spindrift, assuming structure where there may be none. It feels as though I have been here for days, maybe weeks, yet there are no days. Only interminable night. And no sleep and no dreams to break this terrible monotony. To embody and embolden ignorance, make ignorance incarnate, was clearly the intention but I had not expected this – this hermetic darkness. Where are others? Are there others? There must be. But for now I am alone. There is nothing here. Not even ground to move along. No points of reference. Everywhere about me, in every direction, is impenetrable starless night as though I am at the centre of a black void. All is nothing. Nothing is all there is. No features. No sound. I am neither hot nor cold. And there is no one and no thing here, wherever here is. Yet I exist, and have reason to think I do and therefore the best of all reasons. There will surely be others here too. I cannot expect to be unique. To see, hear and commune with through a flavour of physics specific to this new self, and quite beyond Newtonian observation, I suspect. Illogical to think otherwise. This is pure solipsism.

If I assume continuity and alignment I will learn what is

required, having retained planetary knowledge and memory. And what memories they are! Oh, that they had been erased, deleted from the sum of human experience! Except for my childhood years perhaps. Yet, since I have retained my reason I must put it to some use while I am racked on the torpor of inertia. If there are moments. I create them by sequential thinking. I can say a moment ago, I thought this way, and before that, another way. There is time in this non-place. I am and therefore there is time. Though no means to measure it, it would seem. The thought is already in the past and my next inference, whatever it will be, I will pluck from the future. My future. So I have a future. Of sort unknown. And yet these new moments can only be reactive, and reflective since nothing is happening here, in this infernal eternal night. What surprises me is, I am not elated at finding myself still extant in some form after death. Oh, I know I was known for my Deist beliefs and in public it is true I affirmed the existence of God and the immortality of the soul. But if I am honest (and now perhaps finally I can afford to be) in my heart of hearts the observations of my life only ever pointed to the absolute termination of it. No doubt such hypocrisy is not unique to me.

But certainly not this! Suspended in darkness like a dead fish at the bottom of a quarry lake. A stand-alone thinking mind with nothing stirring above or below me. Neither in front nor behind. Nor on any side. If I have sides. And I am not sure I do. Silence is ambient here. And yet . . . I have no fear. I do not understand why, but am grateful for it. To whom must I be grateful? Ah! That I do not know . . . yet. But I am content. I will wait. What else can I do? Extrapolate from my inertia? Make deductions about nothing? Deduce what from what? That eventually I will have the means to move about and join others? If there are others. And if there are may I not anticipate friendship, loyalty, love? Vengeance and hate too. Ah, this new thought grinds out fear. Creates it where before there was none. What if there is only hate and retribution? Then I must be in Hell. And yet without fear of it. But with fear of others. Those who might seek revenge. Oh, when will this overwhelming penumbra lift? Surely there will be a new topography when this cloying night lifts; perhaps mountains and rivers, sea, towns and cities, earth and fire? There is no hint of these yet.

When will this darkness end? When will someone make contact? Will someone make contact? Perhaps I am being tended in my absence. I strain to hear but there is nothing to hear. And nothing to see. And yet, I am largely content . . . for now, existing in this vacuum. I do not say – living. Though I must be living in some sense. All I can do is pass time in thought. Speculation about the state in which I find myself earned not one solitary word of response throughout the millennia man has existed. There was only ever faith, born of a terrifying fear of non-existence. The loss of self. The annihilation of personality no matter its arrogant sophistication. We called it faith but in fact it was only ever hope. A vain hope in something beyond the rot of flesh. But now, it seems to me (now I am beyond death) there is no evidence that faith or hope was ever required. Yet hope has been realised. It has become fact. So why no response? And why does mankind we have to live in ignorance? Why was I denied all knowledge of where and what I am now – existing in an afterlife, but little more than that.

I had no reason to anticipate this. And yet does it not

imply design, purpose, intention? Whose intention? And dare I suppose a who, since I am still me. Or he. As self-consumed as ever. Yes, I know it. I freely admit it. There is no shame in that. How else can it be now – here? But surely I can expect others to come soon. Will this dark silence never cease to deafen? With only myself for company in this all-consuming solitude. Shall I whistle to keep my spirits up? How can I? I have no lips to purse. And yet . . . Ah yes . . . there . . . I hear myself whistling. Can I hum? Shall I hum a tune? I'll hum the Marseillais . . . and there it is. Crisp and clear. Silence no more. I hear myself humming. It will pass the time. Let's see, what other tunes can I remember? At least I have memory for how could it be otherwise? Without memory I would not be me . . .

And now I am bored. Will no one in authority come? Some Tiresian figure perhaps, to explain what I must do, what is expected of me, if anything, what passes for the way of life here. Not King Louis I hope. He will certainly have it in for me. If reprisal is permitted here. Which it may be if this is Hell. Yet I do not feel I am in Hell. Not in Heaven either. Intuition does not seem to have forsaken me. The first question I will ask of whoever comes is, why one state of existence should succeed another? Why has my brief materiate span been supplanted by this solipsistic existence of the mind? And are there accounts to be settled for what I did on Earth; or did not do and should have? So many lives I signed away. Cutting them short for the greater good. Will that be justification enough? Will our religious teachers, in all their various vestments and rites, be proved correct after all? On other words, will I be judged as the clerics preached? How I despised their self-righteousness. Even if my continued existence has settled the question of survival once and for all, they did not know it. No one knew. It was only ever guess-work. Nothing more than that.

But wait! Am I deceived or is the darkness less dark? I have no eyes and yet . . . yes, this black cast appears to be breaking up. There is . . . yes, an up light. It pervades. Gradual but yes . . . I am sure of it: black is now shallow black. Increasingly so. At last! And now I see shapes in the far distance. On the edge of this diminishing penumbra. How do I see them if I have no eyes? And yet I do. In every direction. Amorphous shapes, though upright. Drifting. Like slow flotsam. Clusters. What they are? Demons, angels or spirits? Or simply the inhuman creatures of this wretched region.

And now for the first time I feel cold. A coldness which reaches into despair. My contentment falters. Suddenly I am uneasy. I do not like these strange forms. They have an aura of malevolence about them. This is cannot Paradise. But it may be Hell. Yet why am I in Hell? Did my good works count for nothing - the candles I burned down to guttering flames through solitary nights, drafting laws to protect the nation, championing the cause of slaves, thespians, defending Jews? The commissions and tribunals I sat on dispensing justice with the sword of law. Do they count for nothing? I have not asked for much in life. I have been frugal and moderate in my tastes. Lived a sober, God-fearing life. Yet am I still to fear God? Surely not like this! Confronted by these hideous beings. Their numbers swell. I must hold myself firm. Brace myself. At least it is no longer dark. Perhaps I will soon wish it was.

They are getting nearer now? Yes, I am sure of it. I can see them clearer. They bear the pallor of cerecloth. A sickly sweet smell rises from them. Violets perhaps. Sharp. Fierce. Unpleasant. And yet though they grow taller the nearer they get, they are still unrecognisable. Were they once human? There are hundreds of them! Some hang back. Others drift ever nearer. Drifting because they have no limbs. Neither arms, nor heads yet somehow humanoid. The nearest approach like headless torsos tightly wrapped in bandages. Ah, I fear them! It's as though they accuse me of some terrible crime. Why will no one protect me?

Wait. Those nearest have stopped within the range of stones if I had stones to throw at them; paused as if waiting for the others to catch up. Nothing good can come of this. I am in fear of my . . . life? Existence then. My very being. They must be demons. Malevolent sprites. The Devil's henchmen. And still their numbers multiply. Rank upon rank. A silent claque waiting for the curtain to fall. Or a trapdoor to open. Or a blade to drop. I am oppressed on all sides by violent denunciation and yet nothing is said. At least I hear nothing. And all the while the choking stench of violets . . . and now a new aroma: acrid, metallic and yet not of metal as one of these beings draws close. Approaches relentlessly. So close I see its limbs pinioned by rope. And a stale crimson stain where a head should be. The vile thing is upon me! too close! Too close! It will be as one with me! And I have no means of evading it! Its stench of blood! I cannot bear it . . . Go away! No! No! . . .

It's gone! Where did it go? Did I absorb it! Yes. I feel its weight! As though its appalling energy is at one with mine, crushing my spirit! We are commingled! How terrible! And now another comes at me too. Impossibly close. I feel its fear, its despair, its anger . . . We merge! How terrible! And now it's gone. At a point of symbiosis, when we have coalesced! The thing, whatever it is, is inside me. Added its energy to the other within my being. And I feel their sorrow. It overwhelms me. And now others draw close, following quickly. From every direction. Somehow I absorb their shrouds and in their passing into me I know their melancholy. I have no choice but to suffer their terror. I have no eyes to close, no mouth to scream, no legs to run. And still they come at me! In their hundreds. I am in Hell! I

Yet why must I suffer this? I kept the commandments. I lived a simple celibate life, lodging in a carpenter's house when I could have lived in palaces. I refused to exploit my public office for gain. I made do with my miserable deputy's pay. I killed no one . . . though it's true I signed away hundreds to die, but always for the good of the state. Always in good faith. And their deaths were quick and painless. I stole from no one. I never missed mass unless I was too busy with the nation's affairs. I coveted no one's wife. Honoured my parents while they lived. Gave to the poor. Championed the disadvantaged against the privileged few. I stood out for equality, fraternity and liberty. What more could I have done? Does all this count for nothing? Is no one listening to me? Many died, yes, but many more were saved. Terror was necessary. A swift severe justice. An emanation of virtue. Conscription and the end to the civil war depended on it! The spectacle of public execution was a necessity. The people had to see justice done. They had to know fear. Surely that was reasonable. Ah, mercy! Still they come these hideous templates of death! Is there no end to them?

Didn't I suffer ignominy and terror myself? Exposed to the ungrateful herd whose lives I had striven to better.

Wigless. Humiliated high on the scaffold. My hands trussed behind me. Already in pain from the gunshot wound to my jaw. How I screamed in agony as the executioner removed the bandage to clear my neck for the blade! Was that not enough redress for any wrong I may be deemed to have committed? I do not deserve this. These horrors!

On, on they come! Blood soaked necks torsos. I can do nothing about them. Will this go on for all eternity? There are as many as ever. Surely there will be mercy! Mercy, I say. Have mercy on me! God have mercy on me . . . !

They've gone! Gone! All of them! Gone! And gone from within me too. I am suddenly no longer oppressed. In the instant I begged for mercy. Oh, what joy! What relief to be surrounded by the nothingness again. Thank you, God! God be praised for his blessed mercy? . . . But what mercy did I show? And why does Lucille Desmoulins surface to the forefront of my mind? Camille's, my boyhood friend's wife. Her mother pleaded for her but I did not answer her letter. France must always come before loyalty to friends . . . That must be right, but yes – I could have shown her mercy. I could have made her an exception. Perhaps I should have. Is that why I suffered these vile torments which . . . ?

Oh, my dear God! Not again! Please, not again! Those monstrous shapes are back, regathering in the distance. Multiplying. Drawing near again. More than ever. An army massing as before. Relentlessly they descend on me. Is there no end to their haunting? Have I destroyed mercy so that there is none for me?

TOXIC

FINALLY, THEY DROPPED all the pretences and produced a drug that had no benefits, just side effects. Carlos
told me about it. It's the Chinese. They cook up some new
snortable chemical every day, give it a catchy name and sell it
to twelve-year-olds on the internet. Don't ask me why twelve-
year-olds are chopping up lines when they should be running
around in the sunshine, or doing their homework, or at least
learning basic HTML, so they can get a job someday. I don't
know why things have got so bad. I spend a lot of time wishing
that they hadn't. But that's not going to stop these kids from
getting their rocks off. Nothing will, Carlos says.

I don't know where he gets all this information from. One
of those chat rooms he's always on, or Reddit, or something.
His mother thinks he spends far too much time in his room,
eyes glued to screen. I hate to sound like a bore, but I have to
agree with her. Mostly because she always gives me food and
I'm a little bit in love with her, but also because Carlos's room
itself has gotten so depressing in the past few years. Piles of
horror novels everywhere. Old Coke cans he's been using as
ashtrays. Dirty tube socks peeping out a bin, gone that special
shade of burnt yellow on the sole that the eBay perverts pay
big bucks for. He keeps the blackout blinds drawn most of

the time, which is why he's so pale, I suppose. I don't think he eats too well either. He always had acne, as a teenager. It's still bad.

Anyway, he told me that the twelve-year-olds . . . once the shit has finally passed through their systems . . . they post reviews. These seedy darknet sites, where you can buy drugs and guns, scroll through whores and assassins and weird sex toys and government secrets and all kinds of crap like that . . . they actually have little boxes at the end of the page for comments. It's true. The twelve-year-olds are really into it. Exclamation marks and emojis all over the place. The Chinese collect all the reviews, translate them, and take all the constructive comments into account, before rustling up a new strain of nose candy – an improved formulation – and selling it back to the twelve-year-olds, who waste no time in hoovering it up.

He told me all about it while we were waiting for his mother to fix dinner, drinking a big bottle of Diet Coke, playing video games. I was letting him win, because I felt bad for him. It wasn't the first such story he'd told me, but I got a kick out of the idea. Apparently after the Chinese had completed the process – of making drugs, selling to children, collecting feedback, making more drugs – three or four thousand times, they began to see some weird trends in the reviews. If they made a drug that was a little less potent, a little less euphoric, but cut it up with random noxious powders that were kicking round the lab – resulting in who knows what kind of nasty feelings the day after – none of the kids seemed to mind that much. But when they came up with something that completely eliminated the comedown, everyone hated it. Turns out, the headaches and the shakes were the most important part of the whole experience. Without them, said the twelve-year-olds, it felt like they hadn't even taken a drug at all. Then the Chinese figured they could just save some money by just sending out the poisonous stuff. No need for a buzz, just the blues. That's how they came up with this latest one.

Obviously, we had to try it. As soon as Carlos finished telling me about it, I knew it, and he knew it. We even made eye contact, for a brief moment. This is not something that Carlos and I generally like to do. He is hideously ugly – the spots don't help at all – but his eyes are blue, the kind of clear, cold blue that can look either sparkling or wolfish, depending on the situation. When he's excited, as he was then, it's like another person entirely is staring out from behind it all, the greasy skin, the lank fringe, the monobrow. It's pretty intense.

I was like, okay, so where do we get a gram or two? And he said he didn't know exactly, but we should have a look. And we spent the next few hours going through the weird back-alleys of the internet, sniggering at the porn pop-ups, flicking through the knife and bomb catalogues, scrolling down, down, down, through the endless reviews of substances like 'HXM-PAL-1' and 'GIG-L-S' and also a bunch of stuff in Chinese that we naturally couldn't read or understand. We didn't really find anything, and Carlos looked annoyed and then his mother popped her head round the door and said she had a pizza for us, so we ate that and I imagined that she was feeding me every slice by hand, and her fingernails were glossy and red, like pepperoni.

A couple of days later, after going through all his shady online contacts trying to find this mystery substance, Carlos finally found someone who was willing to sell us some of his stash. Actually, it was the guy's little brother's stash, I think.

The little brother was a twelve-year-old – really we should have thought of that earlier, I suppose. Carlos said he was going to go and meet with him, which meant he had to leave his room, and go outside, and get a bus. Which was a big deal. He's sort of a remedial case, I think. But he did it. He was pretty pleased with himself when he called me that day, with the big news: we had scored.

We decided to do it straight away, that night, but in my room this time. The reason being that, though I wouldn't change a single perfect thing about Carlos's mother, she does tend to burst through doorways unannounced. This is only a nice surprise if you're sitting playing video games and getting hungry, not if you're sitting on the floor, shovelling shit up your nose. My mother is much more respectful of my privacy. And my room is a more of a congenial environment. I have alphabetised my CD collection. I store my novels – spanning a range of interesting and diverse genres – not on the floor but in the bookcase, where they are meant to live. I fold up all my clothes and put them in the drawers. No tube socks anywhere. None.

I didn't have a mirrored tray, or a silver straw or any of that other paraphernalia that you see people doing drugs with, in movies, surrounded by beautiful women and leather chairs and guys with chains round their necks, and guns. So we just cut up the powder ourselves with an expired young saver card on this big book I've never read. An ill-judged Christmas present. Incredible modern homes. Something like that. We didn't really have any other plans that day, so we thought we'd do it all in one sitting. Carlos put on this YouTube video that, he said, all the twelve-year-olds like to trip out to, and then got going with the snorting. It was quite a dense powder, and after four or five lines both of my nostrils were completely blocked, so then we dabbed it into our gums until the taste became unbearable, then got my mother to bring us up some tea (we hid the drug-covered book under the bed when she came in to deliver it) and sprinkled the rest in that, and drank it. Then we sat in silence, watching the video.

As expected, I didn't really feel any different from normal, apart from the blocked nose and the burning gums, and the soapy sensation in my mouth. The video was a collage of lots of other videos, showing clouds rolling over landscapes, a sky-diver falling through the air, wind rustling leaves, ripples on water, that kind of thing. In its own way, it was beautiful, and, though we didn't speak much, the silence between myself and Carlos felt peaceful. We watched the video intently until it was dark outside and then Carlos had to go home for dinner, which was pizza again. He asked me if I wanted to come over for a slice but I said I don't know and he left.

I felt fine the next day, which was a huge letdown. Maybe, I thought, we'd got the wrong thing. I called Carlos. He said he felt OK too. He wasn't happy about it. That was that. I'd taken the morning off work, thinking I might need to sleep in and shake off the after effects. But I didn't have anything else to do, so I went in anyway. My job is pretty easy, mostly just answering the phone. It's the kind of job that will definitely be performed by some sort of robot or algorithm in the near future, which is why I'm glad I learned HTML, and why I worry sometimes about all the twelve-year-olds. Actually, I'm also responsible for restocking the paper on the printer, and getting the meeting rooms ready the way all the professional types there like them. So maybe it will take a while for me to become obsolete. I like the idea of sticking around, for a while at least.

What I hadn't thought through at this point is that the most truly evil comedowns have an incubation period of at least 24 hours. I guess the Chinese must have looked into this phenomenon and coded their wonder-dust accordingly, because it was four whole days before I began to feel a little bit down in the dumps, then another two before the headache kicked in, and then another before the vomiting and dizziness got so bad that I had to call into work and explain the situation. I felt too terrible to lie, so I told them all about the Chinese and the twelve-year-olds, and how there's nothing we can do to stop them living like this. It's scary, I told them, because these little guys are going to be adults some day, and they'll be coming into the office and doing our jobs - until the robots do them - and this is what it will be like, everyone phoning in sick, having this same same conversation. Work was surprisingly sympathetic.

But back to the comedown. It was a real masterpiece, as far as comedowns are concerned. It felt like the earth had opened up. I spent most of it in my room, not a huge change in the order of business because, let's be honest, I spend a lot of time in my room too. But all of a sudden all the things in it, which I had previously admired and tended to throughout my life filled me with a gut-wrenching feeling of disgust and shame. Here was the bed in which my body had revolted against the ageing process, protesting the unfairness of it all with toxic farts and yellow sweat and surprise night-time emissions. Here were the walls I had painted blue, ten years ago, now faded to a dull, corpse-like grey, very upsetting. Here was a bunch of posters - all of stuff that I used to like but was now too old for – that I had always been too lazy to take down. There was the computer, already getting on, designed to be replaced, just sitting there and sucking up useless information, filling itself to bursting. The more I looked at it all, the more I was unable to focus on the individual elements. I could only see, or rather imagine, how it would all look many thousands of years in the future, a pond of gloopy grey mulch through which my bones would drift unseen, the ooze sucking at them noisily. Then I got black spots at the corners of my eyes. My tongue swelled up so I could barely breathe. I started sweating, and my joints hurt, and all over my skin, anywhere I had hair, it felt like ants crawling and rats nibbling and I couldn't stop itching, even when all these places were red and and my fingernails were black with my ooze and sweat and blood.

On the phone, Carlos didn't sound so hot either.

My mother drove me round.

Carlos and I sat in his bedroom, shit all over the place as usual, and watched the YouTube video again, though the mountains laughed at us and the clouds and the streaming sky billowed overhead like some giant clenched fist getting ready to fly at our faces. At some point, I had an attack of vertigo and grabbed on to him, just to have something to hold on to. And then we sat with our arms around each other, glad of the warmth, and the touch, and the sound of each other's heartbeats. It was then that he looked at me again, his forehead touched to mine, and his eyes were crazily blue, so blue that they burned, and he looked at me, too, like I was on fire, and disintegrating in front of him, and his mouth was a wide O that kept opening and shutting and his eyes were watering. It felt a little weird to be that physically close, by which I mean that I'm not sure whether I was comforted or disgusted as I breathed in his stale Diet Coke breath and unwashed armpits, and clutched desperately at his scrawny shoulders and back, and bit my lip, and sighed. He is more than usually sweaty. There were wet patches everywhere.

So that was quite the ride. You have to admire the Chinese for their workmanship.

It took me a while to feel normal, but after a full week of lying in bed with the YouTube video, crying into my pillow, the vomiting had subsided and my chinos and shirts and alphabetised novels didn't bum me out so much and ultimately I felt OK enough to go back to my regular life, to go into work and put the washing out for my mother to pick up and do and to once again imagine the possibility of a future without the slime and the doom and all that stuff. Most of the time, now, it feels like the rift in the ground has closed up, and that everything is back to what it always should have been. But then again, things keep changing, so it also doesn't feel like that at all, and I do wonder.

Carlos's next thing is that he's moving away. I don't entirely believe him, but it seems to be happening. He says he has got himself a job, which is weird because he has never worked before - nor expressed any wish to. And, if I'm being completely honest, I'd have to say he doesn't have any skills, aside from drinking Diet Coke, and playing computer games, badly. I wouldn't hire him. No way. But it's something to do with coding, he says, working with some guy he met on a chat room. They are going to pay him a lot of money, but he can't do it from here, he has to go, somewhere else. Straight away. The whole thing is so sudden that I didn't even feel all that sad, yesterday, as we began to pack all his crap into ugly boxes, and then gave up and sat playing video games and drinking Diet Coke. Didn't care much when his incredible mother came up to hand me the pizza and bent down low, so low, to blow me a kiss and give me a squeeze and a hug, as if we were saying goodbye then and there, rather than in a week's time, when he says he's going. I wonder if I will miss him a lot. His acne seems to be clearing up. My skin is terrible.

Also, weirdly, they have found the Chinese. Or at least, some of them. I mean, I assume they're Chinese. They don't all look it, entirely. It turns out they're not running their business entirely from some crazy meth lab in the far east. Actually, they are local. All this time, they've been working out of one of the supposedly empty flats across the road, which I suppose explains why they were able to adapt so quickly to the market. I can actually see the flat from my room, when I roll up the blinds. It looks normal from the outside: whitewashed walls, slightly overgrown front garden, big 'For Sale' sign hovering above the gate. The window's blocked out, but that's not unusual, round here. Carlos told me they knocked through the ceiling on the ground floor, to create a giant atrium in which they could install their vats and UV lights, and cook up all kinds of horrible garbage for the local prep schools. I saw them being marched out the building, by the police into a van, smoke-blind. They could have been anyone.

Carlos is talking to people on the internet, and keeping me updated about it. About them. He says that they were all taken to a small, grey room, not much bigger than his room, though presumably much cleaner, and subjected to intense questioning, by which he means beaten up pretty badly. While this happened every twelve-year-old in town, Carlos says, was naturally trying to flush his or her stash down the toilet, or throw it in the river, or just get rid of it any way he or she could, in case someone's parents found out. Because of this, Carlos says, now all the shit is in the water supply, and it's highly possible that, in a couple of weeks, the entire borough could be locked up in their rooms, watching the YouTube video, their teeth firmly clamped around their fists, their toes curled and their fingers splayed. I'm a little worried about the consequences of it all.

But Carlos thinks the Chinese, and the twelve-year-olds, are going to get away with it. When the police went in there, he says, and emptied those vats and analysed all those thousands of tight-packed cubes of powder, lying in wait, ready to be bought and cut up and sucked viciously down tiny, perfect, pre-teen nostrils, they couldn't find anything incriminating about it. The substance they were making had no discernable purpose. Not a stimulant, narcotic, analgesic, euphoric, psychedelic, anything. No side effects either. If someone had seen fit to use it recreationally, Carlos says, they would have experienced nothing at all. No sudden release of dopamine, no eventual crushing melancholy. It would simply enter the bloodstream without incident and gently dissipate. Like the tiny bubbles that float upwards in a glass of Diet Coke, and burst on the surface. Or like those thin white lines that planes leave zigzagging across the sky, on their way to elsewhere. Doing it would have been like snorting a haiku, getting high on a riddle. We must have taken something else.

A HAIR CLASP

WE WENT SWIMMING, my daughter and I. She was twenty and a good swimmer. I didn't need to keep an eye on her. I read on the beach while she went into the sea. From time to time, I lifted my eyes from my book and looked at her. She would smile and raise an arm, as if in greeting. Or perhaps she wanted to say, 'Look at me,' as children often do, seeking recognition even when they are past their childhood. The last time I saw her, the waves had grown and the choppy sea tossed her around playfully. One moment she was hidden under the foamy whiteness, another moment she was riding the crest of the waves, shimmering against the glistening surface of the water. I smiled and thought how much I loved her. This happy young woman. I wanted to shout how lovely she looked, but there was no point as my voice would have been lost in the crushing power of the sea. So I greeted her with my hand up in the air and went back to my reading. The next time I looked up, I couldn't see her. I saw other swimmers, a dozen of them, enjoying the waves. I wanted to see her smiling and communicating her pleasure to me so I climbed a bridge next to where they were swimming. I still couldn't spot her. A thought crossed my mind that she may have drowned. I have always been a worrier but sometimes your worst fears come true. I looked harder, I moved around the bridge but I still couldn't see her. My chest tightened with fear. Was this really happening? Then I noticed a beautiful hair clasp, an antique piece that someone must have left there or, more likely, lost. The piece was lying on top of a stone pillar that formed part of the banister of the bridge. Cupping it in the palm of my hand, I caressed the pearly section held by its silver frame. The intricacy of its craft and the smoothness of the object charmed me. As I turned it around, sunshine played hide and seek on its surface. I would have loved to have it but the find was too valuable not to report. But something told me that I had the right to keep it. I clutched it firmly and walked home alone. I will be careful never to lose it.

REALITY

WHEN IONA WOKE up in the house she knew where she was straight away, and she knew she was alone. There was none of that blurry intermediate state of semi-consciousness that people usually get when they're in an unfamiliar place. Everything about the bed, the clean low modern furniture, the white painted walls, the angled light coming in through the edges of the blackout blinds – it was all crisp and distinct. She stretched and yawned and put her feet on the bare but warm floor. She was wearing her second-best sleeping shorts and some long-forgotten ex's heavily faded Ramones T-shirt. It was a low bed, the kind that older people find it hard to straighten up from. But Iona was not old. Her mouth tasted fresh. She couldn't smell her own breath, nobody can, but she could tell that if she were able to, it would smell sweet. The bathroom was en suite. She padded across to it and surveyed the unbranded but obviously fancy modern toiletries. Fine. She did what she had to do to be ready for the day. She checked herself out in the mirror. Good: as often when she'd just woken up, she had perfect bedhead. It was known to be one of her best looks.

The next question was: how to fill the day. What next? The others would be arriving before too long, maybe later the same day, maybe over the subsequent days, who knew?

But soon. So this was her chance to have a good look around and explore the villa and mark her territory. Not literally, obviously. But a chance to get a feel for the place and to make a good impression. She was very aware of being watched the whole time – that was the entire point of this place, that you were watched the whole time, you are not just on show, you are the show – and that this was a chance to occupy all the space. For today, and maybe for today only, she was the sole and only and exclusive star. It was all about her. Well, OK then. She would be the star. Eyes to me!

The fitted cupboard was full of her clothes, except they seemed a bit cleaner, a bit newer. It was clever how they'd managed to arrange that. She opened it and studied it and performed complex calculations about how to play this, about what the audience would want and how to give it to them while acting as if she wasn't thinking about them and their reactions. Act natural – always a tricky one. First thing, freshly out of bed and on her own: the call was probably for sexy casual, but not too casual and the sexy part mustn't seem calculating. Also, the clock was ticking, she realised as she stood in front of the short wall of clothes. If she spent twenty minutes here and then came out looking like she'd just thrown some stuff on, the extended deliberation would contradict the intended effect. She wasn't stupid. OK so it was Lululemon yoga bottoms, the same T-shirt she already had on, and flip-flops.

She hit the switch controlling the blinds. They slid silently up and light flooded into her bedroom. She would look amazing, dazzling, filmed from behind, she knew: a blazing angel. Looking out, she found that she was on the first floor. Outside was a well-kept Mediterranean garden with gravel paths weaving between flowerbeds, with a hedge about a hundred metres away, and nothing visible beyond. They must be in a high place, not overlooked. There would be a pool, Iona felt sure. It was a compound. She could see no way in or out. So perhaps this was the back of the house.

Iona headed out into the stairwell for a bit of an explore. This upper floor of the villa had six rooms leading to a gallery, with stairs running down one side and a skylight above and walls painted white. It was very bright. She knew without looking that the other rooms would be bedrooms, and that this meant there would be six of them in the villa. Three girls and three boys. She couldn't see any cameras or mikes so whatever they did with them must be very very clever, super-clever, because she was certain she was being watched. Her consciousness was – had to be – double at all times: what she was doing, and what impression she would make by doing it. That was fine by Iona: she was used to it, she knew how it worked. She knew the rules of seeming. In accordance with them, she went and tapped briefly on the door of the room next to hers, waited a few seconds, and nudged the door open. As she'd expected, everything about the room was identical to hers. She didn't bother checking the other rooms, not yet. There was no shortage of time.

Downstairs Iona found a hallway that opened out under the gallery and gave direct access to a huge sitting room stuffed with beanbags, a TV room, what must be intended as a boys' room with game consoles and a pool table, a lovely big kitchen with a breakfast bar and dining table. Another huge room opened straight out to the – she'd been right – huge bright blue-green swimming pool, where there were six sun-loungers laid out under umbrellas on one side, six laid out in the sun on the other side, and a pool house at the far end. It looked like, indeed was, a picture-perfect holiday pool. She went out, dipped a hand in the warm water, walked around, felt the colossal fluffy towels in the pool room.

All this time Iona was thinking hard. She wouldn't be on her own for ever. No one would want to watch that. Nobody would pay to watch that! People might be interested in what she did with herself when she was by herself but they wouldn't be interested for long, so it wouldn't be more than a day at most. She must think of it as one day at a time. She must look composed, sexy, self-contained; mustn't look needy and impatient for the others to arrive; must look like someone who can look after herself. While taking care at all times to act natural. What that meant in the short term was that she should make some breakfast. She hadn't checked that the kitchen was stocked, but it must be - it would make no sense for it not to be.

She flip-flopped round the edge of the pool, crossed the room that led from the pool, crossed the hallway to the kitchen, pushed the swing door open, and almost died of a heart attack. A dark-haired woman was bending down and looking into the fridge. Iona's scream made the woman startle and she hopped up and shrieked too, making a dissonant off-beat one-two of female distress. The woman put her hand on her chest and took a breath.

'Jesus! I'm sorry,' Iona said. 'You startled me. I thought I was on my own. I'm Iona.'

'Nousche,' said the woman, who had the trace of an accent - French? Italian? That must be her name: Nousche. She was wearing a light, filmy top and clinging shorts. These looked carefully calculated in a sexy Eurominx style while also being fully deniable, as something she had just flung on in the morning without a second thought. Nousche's dark hair curled round her face, a very sophisticated bob cut. Iona couldn't tell why but she had been sure the next person in the villa would be a man. That was just how shows like this worked – girl-boy, girl-boy. Evidently that was wrong. If it was going to be a girl, though, this kind of girl was perfect: dark where Iona was blonde, petite where Iona was tall, classy-foreign where Iona was relatable-native. Maybe it would be all girls, carefully calibrated to be different, like a manufactured pop group. 'I saw you down by the pool,' Nousche went on. 'I was just coming out to say hello but I wanted to see if there was anything to eat first, I'm starving.'

'Me too!' Iona said, though it wasn't strictly true: she'd been too hyped and energised by the strangeness of it all to think about food. But it would make the wrong impression if she seemed like the kind of girl who was too up herself, too interested in being skinny, to admit she needed to eat. The calculations she was making about first impressions were all changed by the arrival of the second girl. She wasn't creating an image of how she behaved when she was on her own, but giving a sense of what she was like to interact with. Very different. Now it was time for Operation Nice. Well, that was no problem. Iona knew how to do nice.

'What is there?' she said, bouncing over towards the cooking area. She noticed that the acoustics of the kitchen, indeed of the whole villa, were hard and flat – no soft surfaces, nothing to absorb noise.

'Everything,' Nousche said, opening the fridge wider. Something about the way she flung the door open – or pretended to fling the door open, because you can't really fling a fridge door open, not without breaking it - made Iona see that she had a feel for drama; Nousche was one to watch. Good to know. Iona, playing along, peered into the fridge. It was indeed very well stocked, which was a good sign because it meant the others were coming and were probably coming pretty soon.

'I could make us a frittata?' Nousche said. Damn, thought Iona. So Euroskank gets to be the practical caring helpful one, while also avoiding carbs.

'Super!' said Iona. 'You know what, while you do, I'll just check the other rooms, because if you're here and I didn't realise, maybe some other people are here too, you know, and we can ask them down?' This would serve the dual purpose of making her look caring and thoughtful too, while also getting her out of Nousche's blast area for a bit so she could formulate a plan. It was always easy for an observer to pick up on overt bitchiness, snark, eye-rolling, and you didn't need to counter it, because the cameras and mikes countered it for you. But this was much more subtle. Nobody would have seen anything yet. They wouldn't know what was happening.

'Unless they need a lie-in?' said Nousche, counter-thought-fulling. Oh, OK bitch, so this is going to be war.

'Well, I'm sure your frittatas are delicious, it would be a pity if anyone missed them!'

Nousche did a weird thing closing her eyes and raising one shoulder. It seemed to mean something along the lines of: oh all right then, if you insist on flattering me so, please by all means go ahead. Iona went back to the main staircase and started heading up. Part of her wanted to change clothes, to signal to herself that the game was different; but that made no sense. In fact it would just look a bit mad: girl meets other girl in villa, changes outfit. No, Lululemon had got her into this, and Lululemon would have to get her out. She got to the top of the stairs and went past the door she had already checked to the one after it – and just as she was reaching for the handle, it opened from the inside and a man stepped out. Iona didn't give a full scream as she had when startled by Nousche, but she did emit a squeak. The man had curly red hair, lots of it, and was of medium height and compactly built, a fact it was simple for Iona to verify because he was naked from the waist up. A gym bunny, it was easy to see. He was carrying a towel in his left hand, and now flung it across his shoulder to cover himself partly, like an impromptu toga.

'Whoa,' he said. Semi-posh accent, a bit like Iona's own. 'I thought I was alone. Harry.' He held out his hand.

'Iona,' said Iona. 'I thought the same thing. But you're the third. And maybe there are more, I haven't checked. Nousche is downstairs, making omelettes. No, frittatas.' This was, Iona thought, so much better. While Harry wasn't her type – nothing personal, she could see he was attractive, just not for her – there was no denying that this was much more like it. Balance and order had been restored to the cosmos. It would surely be half boys and half girls now, anything else would make no sense. On this terrain, she was sure she could prevail.

'What's a frittata?' said Harry.

'It's an omelette that's gone wrong on purpose.'

'Cool,' said Harry. 'I mean, I'm allergic to eggs, but still, you know, cool.'

In that moment, Iona felt that she loved him very much.

Harry gestured back towards his room. 'I'll just, you know, clothes,' he said.

'Absolutely!' Iona said.

So they had breakfast together. Iona ate just enough of Nousche's frittata to show she was a good sport but left just enough to show that it wasn't particularly good. Nousche did an I'm-French, I-eat-everything-and-never-put-on-an-ounce thing. Iona (caring, practical Iona) made Harry a bacon sandwich. They chatted about this and that, but mainly about when the others would arrive and who they would be and what they would be like. It went unstated that they would be attractive young people, because, well, it was obvious that that was the whole point. They talked a bit about what they did before. Harry was a model. Nousche was a 'gallerist', whatever that was. Iona thought about asking her but her instinct was that the query might not come out right - might sound like an attack, which was problematic, because of course that's exactly what it was. So she would save that for later when the lie of the land was more clear. Iona told them she was an actress, because if she said she was an actress slash model slash influencer ('classic triple threat', according to her agent) that would make two models out of three and would thereby hand Nousche an advantage.

Just as they were finishing breakfast, Eli walked into the room. Iona had screamed when she saw Nousche and squeaked when she saw Harry, but honestly, when she saw Eli, she almost fainted. He was so far past handsome it was like they needed some other whole vocabulary for it. He had long black hair which was at risk of being cut by his cheekbones, dark brown eyes, and was wearing a white linen shirt which did an exceptionally bad job of hiding just how ripped he was. Best of all, he carried himself as if he wasn't aware of any of this - just, you know, moving through his day, nothing to see here, it's normal for girls to cross their legs and become unable to speak, I'm sure that was what it was like before I came in. Iona wasn't sure how they got through the introductions and all that: all she could hear was the blood in her head. Crucially, she could tell he preferred her to Nousche. Nothing specific, she could just tell. Ha!

Eli was a photographer. Not a fashion photographer, the other sort. You know, warzones. Of course he was.

After breakfast they went for a swim and to hang out by the pool for a while. Iona was a very good swimmer – a very elegant swimmer – and had been looking forward to this being a point of difference, but it annoyingly turned out that Nousche was a star swimmer too. Still, Iona knew she was on strong ground with the impression she made in a bikini. She did a few laps, then got out and dried off in the sun on a lounger next to Harry. He was lying on his front to tan his back, but when she lay down he turned over and flipped his Ray-bans down over his eyes.

'Dude, gonna be honest, I could get used to this,' he said.

It was too bright to open her eyes and too warm, in the direct sun, to think or speak clearly, so Iona made an affirmative grunty noise. The problem of how to fill the day, this first day, had been solved by the new arrivals, each coming as a pleasant surprise, unexpected to her and no doubt to the viewers too. Or maybe the viewers already knew? No – no point thinking about that too much. The trick for dealing with the viewers would be to have them in the back of your mind but not the front of it. If you were constantly trying to second-guess them, to see what they were seeing and finesse or manipulate it, you would go mad. And also you would be obvious about it and that would spoil the whole thing. You can't be seen thinking about how you seem – fatal.

Still, it was tempting to wonder if they knew what was coming, who would be next through the pool-patio room, who would be next to do the self-conscious walk, the self-conscious wave, to reach up and flick their long black hair out of their dark brown eyes, to pull off their white linen top and . . .

A tall black man came out from the house and stood in the doorway by the pool squinting over at them with his hand held up to shield his eyes from the sun. He was wearing a grey T-shirt and black sweatpants and he too was super-ripped, even more so than Eli and Harry, which Iona wouldn't have thought was possible, but this guy was something else, it was like his muscles had muscles. Also he seriously knew how to make an entrance. He did a slow look around and then walked over towards them. Nousche stopped swimming, came to the side of the pool and draped her arms over it, the skank. He went towards her, crouched down on his haunches, held out his hand and said:

'Liam.'

Nousche held out her hand in an unbelievably pretentious way, wrist up, palm drooping down, like she was the fucking queen or something. She said her name. Liam did a squinty smile and – this too was unbelievable and was all Nousche's fault – briefly bowed his head down and kissed her hand. Iona felt she might throw up in her mouth. Liam straightened up, not without a lingering flirty smoulder towards Nousche, and came over to Iona. Get up, don't get up? But if Nousche had done an I'm-a-duchess number the thing to do was go the other way. Iona hopped up off her lounger and walked towards Liam to introduce herself. Harry, nice manners, got up too. Harry was closer to Liam than she was so they greeted each other first, Liam offering a fist bump and a 'hey man' that couldn't be more precisely calibrated to be Harry's shtick. This new guy was a very quick reader of people. He came over to Iona and said hello and then, genius move for people-pleasing people-person, I'm super-pretty-but-I'm-so-friendly-you-almost-forget-except-not-really Iona, came in for a quick unsexy people-person's hug.

'Well, this is weird,' Liam said. They all agreed it was weird. 'Is everybody here?'

'I don't think so,' said Iona. 'Six bedrooms. Five of us so far. Three boys. So I'm guessing another girl? But I don't know any more than you do.'

'I doubt that's often true,' said Liam, giving her a private smile. Iona knew enough about players to know how it works: you flatter the clever ones for being pretty and the pretty ones for being clever. And yet she still felt a complimented glow. Would it be so bad if it stayed at five in the villa, three boys and two girls? Would that be so very wrong?

'I wonder when it'll start,' said Harry. 'You know, tasks, whatever it is.' He flexed his shoulders, thinking about tasks.

'Me too,' Iona said. 'What did you do, what do you do, out there?' she asked Liam, trying to guess: athlete? Not another actor, he was the wrong kind of vain.

'Money,' said Liam, with a smile. 'I do money stuff.' That meant banking or finance or something, and don't bother your pretty little etc. Nousche had kept swimming, but she must have realised she was being left out of the chat, so she got out of the pool, wrapped a towel around her head and came over.

'We're just talking about when it will all start,' said Iona, being the friendly one, because she could, in the patterns that she could sense developing, sense that that would work for her. 'You know—'

But Nousche knew what she meant. She was nodding vigorously.

'Tout à fait,' she said. 'I was wondering—' and then she was interrupted by a loud female voice coming from the pool patio.

'Wahey!' it said. 'Room for a small one?' A tall strong-looking girl in a black tracksuit and baseball cap came bouncing, no other word for it, out of the villa and crossed to the pool. Iona instantly thought: here comes the noisy one, the extrovert, the catalyst. The new arrival came over to where they were standing and said:

'Oi oi! I'm Lara but everyone calls me Laz.' They introduced themselves in turn and, in turn, Lara/Laz came in for a full hug and double-cheek kiss, including with the still pretty damp Nousche, whose expression was that of a person having second thoughts.

'Cor, you're soaking!' said Laz. 'Mind you, I am too now. I should tell you, I'm mainly straight, but I'd be lying if I said I don't sometimes like a bit of both!'

All the men suddenly looked interested. Nousche looked as if she might be about to burst into tears. Iona said: 'Shall we go inside and have a cup of tea?'

They spent the afternoon wondering when the tasks would start, what they would be like, when the evictions would begin. The format is always that some time will pass before the first evictions, at least a week, maybe more. It might be two weeks or could even be as long as a month. Of course they would be watched and listened to, monitored and judged and assessed, all the time. It was the nature of these things that some of the tasks would be humiliating, physically or psychologically. Break the six down a bit, get a sense of what they're really like. Or – to put it as an opportunity rather than a problem – give them a chance to show a bit of grace under pressure. Just as a hint about the nature of the process, the huge library of DVDs, which looked so promising at first glance, consisted exclusively of box sets from reality TV shows. It was the British Library of reality TV. Talk about a strong hint of what was to come.

The thing was, though, that the tasks hadn't started. The housemates talked and talked and thought out loud and ran alternative scenarios about what might be going to happen to them, but none of it did. They were all wondering when it was going to start. Perhaps the problem was that they were too self-aware, too aware of the setup; perhaps the problem was precisely that they were talking about it so much? It could be that there was a taboo on asking these questions out loud; it was making them seem too needy, too aware of the audience. In short, maybe they were doing something wrong. It was vital to think about the viewers all the time. It was also vital not to seem to be thinking about them. To Iona this was an interesting conundrum for the first day or two, but gradually more oppressive. She was having to work hard at it and could tell that the others were too. She had a theory, one she hadn't shared with the others yet: that this was a new kind of show, one where there was no interaction with the producers or the viewers, no games or tasks or challenges or external organisation, no structure. They wouldn't be told what to do. They would just be evicted, expelled, one at a time. It could start at any point. They were waiting for it to start, but perhaps it had already started. Just a theory, but it could be true, and if it was true, Iona had figured it out but was pretty sure the others hadn't.

The pool was OK, because you could just lie there, or dive in when it got too hot. Her room was OK, a sanctuary, the only place in the villa where she felt she could just be herself, by herself. Though that of course wasn't entirely true; they were all being watched all the time, and the moments when you were on your own could reveal a lot about who you were. You had to be particularly careful about the amount of time you spent primping and floofing. You didn't want to underdo it so badly you looked like you'd been dragged through a hedge, but on the other hand you didn't want to be caught seeming vain, taking too much trouble, pouting and striking poses. And there was also the fact that you weren't winning anyone over while you sat or lay on your bed. Nobody changed their minds about someone because that person was sitting alone in their room. You need to get out there. So Iona did get out there.

It was the kitchen and dining room that were difficult. The issue she had noticed on the very first morning, about the noise, was more and more prominent. It was the flat hard reflective surfaces that caused the trouble.

Iona's father had been a poker player in his youth (a very good one, according to him), and he had once said that the best way of telling whether someone was telling the truth was to listen not to what they were saying, or even to the tone of their voice, but to the echo of their voice. As time went past in this sharply echoing indoor space, a cool room where they spent more time together than anywhere else in the baking-hot villa, Iona began more and more to notice the sound not of the other contestants' voices, but their echoes. The voices would often be lifted, bright, happy, joking. The echoes sounded flat and angular and full of silences; full of holes, contradictions, meanings that weren't supposed to be there. Positive greetings – 'Hi!', 'How are you!', 'Love the outfit!', 'Looking good!' – sounded like curses or lies. The echo of a joke sounded like an insult. The echo of a friendly question sounded like a jeer. The echo of a friendly comment dripped with loathing. They spent lots of time in that kitchen. And yet when you spent time there you came to think that everything about the villa was the opposite of what it seemed to be: that good feelings were full of hate, that friends were enemies, that laughter was violence, that there was no such thing as love.

On the morning of the seventh day, Iona woke early, a shaft of light from the corner of the blind catching her eye as she rolled over in bed. The spectacular Balearic light was one of the principal characters in the villa. In the morning it was slanted, yellow, insistent: get up! Show yourself! Act natural! It wasn't the kind of light that made it easy to lie in bed. Nobody came out on top in a contest like this by lying in bed. The morning sun here reminded you of that. Then, as the morning wore on, the light gradually hardened. From midday through the early part of the afternoon the light was so bright it was almost metallic. It gave you thoughts of escape, because you knew there could be no escape. The sun was like a giant staring eye. There was no colour to it, just pure light. It was so bright, so hard, it was frightening. However much sun cream you put on, you could feel yourself cook. Getting out of the pool into the sun you felt like a lobster climbing into its own pan, fizzing and sizzling.

The way you could tell this part of the day was coming to

an end was by seeing colour start to return. The white sky went blue, the blazing vertical light started to tilt and turn silver, then yellow, then, as the day turned to evening, gold. The colours of the garden and villa and the contestants and their clothes looked like themselves, only more so. Everything was lovely in that brief period of glow, especially the six of them, during that golden hour which here was shorter than an hour; but they were never more aware of being filmed, surveilled, watched and judged and assessed and ranked for popularity.

Allegiances and alliances were covertly forming. You couldn't say anything explicitly, of course, but you could do a lot with body language and eye talk, with grunts and nods and even silences: silence of assent, silence of letting something hang there, amused silence, disgruntled silence, disbelieving silence, drawing-someone-out silence, silent disagreement and disobedience. Iona always got on best with intelligent people. That meant the person she should be getting on best with in the villa was Liam, who was clearly and self-evidently bright, and, it made her grit her teeth to think this, Nousche. But that didn't work. Liam was a game theorist, an angle-player, a manipulator and reader of rooms, and to make it worse the person he got on best with – was always having tiny muttered colloquies with, side-of-the-mouth – was Nousche. As for Nousche, well, she was still and always Nousche, still her incredibly annoying, permanently calculating, dissembling, sneaky, undermining Eurosnake self. So the people with whom Iona would normally have clicked most easily were not only not her friends, but were in an unnerving alliance with each other. As for the others, Harry in a sense didn't count. He was good-natured and weak and not very bright. They got on well but Harry was like a dog: he would get on well with anyone who petted and fed him (which incidentally was something they had to do, since Harry was the only person in the villa who never cooked anything; you wouldn't trust him to be able to make toast). She was left with Eli, who was so good-looking it was distracting, and was one of those men who have never had to learn how to talk, because women are always fainting and falling into bed with them on sight. So he was off-the-scale attractive but also exhausting since you had to do literally ALL the conversational work. This meant that the person she got on best with was Laz. That would be a surprise at first sight, but it was much less so once you'd seen Laz at close quarters for a day or two. She was noisy and up-for-it to compensate for a secret self that was private and shy.

When Iona got downstairs to breakfast on that seventh day, Laz was already in the kitchen, stirring something on the stove.

'Oi oi,' she said, but quietly.

'Oi oi,' said Iona, also quietly. 'What are you making?'

'Porridge. "Keeps me regular,"' she said in a voice which made it obvious she was quoting somebody, even though there was no possibility that Iona would know who it was. That was one of Lara/Laz's habits and it meant that at times, for all her outgoingness and good nature, you couldn't tell what she was saying, beneath the various layers of impersonations, special voices, ironies and mini-playlets. 'No carbs for me,' she now said in a different voice, one which could, just possibly, be an impersonation of Nousche, in which case Iona officially thought it was hilarious.

'Moi non plus,' Iona said, joining in the anti-Nousche moment, but not too obviously so, just enough that only clued-up viewers, and Laz herself, would know what she meant, if that indeed had been what she meant.

'Are we the first up?'

'Herself and Liam are doing laps,' Laz said, making vague waving gestures with her arms, possibly indicating breast-stroke. By using 'herself' to mean Nousche, it was clear that she was drawing lines. This was an escalation. Oh, it's on! Iona came over to the breakfast bar and sat down at the counter. She was having a little think. The best move was probably to egg Laz on while not appearing to, while also sending signals that she was on the same side, but not coming across as too much of a mean girl. Bitchy but deniable.

'Laps before breakfast,' Iona said, her tone making it both a question and a statement. 'Laps after breakfast. You know – bit of curd. A few berries. "Breakfast."' This last word in broad Australian. Iona didn't roll her eyes but she flared them slightly, in on the joke but subtly so.

'Fancy some porridge?'

'Why not?' Iona said. Laz put the saucepan she'd been stirring on the breakfast bar, then followed it up with bowls and spoons and sat opposite. She dolloped porridge into the bowls, pushed one across to Iona and started blowing on the bowl in front of her.

'I vant some berries,' Iona said in a German accent, for no other reason than that she thought Laz would find it funny, which she did, very.

'Get your own focking berries,' said Laz, also in a German accent. They snorted and giggled together and the noise (and entertainment) they were generating was enough to distract them from the arrival of Harry, who had come downstairs and into the kitchen barefoot and topless. In a villa full of good-looking, not-shy people, Harry stood out for his uncanny, almost supernatural body confidence. He wore a shirt in the evening, when the temperature dropped a few degrees, but in the day he wasn't usually wearing more than a single garment on his lower body, most often shorts or swimming trunks. There was a shower room over in the pool house, and Harry could not be relied on to lock the door.

'Guys,' he said, as a greeting.

Iona held up the saucepan, offering the porridge Laz had made.

'Um – yeah, cool,' said Harry. He got himself a bowl and spoon and helped himself. His arrival threw the dynamics out a little, since he could be absolutely relied on to miss all the nuances about trash-talking and ganging up on Nousche while pretending not to. He didn't speak while eating his porridge but gave little nods of appreciation.

'Man, that was great. You could like, open a restaurant,' Harry said when he finished.

'A porridge restaurant,' Iona said, giving Laz a look. But Harry, while slow, was maybe not as slow as all that, because he immediately said: 'Is that funny?'

'No no,' said Iona, flustered, cornered, stalling. 'No, it's only—'

'Because lots of restaurants do nice breakfasts. Brunches. People love it.' Harry said this sulkily. The encounter was turning into a disaster. Iona and Laz were being turned into the mean girls, which was completely unfair – well, OK, it was a tiny bit fair, but they weren't specifically being mean to Harry at this point, they'd just got a bit carried away over their bonding.

'People love breakfast!' Iona said, maintaining eye contact

with Harry while as it were directing her mind at Laz, who was supposed to pick up on this new tone. 'I just thought it was funny to have a restaurant that only did porridge, you know, like for the Three Bears or something. You could call it the Three Bears.' Again, there was that thing with the echo. Her voice sounded normal when you listened to it, but if you paid attention to the echo, you would think you were hearing a soul in torment, pleading, angrily begging, for release. A terrible noise. Harry, though, had a ginger's trained awareness for when he was being picked on. He didn't say anything, just took his bowl over to the sink, washed it, put it on the drying rack. Iona and Laz looked at each other and Laz gave a tiny eye-shrug. This one wasn't reparable, not immediately. Iona was thinking hard about how this would look, about what her next move or gesture should be, but before she could come up with anything, Liam, dripping slightly, came in from the pool with nothing on but swimming trunks. He was rubbing his hair with a towel. He had the air of a man who knows perfectly well that this sight is to be considered among the eight wonders of the world.

'Sup,' Liam said, not really making it a question, still towelling away.

'The usual,' said Harry, his tone neutral on the surface but, again, if you listened to the reverberation, it sounded different: it had a hissing, bitter edge. Liam gave Harry a look that showed he knew perfectly well what Harry was talking about. He nodded. Iona realised with horror that 'the usual' meant her and Laz ganging up, being the baddies, the bitches, the self-appointed alphas. This could only mean that Harry was already aligned with Liam and Nousche! They had thought they were being careful: they hadn't been anywhere near careful enough. Oh this was a disaster! If that was how it seemed to the housemates in the villa, for the viewers it would be a hundred times worse. Everything would be magnified, blown up, replayed, commented on. It was literally impossible for this to have gone more badly wrong.

And then it did, because Nousche came in from the pool. Having done the look-at-how-little-I-care-about-being-seen-with-wet-hair thing on the first day, she was now a genius at always having her hair completely on point. Of course that style, the Louise Brooks thing, was easy to manage, but . . . Iona could feel herself getting distracted and forced herself to snap out of it. This was a crisis. She could die on a raft with Laz or she could maybe, just maybe, cut herself loose and oat to safety. Groups of this sort often have an official scapegoat and outsider. New name for that person: Laz.

'I wish I hadn't had that porridge,' Iona said, puffing out her cheeks, making a fat-person face. 'Bloat city.' Nousche didn't stoop to answering that observation, not with actual words, but she did make a tiny little moue, a sub-pout, of agreed amusement. Iona thought: this could work. Don't overplay it. Subtle. That's how you crush it, in a situation like this – with subtlety.

'Yeah, you sure don't want to live there. Bloat city,' said Laz, doing one of her silly voices, her cheeks puffed out the same way Iona's had been, and Nousche laughed, and then the others laughed too, including Eli, who had come downstairs during all the breakfast drama without Iona realising he was there. Iona started to join in the laughter, even though in truth she didn't fully get it, and then she realised that Laz's silly voice was actually an impersonation of Iona, and she saw, with a feeling that the floor was sliding down from beneath her, actually physically sinking down and down and down, descending into the earth – she saw that all of them were laughing at her. Laughter, that was what it was supposed to be. And yet, if you listened to it in the new way, by paying attention to the echo, it didn't sound like laughter at all. It sounded like the noise made by souls in torment; by beings undergoing torture; it sounded like screams of pain and anger, like nails on a blackboard but in physical form; it sounded demonic. There was nowhere to go outside this noise. The laughter grew louder. Iona moved towards Nousche and then past her and stood in the doorway to the pool and turned to face them. All the housemates were standing in front of her. Nousche was closest and the others were behind her. The light had taken on its harsh, burning, middle-of-the-day flatness. The laughter had taken on its own momentum, they were still laughing, were laughing harder than ever. What did this mean, where did they go from here? What would the viewers think? How would this look? How would they be judging her? And still they kept laughing at Iona, all of them lined up, as the laughter and the sound of torture grew and grew, the sound of souls screaming in pain grew louder and louder, as they stood there, all of them – Iona, Nousche, Harry, Eli, Liam, Laz – and then with that feeling of dropping through the floor, free-falling, nauseous, the rollercoaster plunge in her stomach, the noise of torture in her ears, she got it: Iona, Nousche, Harry, Eli, Liam, Laz.

They could all see her distress, indeed they seemed to be actively enjoying it, but of all people it was Liam who broke things up. He came over to her and put a non-sexual arm on her shoulder. Nousche came further into the room. Harry moved out towards the pool. Laz was doing something at the sink, Eli had turned and gone back upstairs. The room broke up and, as with a shaken kaleidoscope, the old pattern had been permanently erased. Iona must have been imagining things, imagining the feeling in the room, and everything else too.

'Hey,' Liam said, his voice low, 'you OK?'

Iona didn't think she was, but she nodded. And in truth she did feel a bit better. The others were talking, not loudly and not consequentially, just chat, and it was helpful to listen not to the echo but just to the words, not the undertone but the tone.

'It'll begin soon, OK?' Liam said. 'The tasks and evictions, they'll begin soon. It's not as if this will go on for ever.'

She listened hard to his voice, just the words on his lips. The difference between forever and for ever: she'd been taught that at school. Forever, as in someone is forever going on about something. For ever as in endless, lasting for all time, continuing for eternity. For ever. She listened to what Liam was saying and felt herself believing it, they'll begin soon, it's not as if this can go on for ever. Nothing goes on for ever. Does it?

ON THE WAY TO
THE CHURCH

THEY HAD DRIVEN down from London late the night before. Even before they set out they were exhausted. All the way through the business of leaving their house – locking windows, switching off lights, carrying the bags and the howling baby out to the car – they had argued, bitterly, furiously, until they lost all notion of what it was they wanted from one another and only a sense of miserable, injured, short-changed grievance remained. Most of the five-hour drive passed in silence.

The weather seemed to pick up their mood and magnify it. Rain battered the windscreen. Gusts of wind shook the car. Sarah was afraid they would overturn and be thrown into the whirling, sticky blackness. The usual signs flashed by: Hungerford, Maidenhead, Bristol, Cardiff. Hard to believe such places still existed when they were in the middle of such darkness. For long stretches there were no lights along the motorway and then it felt as if the road itself had been abolished. They could have been driving under the sea or stalled, just a set of headlights drilling into oblivion. And through it all the poor baby slept in his cot on the backseat, unaware that his world was coming undone.

People found it bizarre that they should become parents now, after fifteen years of marriage. Why wait so long? they'd say, or, Whatever for? 'It was an accident,' she'd say. 'We thought we couldn't.' Most people laughed at that but some looked disappointed, as if they wished she'd invented a prettier story. Still, it was the truth.

Now and then the car wavered in its lane. Sarah felt John's strength falter and she understood the effort it took to keep the three of them on this road. She wondered, not for the first time, whether this was the cost of her choice to go ahead with the pregnancy. She was 43 and he 50 – far too old to be having babies.

By the time they reached his mother's place it was one in the morning and the town was shuttered up for sleep with only a few late-night stragglers stumbling home. Ann was at the door as soon as she heard their car, greedy arms outstretched.

Sarah and John put on a show of being on speaking terms, but Ann wasn't interested in them. 'Give him to me,' she crooned. 'The babe, the babe. Let me hold him. Come to me, my precious.'

The next day was freezing but bright, rinsed clean by the storm. To Sarah's relief, her mother-in-law set out early with one of the neighbours to be sure of getting good seats in church. Sarah and John got ready in silence. When it was time to leave the house John went ahead without a backward glance. Sarah followed with the pram. There was no traffic so they walked in the middle of the road. Fifteen years. His face was so familiar to her that she could hardly even see him, and yet lately he'd become a stranger.

She had given up her job in order to spend the first year with the child, but at times like this she felt she'd made a terrible mistake. She had made herself dependent just when John became undependable. There were moments of great joy, but she was always responding, always governed by the machine-gun tattoo of the child's needs or John's moods, supplying whatever seemed to be required. Now. Now. Now. Some days she felt that 'accident' was the most accurate description of what had happened to them and that everything she'd ever known and valued had been consumed in the wreckage.

A pigeon flapped by overhead and the baby gave a wordless exclamation of pleasure. That was new. She smiled down at him, admiring the curve of his head, the kiss-curl on his brow, those fat, perfect little hands fiddling with the tassels of his blanket. She leaned in to straighten the neck of his christening gown. He caught a hank of her hair and tugged it like a bell-pull. She laughed. The feeling of dread inside her lifted a little. It was 9.15 am. They had fifteen minutes before the start of the service.

She walked on.

Each street was much like the next, rows of two-up, two-down houses, mostly pebble-dashed and double-glazed. Outside Mitzi's Hair Salon John had paused, waiting for her to catch up, though still with his back turned. He was talking to an elderly man with a terrier. Sarah slowed her pace, hoping that the man would be gone before she got there. She wasn't in the mood for small talk.

Now John turned around, beaming, as if no cross word

had ever passed between them. 'Sarah, come and say hullo. This is Rhydian. Rhydian, this is my wife. And this . . .' John looked down at the pram with a faintly surprised expression. '. . . this is my son.'

They all stood and gazed at the child. How could such a gleaming creature have sprung from two such worn and bitter bodies?

'I've known Rhydian all my life,' John was saying. 'I remember during the miners' strike, we'd be out in front of Woolworths collecting for them. Isn't that right, Rhydian?'

'Aye.' The old man nodded.

'That's, what, twenty years ago, now?'

'Thirty, more like,' said Rhydian, wheezing. 'You were still a bit wet behind the ears back then.'

John shook his head. 'Terrible. All those pits closed in the end, just like we said.'

'Aye,' said Rhydian. 'And Woolworths.'

The baby had begun to fuss and wriggle under his blankets.

'We need to get a move on, John,' Sarah whispered. To Rhydian she explained that Ann was keeping seats for them in the church. She nodded at the child. 'He's being christened today.'

'Mustn't keep you, then,' said Rhydian, patting John on one shoulder. 'Give my best to your mother.'

They walked on. Soon the high street was in view. Groups of mostly elderly people in their best clothes were making their way up the hill towards the church. But John was looking in the opposite direction, down a side road.

'When I was ten I fell off my bike over there,' he said. 'Skinned my leg all the way from the ankle to the knee. And when I was older, sixteen or seventeen, I remember I persuaded this boy to let me try his motorbike along here. But he didn't tell me how to stop. I had to crash into a wall.' The meeting with Rhydian seemed to have tipped him back into the past. 'When I went up to the grammar school, I used to travel with a boy who lived on the left, there, Gareth Mason.'

Sarah chewed her thumbnail. Somehow she had to get him to hurry up without triggering a row. Ann would be counting the seconds by now, eyes fixed on the door at the back of the church.

'Gareth Mason, eh?' She forced a smile.

'Yes, he lived along there at number twelve. He was abroad for years, working for one of the big oil companies, but he's been ill. My mother was telling me he's moved back home to recuperate.'

Sarah kept the smile going though on the inside she was raging: that she should be forced to behave like an airhostess with her own husband and, worst of all, that John seemed to prefer this fake, grinning persona to her real self.

'Tell you what,' he was saying, 'I'm just going to knock the door and see if Gareth's in. Just a quick hullo. We've got plenty of time.' He took the pram away from her and set off down the side street. Sarah hurried after him. What will we do after today, she wondered? The road keeps running into sand.

A gaunt-looking man answered the door. There was laughter and back-slapping, then to Sarah's dismay the two of them began to pull the pram into the house. Had John lost his mind? The service was about to begin. They had seven minutes to get the church.

'A baby, eh?' said Gareth Mason, looking everywhere but

at the child. He showed them into a warm, cluttered sitting room where a game of football played silently on TV. 'I'll make some tea.' He left the room.

'We don't have time for this!' Sarah hissed. She yanked the pram handles in her temper so that the baby gave a soft cry of protest.

John didn't seem to hear. He was kneeling on the floor, looking through Gareth Mason's vinyl collection, murmuring with pleasure at various albums he recognised.

Gareth came back and leaned in the doorway while he waited for the kettle to boil. 'They were up in the loft for years,' he said, nodding at the stack of albums. 'Mam never throws anything out.'

John pulled out a David Bowie album. 'Unbelievable, isn't it, to think he's gone?'

'Shocking,' said Gareth.

'He always looked so alive. So indestructible. Though mind you, he had a heart attack in the noughties, didn't he? He nearly died on stage.'

John began to read through the song titles under his breath. 'Changes. That's him in a nutshell, isn't it? He reinvented himself so many times. So many lives he lived.'

Gareth opened his mouth to say something, but the kettle whistled in the kitchen. He went out.

Sarah was lurching between panic and a white-hot fury. She began to turn the pram around towards the hall. 'John, your mother is sitting there in front of the whole congregation waiting for us. We have to go right NOW or we'll miss the start and she will never, ever forgive us . . .'

John had pulled another record from its sleeve and was running one finger lightly around the outer rim.

'Did you hear me, John?'

'Let's not rush,' he murmured. 'It's just a normal church service to begin with. The christening bit isn't till the very end.' And then, almost inaudibly, 'There's something I need to tell you.'

'Oh.' She let her hands slip away from the pram. 'Right now?'

'There's never a good time, is there?'

A chill spread through her. I knew it, I knew it, I knew it. He's leaving. He's met someone who isn't constantly covered in baby sick, someone who finishes their sentences, who isn't always too tired for sex. She took a few faltering steps into the centre of the room, then retreated to the sofa so that when it came – the end of the road – she wouldn't have too far to fall.

'Go on.'

In the kitchen they could hear the ring of a spoon on china. Something metallic fell with a crash.

John put the record away. 'So,' he said. He scrubbed his mouth with the back of one hand. 'You remember I had that hospital appointment last year about the deafness in my right ear? Remember? And I never heard back from them so I assumed . . .'

This was not what she'd been expecting. Not at all.

John was still speaking. He was using words like: 'scan' and 'tumour'. Sarah wanted to respond but all she could manage was strangled noise at the back of her throat.

'. . . they put the result in the wrong pile, apparently, or they misfiled it, or lost it. Something. They should have called me in sooner,' he said. 'But anyway, they're on the case now. And it's not too late. It's a slow-growing one, apparently.

So they're going to open up just here.' He indicated a place behind his ear. 'And whip it out.'

Sarah sank backwards into the sofa. Motes of dust tumbled in the stream of winter sunlight from the window behind her. She felt she might never get up again.

John came and sat beside her. 'You mustn't worry, Sarah.' He took her hand. 'The surgeon does these operations all the time. I googled him. He's world class.' He laughed. 'Funny, isn't it? All that time when you were pregnant, I was growing a tumour. Like a competition.'

She turned to him in a daze. How long is it, she wondered, since I've heard him laugh?

Gareth Mason came in clutching three mugs in his trembling, skeletal hands. 'I put milk in all of them,' he said. 'I wasn't sure.'

'Good man.' John's face was open and relaxed. You could see what he must have been like, Sarah thought, when he and Gareth Mason were friends.

Gareth gave Sarah her tea, then went over to the stack of records and fished out a cinnamon-coloured album. 'Remember this one, John? 1977, *Low*. Let me play you my favourite track.' He bent down and fiddled with the stereo.

'It'll be all right, Sarah,' John whispered. 'I promise.' And then, 'Sorry about the things I said last night. I didn't really mean any of it.'

'I love this one,' said Gareth, dropping the needle onto the disc.

There was a brief crackle like bacon in a pan, then David Bowie began to sing 'Always Crashing in the Same Car'. Gareth Mason hummed along. John drank his tea. The baby rubbed his ear and grew sweaty and fell asleep. And Sarah closed her eyes and went hurtling into the welter of possibilities ahead, hoping that John would be right, that they would be lucky - luckier than the miners, luckier than Woolworths, luckier, even, than David Bowie with all his many, many lives.

CLUSTER

THE MAN TWO doors down pursues a secret hobby in the dead of night. This is one of your first discoveries.

You've seen him around, in the daytime, in the time before, but only to nod to. He's a solid man with a mild demeanour and you've always assumed he's a postman, or a hospital porter, or a refuse collector; that he is engaged in some stolid, civic-minded profession. Surely a man like him should have no trouble sleeping. But just a few nights in, you find him out. You haven't slept at all. The nightlight is a small crescent of brightness in the dark blur of milk and skin and adrenaline that night has become. There is a sound outside. Something clangs as it drops onto the ground: metal against concrete. Shuffling, shoe scuffing, a mechanistic clacking. None of these noises would be loud enough to wake you, if you were fast asleep. But in this new nocturnal world, they are more insistent than daytime sounds. They are intimate, in the same way that voices on the telephone whorl into the dark of your ear, closer even than someone speaking next to you.

You glance at your phone, which now sleeps under the corner of your pillow. You tilt it, make it glow. Three twenty-five. There have been letters from the police, opened by the people in the flat downstairs and left on the table in the shared hallway, letters about burglaries in the area. You should get out of bed and check on these sounds. Even the thought of witnessing a crime is poor motivation, but you make yourself move: you rise up past the Moses basket, make your way to the window. You move the curtain, just a fraction. You look out over two lines of backyards and the black river of cobbles that bisects them. You stand very still, waiting for another sound. It comes again: the jangle of metal, the sound of someone about some secret business. You survey the terraces until you locate the source: two doors down, there's a small tilley lamp at the end of a yard and a man crouched down beside it. It takes a while for the scene to sharpen into coherence. A man crouches over a wheel, spinning it. A bike is upside down, and the man stoops over it, working on something at the wheel-hub, adjusting it, then spinning the wheel again. You watch for a while. The man's movements are slow and full of care. He works over the body of the bike with a soft cloth periodically; stands back and puts his hands in his pockets. You let the curtain fall back into place. All this detail, all this secret work, is folded back into the dark. After that, you listen for him in the nighttime, when the baby frets and whinnies awake, over and over again, startling out of sleep as though she is falling, falling, into something terrible, her tiny limbs twitching, her mouth a worried beak; the baby who does not yet know what sleep is, who does not know its softness. You listen for the man when you scoop the baby up again and again and rock it and try to teach it how to sleep, whilst beginning to forget how to yourself. You listen for him moving around, or the creak of a bike chain, like a reptile in the night; you listen for his nighttime industry, a shadow of yours.

⚜

Callum sleeps. He sleeps through all of it, even just a few days in. How can he, you wonder. The baby makes such noises, such terrible tiny rasps and rattles and sighs, as though breathing is altogether too difficult, as though she might give up on it at the turn of each breath. Fifteen days old, the creature at your breast. The nightlight glances off her darting eyes: half-blind eyes that can barely see beyond your face, but they flicker wildly when the baby latches, as though she is checking sideways for competition or predators. You hear scuffling outside: the secret mechanic, you think. But this is not him. The scuffling is more persistent and less careful. There is laughter, and then there are low voices. Earlier in the night there was bellowing and singing, the voices of groups of people veering wildly as they stumbled home from the pub. It's Friday night, you remind yourself; the weeks have lost their shape now that the nighttime lasts so much longer than the day. Today you took the baby to a class, a class for new mothers in the city centre, so you know that it was Friday today. At the end of the class there had been an opportunity to ask questions. You'd all sat in a circle on beanbags, your babies bundled in blankets. The other women looked variously blissful or alarmed or stupefied by the creatures in their arms. I read a story about a bottle of baby powder exploding and the baby choking on the dust, one woman said. Is it true? Can talcum powder kill them? Am I not supposed to be powdering him? God, another woman said, there are stories about everything. Try to relax a bit. This one's my second and the older one, she's five, she came home from school yesterday and said, Mum, what's terrorism? Just you wait until that happens, then you can really start to worry. This is the easy bit. Some of other women in the circle had begun to fidget then, to shift uncomfortably on their bean bags, whether from their episiotomies or from the talk of terrorism or from the thought of all of this being easy, it was difficult to say. You resolved never to go to a mums' group again.

The murmuring continues outside. The baby is still at your breast. The baby has been at your breast all night. Cluster feeding, the health visitor who led the group had explained, is very common in the early days. The baby might feed for hours in the night. Hours and hours. It's clever. It knows when to seek its mother out, with the best chance of her un-divided attention, with the best chance of her body guarding it against the cold, and snakes, and raiders. But we don't have snakes in South Leeds, do we, one dazed-looking girl had said. Oh I know, dear, the health visitor said, I'm speaking *ev-o-lut-ionarily*. The new word flickers in your mind as the baby's face repeatedly shivers into your breast, searching and finding. Cluster feed. Cluster fuck. Cluster bomb. None of the associations are exactly encouraging.

You're listening to the voices but you don't move. There's a bit of back and forth out there; some sort of negotiation is taking place. They've settled in one spot, close to the back of the house. You scoop the baby up, keeping her latched, when you finally move to the window. You move the curtain just a fraction. There are three of them in the back alley, three lads. Two of them are jittering about: moving from foot to foot, pushing hands into pockets, taking them out again, pushing them back in. The other man is making a show of not being nervous. He's wearing a bulky jacket and he leans back into the light cast by the street lamp at the very end of the alley so that he can count their money. He's selling: he passes something over to one of the lads. Then he's off, leaving the pair of them to lean into one another, to unwrap their tiny parcel.

This network of Victorian alleys at the edge of the city is a gift for buyers and sellers. There are often needles in the gutters. Sheila in the ground-floor flat has called for an ambulance several times; young lads and old, wiry men alike, not able to make it home before necking what they've bought. What city doesn't have a drug problem, Callum said, when they looked around the place. And anyway, that's why we can afford a flat with a double-bedroom, so don't knock it, love. You're not knocking it; not now. You're glad of the company, however distant, while the baby *clusters*. You lie back in bed, and the baby tilts back her head, swooning with milk. You listen to the lads staggering off, finding their own comfort, their own protection from snakes and raiders.

Sometimes there is singing. There's a couple whose voices you have come to recognise. They stumble home together from the pub a couple of nights a week. They're both loud and hoarse and boisterous. Some nights they sing together, '90s Britpop anthems, blundering through the words, compensating for in-accuracy with volume. Tonight it's mostly the woman singing; her voice cracks when she reaches for the high notes. You don't recognise the song. The man whoops when she finishes. As their voices recede and the street settles back into quiet-ness, the distant city sounds skitter across the sky. A freight train echoes for minutes, its rhythm on the tracks repeat-ing over and over – huckle-berry, huckle-berry, huckle-berry. Silence. A faraway siren swooping. A sudden whoosh from the motorway. Silence. When the baby finally falls asleep in your arms, you are too afraid of waking her to put her down.

A blackbird breaks the quiet outside. When you check your phone, dawn is still far off. The bird is misfiring in the dark. That's another of your discoveries: the sounds of birds. You listen to them as daybreak approaches each morning. There are so many of them, clicking and cooing and calling out to one another across the dark rooftops, telling one another of the light beginning to crack open the distant horizon. You've begun looking for them in the daytime too, trying to identify them. There's a pair of blackbirds nesting in the privet at the front. They seem to be doing things so carefully and so equitably. The nest is hidden deep inside the hedge and each parent, when it is time to leave, darts suddenly out, leaving any watcher uncertain of the exit point. Then they return, they initially stand some way off, on the top of the gate for example, with a morsel in beak, checking and checking once again that no one can see where they are about to go. You watch this from the front window, as you walk with the baby, watching the birds take turns all day long, so prudent and so diligent. They're wise to be careful. The mangey white cat from next door, its fur yellowed at the paws as if by nicotine, waits on its own front-door-step, licking its claws until it's time for fledging.

Over the road, where the houses have small front gardens, two ducks have made their nest a surprising distance from the river, a clutch of thirteen eggs hidden underneath a shrub. The man whose garden they have chosen fills an ice-cream container each day with water for them, and sometimes the dawn chorus admits some quacking. This afternoon, the old man stopped you on your walk out with the pram to tell you that a plumber's merchant has run over the drake – the man has had to scrape him off the road with a spade – and now the female is circling her eggs dementedly, giving the whole game away. The foxes will surely come. What should he do, the man asked you, as though the pram qualified you in some way to give advice. I don't know, you said, what can you do?

You tried not to think about it as you walked the streets, the baby whimpering under gunmetal skies and falling blossom. But now that the blackbird has gone off at this early hour, you can't help but return to the thought of the nest. Can a blackbird be insomniac? Or is something afoot? Is the fox about, stalking the lone duck for her eggs? All is quiet again. Even the baby is silent. But you continue to listen, and a memory materialises vividly in the dark: an experiment you were forced to take part in at primary school. Each of you is given an egg, a hen's egg, at the start of morning class, and is asked to keep it safe, to guard it all day long. The lesson is about the difficulty of looking after something precious and fragile, about how much care is needed. Most girls put the eggs in their pockets, curling their fingers around the grainy shells and hoping to see it through to the end. You make it to lunchtime, when a brief lapse in concentration and a desire for more pudding results in you leaning over recklessly and crushing the shell against the serving table. The crack is initially hardly visible, but then tiny chips begin to come away along its fine line, and when you see the white skin inside and know that the game is up. At the end of lunch, you drop the egg into the dining room bin, with the slop of leftover custard and chocolate sponge, and it makes a sad little plop of defeat. One girl in your group, Leanne, whose hair is always dirty and whose life is already marked by loss, smashed the egg almost immediately, hurling it against the playground wall: I'll only end up breaking it, she said, might as well do it now.

It's the couple again, on their way home from the pub. Tonight they're heckling each other mercilessly. It's the woman you hear first. She's jeering, almost singing her insults at him. The thing about you, yeah, is that you don't know when to shut up, do you? On and on about boring shit. No wonder Paul left. With you going on about your dogs. No one cares about your pedigree bitch, Johnny – she shrieks. Her heels clatter; she's stumbling around, winded by laughter. Yeah, well the thing about you is that you don't have your own friends, do you, Shell? You're only friends with the blokes you're shagging, aren't you? Not exactly known for your conversation, are you? His voice is lower and rougher, but it's still got a playground, sing-song cadence. Yeah, yeah, well at least I don't walk funny. Look at you, look at the fucking state of you! Bow-legged, walking like you're from Manchester, she shouts back. Yeah, right, then why are you shagging me, love? You can't get enough of my amble. And look at the fucking state of you. Look at that fucking fringed monstrosity you're carrying. What is it they say about handbags? Meant to be like a girl's cunt, aren't they? Peals of laughter. Howling. Singing. Silence.

In the middle of the night, in the time before, if you found yourself awake for long stretches of time, you would sometimes get to wondering what it would be like to die. Imagine, your brother used to say to you when you were a child, late at night, a torch up-lighting his nostrils and teeth, imagine, our Ri, how many people have died in this house. It's over a hundred years old, you know. And aren't there meat-hooks in the cellar? Do you think they were only used for animals? And what was that creak in the hallway?

Redbrick terrace houses; you are always awake in redbrick terrace houses. The council-owned back-to-back in Meanwood you grew up in, and now, here you are, back in your hometown; another Victorian slum on the other side of the City. But tonight, as you lie awake listening to the baby scratching the sides of the crib-basket, you don't wonder about who has died here, over the years; you think instead about how many people might have been born in this house. How many tiny creatures have spluttered into life, here, in front of the old fire-place or drenching the sheets of an old bed? People seldom give their consent to die; but no one can ever give their consent to be drawn into life. And endings seem more comprehensible, now, than something beginning. After all, no one is really responsible for death; even a murder is only foreshortening. But a birth? Conjuring something into being, into blood and bone and nails? You were truly culpable for that.

The girl in the flat next door goes out every Thursday night. There is music beforehand, loud laughter, screaming, ferocious and repetitive swearing. Sometimes, in the early hours, you hear the girl return alone, closing the front door carefully, padding up the stairs to her studio, starting a film on her laptop, American voices pinging at one another indistinctly through the party wall. Tonight, the girl returns with another girl. You feed the baby, you feed the baby for more than an hour; the baby rests briefly, her head lolling back, and you think that you might be able to lie down, to rest for just a minute or two, but then the baby's head lifts again, eyes soft and closed like a tiny bat's, and she blindly latches back on, still hungry, clustering her tiny soft mouth. Callum turns suddenly in the bed; sighs; settles back into sleep. You listen to the girls next-door as you continue to feed. They keep trying to whisper, but their voices speed one another along, rising, giggling, shrieking. Eventually their voices taper off into silence - only to re-emerge in the darkness as long, soft, lush moans.

It's the couple again. The baby has just gone down in the basket when you hear shouting from the end of the street. They're rowing. But he's louder than before. There's no laughter and now the woman's not making any comebacks. By the time they're close to the house, he's going full throttle. Don't think I don't know about it, you and Jimmy, you fucking slut. Don't you stop here, don't you think you can stop here, don't you think you're not going to get what you deserve. Get up. Get up. You can fucking walk. You move to the window, push aside the curtain. Someone turns a light on in the house opposite. They can call the fucking police. I don't give a fuck. The woman's down on the pavement. She's in tight white jeans and a white top that has ridden up as she's dragged along. She's not making any sound: she's playing dead, trying to make herself as heavy as possible. Fucking get up, you cunt. You're coming home with me.

Stay on the line, another voice in the darkness says to you. The police are on their way. Can you keep them in your sight? I'm inside my flat, your voice says, and they've just started moving again. Can you go outside? the other voice asks calmly. Can you follow them at a safe distance?

You turn to the Moses basket. The baby is asleep. Callum is asleep too. But he's close by. He'd hear, surely he'd hear the baby and he'd wake if anything were really wrong. If the baby needed him. You can go outside. You can leave them together for just a moment. The idea is terrible and wonderful.

I'll try, you say. You get a coat from the hallway and leave as quickly as you can. You can't have taken even a minute but when you open the door, there's no sound: the couple has vanished. You step out onto the street and the night is darkest blue and as cool and deep as a sea. You walk up and down, check the turn-offs and the mouths of ginnels. But there's no sign of them. I've lost them, you tell the call handler. I'm so sorry. Can you keep checking? the voice says. We've had a number of calls. The police are almost with you. There are lights on in some of the houses around you. Other people have called too. Other people have been awake, or woken, and heard too. You turn back towards your flat. The sky above it is clear, the stars glinting coldly in the darkness. This is the first time you have been outside alone since the baby. You feel giddy. And you feel bereft.

You linger for a little longer on the street, even though the trail's gone cold. You think of the woman, somewhere close by, but hidden from you. Will somebody else hear her again in the dark, someone who can help? Maybe there's someone listening for the woman right now, someone who will answer when she cries out, wherever she is. You think of the first time you heard the baby's heart-beat in the black-ness inside you: your own slow, low pulse answered by this new one, quickening. You listened for her so intently, with such care, hearing her inside yourself even before you saw her.

A police van approaches slowly. You flag it down. They were heading that way and then I lost them, you say. I'm sorry.

Tonight an owl breaks through the darkness. At the same time, the baby laughs in her sleep, a goofy breathy laugh, her cheeks dimpling, her lips wet with milk. Your heart feels like it might be about to shatter. You cry often these days. Maybe it's that thing they talked about in the class, Ri, the baby blues, Callum says. You could ask the doctor. Or we could try your Mum again. The baby might help, if she sees her. She'll sort hersen out, one day, she will. We have a beautiful little girl, Ri, there's nothing to be sad about.

But it's not sadness. Not exactly. The thing is, you now think, is that you've lost all of your conditioning. You learned about Pavlov's dogs at school: conditioned to associate a bell with food, they slavered whenever it was rung. But the lesser-known fact, the teacher had said, was that when Pavlov's lab flooded, the dogs lost their conditioning. A trauma, a shock, a revolution: you can lose everything you've learnt that way. Since the birth, you've forgotten all of your passwords; your days feel like waking dreams; you don't know how to talk to people without being honest, or how to pretend you're not terrified; you can't remember how to forget all of the things that have hurt you; you can't remember how to forget that all of the things that should be joyful have also hurt you.

The owl screeches again. The baby raises her small, fat hands in the air, twists her wrists and points her fingers as though she's conducting an orchestra in her sleep. It's the caring that has been the trauma; it's the caring and the being cared for that has been the shock. After you gave birth, the midwife who was about to sew you up stroked your hand. I'm going to be ever so careful, love, she said. I do needle-work at home. And you felt like a precious, embroidered glove. Or you felt how it might feel to be a child with a mother who cares for her. It is the tenderness of the details that has broken you apart: the tiny scar at the baby's belly button, the tuft of hair at the nape of her neck, her tongue, Christ, the baby's tiny, perfect tongue, rough and clean as a kitten's. And that woman in white, it's the detail of her top riding up that you keep thinking of, keep caring about. You didn't even see her face, just her pale naked torso, and the line of dark fabric that must have been her bra. Was there anyone else to care about these things? Are you the only mother of them? Other people called 999 too. There were other people who had heard in the middle of the night; other people who surely cared.

The baby has settled into a deep, silent sleep in your arms. You look at her: at the feathered veins of her eyelids, finer than lines of purple silk; at the tiny creases in her dark lips. Have I not numbered each hair upon your head? Have I not picked off each flake of cradle cap, scooped out the soft wax from your new ears? You listen for the baby breathing; and when you cannot hear it, you pull her in closer and then you feel her breath against your own chest, you hear the tiny rasp of her inhale. You turn off the light from your phone. I heard you before you were born; I hear you still in the dark. You reach one arm under the duvet, find Callum's warm belly, rising and falling. This. This breathing, together, in the dark, the night an echo chamber for the owl outside and a distant siren and the first street-cleaner and your own mother, some-where, close by or far off, in a back alley or on a stranger's sofa, comatose perhaps, but breathing in this darkness with you too. And aren't you all asleep, or awake, together, under this same night sky, with no god but you – all of you – to care about this cluster of details.

SMACK

THE JELLYFISH COME with the morning – a great beaching, bodies black on sand. The ocean empties, a thousand dead and dying invertebrates, jungled tentacles and fine, fragile membranes blanketing the shore two miles in each direction. They are translucent, almost spectral, as though the sea has exorcised its ghosts. Drowned in air, they break apart and bleed their interiors. A saturation, leeching down into the earth.

People claim they are poisonous – Sea Nettles, Lion's Mane, Portuguese Man of War. Bringing their phones down to the beach, they snap pictures, send them into nature shows. One photograph makes it into the local paper, another fills five minutes on a regional morning show: '*And in local news, a shoal of jellyfish has been causing consternation for tourists at one of the more popular pleasure beaches. Certainly not what you'd expect, coming up for a long weekend, is it, Cathy?'* – '*Actually, Tim, I think you'll find a group of jellyfish is called a "smack".*'

The provenance of the jellyfish remains a mystery. People argue amongst themselves, message links to articles back and forth. They are the result of global warming, of toxic-waste disposal. They are a sign of a change in worldwide migration

124

patterns, rising sea levels, El Niño. They are Californian and a long way from home.

From the back porch, Nicola watches the clean-up for the best part of the afternoon. She has been in her dressing gown since the previous evening, sharp with yesterday's deodorant, caking of toothpaste in the corners of her mouth. She watches men with rubber shoes and litter-pickers moving down the beach, scooping up the glutinous shapes with pails and trenching shovels, dumping them down. The day is hot – white summer, restless with foreign birds. On the deck, she sits with one ankle hooked over the other and eats croissants, stale since Tuesday morning, slugging coffee black because the milk has turned to yellow curds.

Beneath her dressing gown, she is bloody with mosquito bites. Unrazored beneath the arms, unplucked, unmoisturised. The yeasty smell of unwashed bedlinen, salve on childish bruises. Last night, she ate outside – pre-cooked garlic prawns, torn from the packet – and the plates have been left to moulder in the heat of the day. Vulture-like, gulls circle the deck. Dark wails across a melted sky.

'You'd set yourself on fire, if you ever tried to live by yourself,' Cece had once said. 'Two days, tops. You'd boil an egg and burn the kitchen to the ground. Either that or we'd find you three weeks later, suffocated under piles of your own mess. You're not a natural housekeeper, sweetie. You're not that type.'

'Only because you've never let me try.'

Cece's expression – sag of irritated eyes.

'Any time you want to, sweetie. You just be my guest.'

Her phone has been dead since the weekend. A blessing, in many ways. The power in the house is off, has been off since she arrived, and she has no idea how to turn it on. The fuse box in the cellar is unknown territory. She makes coffee on the gas stove, eats shrink-wrapped ham and bread and butter, pickled onions from a jar. In the evenings, when the sun peels away from the easternmost parts of the house, she retreats by degrees to the brighter rooms until there is no more daylight, and then she goes to sleep.

She cannot watch television, though this is only a minor irritation as all she ever really watches are the shopping channels and the twenty-four-hour mediums. *Call now for a personal consultation with an experienced psychic in the comfort of your very own home.* Her type of television is the sort that Daniel says speaks to a weakness of character (although admittedly a lot speaks to Daniel of a weakness of character: a fondness for jelly sweets, the refusal to give dogs human names, hair grown past the shoulders, the Tolkien books). He has, in the past, tried to educate her, turning on the History Channel, documentaries about beluga whales. The first time, walking in on Nicola watching QVC in bed, tangle of orange peel in her lap, he had cocked his head to the side and squinted at the screen.

'What's that they're selling?'

'Fabergé eggs.'

'Not real ones?'

'I don't know. If you buy half a dozen, they send you a hutch to keep them in.'

She had an itchy dialling finger, an overzealous eye for a bargain. The weekly thud of pink-wrapped packages in the letter cage had quickly become a source of tension, Daniel stiffly handing over boxes containing pizza scissors, ceramic knife sets, printed scarves, cultured pearls set in abalone.

'What have you bought this time?'

'It's a hand-carved set of wooden fruit. I thought we could display it in the hall.'

'I keep the Japanese maquettes in the hall.'

'I know, but there's space for two things.'

'What's that?'

'I think that's a kiwi. I don't know. They don't look quite how they looked on TV.'

On the beach, a red-haired woman is walking a child along the sand on a pair of elastic reins. The child can be no more than three, jangle-boned, with the shambling, drunken gait of one whose legs have only very recently been introduced to one another. Lashed to the red-haired woman's wrist, he drags towards the headland, where the men with litter-pickers have now paused to inspect their haul. It is low tide, the sea pretending innocence. Squinting down along the line of the shore, Nicola watches the gentle pull of outgoing water, the glassy sink and swallow, waves drawing back like lips revealing teeth.

There is a sudden commotion, the tethered child making a lurch towards something in the sand – a jellyfish, split open and unbodied, a mess of tentacles and bells and polyps that the men running clean-up operations have failed to sweep away. The red-haired woman gives a mighty tug on the reins, enough to haul the child back and halfway off his feet, at which surprise he stumbles over and starts crying. From the deck, Nicola watches as one of the men from the clean-up crew approaches to assess the situation, the red-haired woman already yanking the child up by his wrist and shaking him – the twist of nails in skin. The man holds up his hands, litter-picker swinging jauntily outwards: *what seems to be the problem, ma'am?* The woman turns on him, jabs a finger into his chest, gesturing first to the litter-picker and then to the jellyfish. The child, wrist still grasped in her other hand, staggers back and forth with her gesticulation, snivelling quickly curtailed by fascination at this sudden opening of hostilities. The man drops his hands, drops back. He swings his litter-picker down, planting it in the sand before changing his mind and looping it upwards, tapping it into his palm like a policeman with a truncheon.

The two of them argue, duelling pointed fingers. The crux of the matter seems to be that the red-haired woman holds the clean-up crew responsible for the child nearly stumbling on a jellyfish, while the man holds the woman responsible for not purchasing a shorter set of reins. The woman jabs at his chest twice more, the man parrying each time with the litter-picker. In her head, Nicola constructs bits and pieces of the conversation – argues both cases, for and against. Meanwhile, the child, working his wrist free of his mother's grasp, totters back towards the jellyfish with renewed purpose, as the voices of the adults are lost to an easterly wind.

She has been here over a week now and still considers herself to be essentially engaged in a siege situation. The food is not holding up quite as she had imagined: two pints of milk, one already curdled; a bag of oranges, three eaten, six rotted; six tins of tuna, one of sweetcorn; two packets of ham, two of prawns, two salami; a pineapple, impenetrable; the jar of pickled onions; a multipack of crackers; a block of cheese; a bar of chocolate; a loaf of bread turned white with creeping mould.

If she were Cece, she would have brought along pasta or potatoes, food suitable for long internments with only a gas cooker for company. If she were Cece, she would have thought to bring a can-opener too. By the third day, she is roiling with pickled onions, sore-gummed from shards of cracker. The unrefrigerated ham is growing an odd, oyster-coloured film along its rind.

This ignobility of rotted bread and milk is not what she would have hoped, though she can't deny it adds something bohemian to the situation. The house – dust-sheeted, its swimming pool drained – seems oddly suited, in its current state, to meals of Sun-Maid raisins and orange cheese eaten on the floor. In the afternoons before the sun runs out, she sits in the dining room overlooking the steep incline of cliffs, stacking miniature towers of crackers which she then covers with marmalade and eats over several long minutes, pretending entire banquets from her customary place at the table's head.

Daniel has already gutted the place of anything really worth taking. The majority of the furniture sold at auction as long ago as November, and most of the blue and white also seems to have been snaffled up around that time. Faded patches where the paintings used to hang – a common phenomenon for which Nicola was once startled to realise there is no formal name – disfigure every room in the house. An exercise in barefaced deception. Daniel had gone ahead and sold the Persian rugs and a good percentage of the silver even before asking for a divorce.

What remains – somewhat pointedly, in Nicola's opinion – are many of her QVC acquisitions. A shelf of Russian dolls painted to resemble the Muppets. A machine for counting change. A large pottery cat in whose hollow skull umbrellas can be stored. Between the empty spaces left by Daniel's confiscations, her personal effects remain like a series of insults. A lamp shaped like a goldfish bowl, an egg timer filled with indigo sand. These objects sit around the house like a dumping of useless artefacts, archaeological pieces too mundane to be brought back from the dig.

The divorce has been in the works over six months and Nicola has given up trying to keep track of where things stand. Her finger has mottled up around her wedding ring, a swell towards the knot of the knuckle like the time she ate rock oysters on her fifteenth birthday and had to be taken to A&E. Every morning, before the heat of the day takes her body and makes it sticky and intractable, she grasps the ring and circles it, twisting back and forth in a vain attempt to take her finger by surprise, slip it up and off before the swelling can stop her. It never works – her left hand is too clever for her right.

'Bacon grease,' Cece had said on the telephone (this was some months before Nicola stole Cece's car to drive down to the beach house and summarily surrendered her right to good advice). 'Or soak your fingers in salt water. It pulls the moisture out of the skin.'

'I tried that,' Nicola had replied. 'And grapefruit balm and salt scrub and keeping my hand elevated fifteen hours a day. Nothing works.'

'Well, I don't know, then.' Cece's children in the background barked instructions for a game of Twister – *left hand red!* 'Cut your finger off or just don't get divorced, I suppose. What do I know.'

Ball lightning hits the patio doors. Wild blue bounce, like a tumbling of hailstones. She watches the storm from the kitchen windows and wonders whether the buffeted sea will soon expel more bodies. Her telephone psychics would be helpful here. *I'm sensing some sort of invertebrate, a whole lot of them, in fact.*

The night she and Daniel met, there had been a thunderstorm. A feeble happening, in truth, three cracks of lightning and a drop in pressure, though still enough to keep Cece's dinner guests entertained. Cece had not seated them together, more concerned with fixing Daniel up with a friend of hers who sold Mannerist art and owned a pack of shih-tzus named for the phases of the moon. *Gibbous is a little scamp, he keeps Crescent and First Quarter on their toes.*

'My sister's the pretty one,' Cece had announced, by way of introduction when Nicola first arrived. 'Our father called her the precious cargo. So everyone be on your best behaviour.'

She had seated her next to an older man who had lectured her on jurisprudence for the duration of the fish course and then excused himself for the lavatory with an expression which very much suggested that Nicola had been the one boring him. It was at this point that Daniel had slid in beside her, leaving the shih-tzu owner, as Cece would lament some time later, quite humiliated five seats down.

'You looked in need of rescuing,' had been his opening salvo. The sudden vastness of him, dark block against the lightning spill.

'I can take care of myself,' she'd responded, squaring shoulders, though he had only shaken his head.

'Can't leave a lady in danger, as my father used to say.'

He had driven her to the beach house that very night – three hours of frantic getaway in a vast September dark. She had let him carry her off, very much as a prize from a captured citadel, let him talk in circles about showing her this place he thought would suit her, a refuge from the pressures of the world. Holding her hand to steer her out of the path of some fox mess in the driveway, he had murmured, 'Watch your step,' in a manner both cautionary and imperative. He had kissed her in the hallway, led her out onto the deck.

Of course, divorcing had been different. No thunderstorm, only a spiralling wind.

She doesn't sleep well. She tries honey, pulls up lavender from the bushes that straggle through the slats of the deck. Daniel has had the bed removed, yet still she sleeps within its confines, rectangular phantom in the centre of the room. From this pretence of space, she can play-act other nights, other weekends, when the house was furnished with more than the memory of things.

Midnight in a hot September, beat of moths against the overhead lamp. July, slick with sweat, Daniel mixing prairie oysters and complaining about his eyes.

A month after they were first married, they had driven up to the house in a sultry twilight, car lights on the water dimmed to white. Crashing in, stumbling to the bedroom, she had pushed him backwards, bared her teeth like knuckles, accused him of driving drunk.

'Speak for yourself,' he had snorted – the furtive joy of him, grabbing at her hair. 'Orange juice all night. Someone had to be the designated driver if you were going to get all drunk drunk.'

'Drunk drunk,' she had repeated, enjoying the sound of it. The dense forgiveness of his expression, the hard clasp of hands on her waist.

In the morning, she had woken to a drifting of summer rain. Heavy arms around her, tricky to escape. Rolling out, she had considered Daniel, snoring gently, glaring in his sleep, as if in disapproval. She had known him then, seen his were-wolf skin beneath the surface. Without waking him, she had left the room and wandered out onto the deck in her dressing gown, bare feet slippery on the slats. Beyond the sand, the water had frothed with animation, as though rising up to meet the rain. The tide had been on the wane, the beach filled with the everyday litter of ascophyllum, cuttlebones and beer cans. The spider crabs had emerged from their hiding places and made for the relative safety of the flats.

There has been no knocking since the third day, when someone from the offices of Daniel's lawyer had driven down in a Prius and camped outside the house.

'The point is to nip this in the bud,' he had called through the letterbox, fanning fingers through the copper flap like some encroaching insect. 'We can sort this out quickly and quietly. Call it a brief lapse in judgement. It's been an emotional time. Tricky business, difficult decisions. No harm, no foul. Et cetera.'

Sitting at the bottom of the hall stairs, she had nibbled on salami and pictured Daniel's lawyer - his almost uncanny hairlessness, as though he had been dipped in lye. At their last meeting, he had leant over the table towards her and she had watched a bead of sweat travel in a seamless line from his crown to the centre of his lip, where he had halted it with a quickly darting tongue. *Do correct me if I'm wrong, of course, but both my records and my client's testimony state that you have actually never worked, Mrs Carmichael. That you have*

*in fact been dependent on the generosity of others your entire
life – is this the case?*

At the letterbox, the fingers had flapped, retracted, the
voice behind the door becoming irritable. 'Mrs Carmichael, I
don't know you but I can't imagine any sane woman would
want to be stuck with an injunction, let alone a charge of
trespassing, and that's what's going to happen if you continue
this stunt. If you just open the door and talk with me, I'm
sure we can sort this out.'

Shrugging a shoulder, Nicola had crossed to the door –
barricaded with a scuttle of chairs – and posted the remainder of her salami out through the letterbox before wandering
away. (She regrets this gesture now, a little. With the ham
on the turn, there is scant protein left amongst her rations.)

Whether or not the threat to return with an injunction was
a serious one, there have been no visitors since the first. Of
course, there may well have been phone calls but she is thank-
fully in no position to say. She has, it is true, half-expected
Cece to come chasing her, but perhaps her sister's current lack
of a car is owed something for that delay.

In the dining room, between marmalade-slathered crackers, she acts out scenes of high drama, imagining scenarios,
gesticulating to the blank spaces on the walls.

'What did you think you were achieving?' her sister would
say – her narrow limbs, ponytail cuffed in Hermès. 'Daniel
takes the beach house in the divorce so you immediately drive
down and barricade yourself in? You know my children prac-
tise better conflict resolution than you.'

'He doesn't even want it,' Nicola would reply. 'He owned
it before we met, he never used it. And yet now he's threaten-
ing to sell it. Just because he knows I want it. He's like a child

who wrecks a toy he never plays with when his mother tries to give it away.'

'That is ten-pence psychology,' Cece would say. 'You don't know what you're talking about. If anyone's being childish here it's you.'

'You're supposed to be on my side,' Nicola would whine – whines aloud, too, in the dining room, to no one.

The jellyfish return again the next day. Flooding the shoreline in the early morning like a littering of plastic, the beach foul-breathed after a stormy night. The summer is becoming unpredictable, rain-swollen – a white, fetid season, filthy with cloud.

From the deck, Nicola watches the commotion. Teenagers with their phones out, filming videos of one another poking jellyfish with sticks. Towards the foreland, an elderly couple are walking arm in arm, in matching jackets. The woman is bent over, great chin and wattle hanging down beyond her breastbone. The man, though tall and relatively sprightly, walks bent over to the same degree, keeping pace with her halting step. As they approach a jellyfish, the man rears upright, just long enough to scout a clear path around the obstacle, before dropping back into his imitation hunch and towing the woman safely up the bay.

Throughout the morning, Nicola watches for the red-headed woman and her tethered child, although neither one appears. Around noon, a television crew arrives to shoot a brief piece – the hosts of a general-interest show Nicola half-remembers Daniel watching, talking genially to each other with their shoes encased in plastic bags. '*Potential tourist attraction, yes – but is this plague symptomatic of something* more serious, Cathy?' – 'Actually, Tim, I think you'll find that "plague" is a word usually only applied to insects.'

Behind them, the teenagers dance about for the cameras, sticking out their tongues and waving until the director has to pause filming to ask them to settle down.

In the afternoon, she sits in the living room and tries to ignore her growling stomach. She is approaching emergency levels with her rations but the prospect of leaving the house to search for food seems only to invite invasion. If she were Cece, she would have brought a cooler. If she were Cece, she would have thought this through.

She sets up the plastic chess set and plays herself with a jumbled, Ludo-like approach to the rules, jumping bishops over knights and moving queens with abandon. Early on, Daniel had showed her a photograph of himself at a junior school chess tournament – ten years old, top-heavy with braces and a nose to grow into, sourly clutching a participation prize.

'I hadn't cracked the code yet,' he had said, laying the chess set out between them, and she had loved him for his straight teeth and strident nose and the fact that he couldn't bear to lose at anything. He had taught her chess strategies and combinations, smacking her hands away from impulse moves.

'There are safer ways to get there,' he would say, time and time again, repositioning her pawns around the king. 'You don't have to be silly about it. There's never any need to lose, if you only use your head.'

Daniel's lawyer has a voice like unguent. As he speaks through the letterbox, she imagines him licking up sweat with the moist dark dab of his tongue.

'Mrs Carmichael, I have here written instruction for you to vacate the premises no later than tomorrow afternoon. We're not playing games here, girlie. This is legal imbroglio. You have to think about where you stand.'

He posts the papers and retreats, though regrettably she has now run out of salami to post back out. Picking up the collection of envelopes, she moves immediately to one addressed in Daniel's handwriting, though the note inside is only a typed rehashing of all the offers he has made her over the past six months: the Alfa Romeo, a sterling-silver knife set, a collection of Danish miniatures, half the books, half the frequent- flier miles, all the jewellery free and clear.

'My heart bleeds,' Cece had said, looking over a similar list only weeks after the divorce was first floated. Slicing blue cheese. Smear of apricot jam at her lip. 'He takes the car so you only get the other car. He takes the credit cards so you only get the gold bullion and the diamond mine.'

She takes the envelopes through to the kitchen and wanders out onto the deck. For the fourth or fifth time, the jellyfish have flooded the shore, but this time the men from the clean-up crew have hit upon the idea of building a bonfire. Not far from the headland, a great tower of bodies is forming – headless, shapeless things stacked one and another, the flimsy outlines of creatures drained of all substance, souping down into the bedrock of the shore. The television crew has returned and is filming a walk-and-talk along the ridge of the dunes. '*And what I believe we can expect in a matter of minutes, Cathy, is an inflagration potentially unlike any we have seen before.*' – '*A conflagration, Tim. Inflagration isn't a word.*'

Nicola watches the small crowd milling around the bonfire, men heaving shovelfuls onto the pile. The fire, when it goes up, is a faint and queasy blue, filling the air with the smell of something boiling. On the deck, Nicola folds in half the typed page she is still holding and finds a further scribble in black biro overleaf.

Nicola for God's sake, grow up.

She is out of food, except for crackers, which have grown soft from being left unwrapped. With nothing to occupy her, she falls asleep on the floor of the bedroom in the early afternoon. She dreams first about her wedding: the prawn cocktails in martini glasses and Daniel swinging her around to 'Try a Little Tenderness'. Cece had given a speech about her little sister – We *always knew Nic would find someone dependable* – and Nicola had tried to make her own toast, although at this point, the dream changes and she imagines herself a jellyfish – a blind thing, tearable as paper, sinking down beneath black water on a moonless febrile night.

Before their father died, he had called her the princess, the precious cargo. Pressed his hands together and mimed an attendant's bow.

'There is a lack of self-preservation about you,' Cece had said, midway through their father's funeral, 'which is frankly a vanity. You assume other people will care enough to look after you.'

In asking for a divorce, Daniel had told her he knew that it was at least partially his fault. Leaning over with his hands on his knees, he had spoken to the floor of the deck, explaining that he hadn't considered the pitfalls inherent in really taking ownership of someone. She had told him, as she had that first night at dinner, that she could actually take care of herself, though he had only shaken his head once again and taken his ring off, easy as pie.

In the evening, Nicola leaves the house and walks down the narrow jag of path onto the beach. The bonfire has burned itself out over the course of the day and what is left is only skeletal. A coil of indigo smoke. The shore is quiet, clean, the way it had been when Daniel first walked her down it, holding her hand and her elbow to guide her over divots in the sand. She navigates her own way now, turns her ankle only briefly on the slope.

Up over the dunes, she can see the deck that wraps around the house, the plates and cups she has left there, the dressing gown she has abandoned to the back of a chair. Daniel's lawyer will not, she imagines, appreciate the mess when he returns tomorrow, nor will he appreciate the empty house or the fact that she has left the front door open, thrown the windows wide on both the north and southern sides, left the key under the mat.

The evening is soft now, wheel of night gulls on the water. In her bag, she has the Russian dolls from QVC, the egg timer filled with coloured sand, the machine for counting change. The pottery cat she has had to leave behind, being too unwieldy to lift.

It is just after ten in the evening, no particular rush to be gone. She sits down in the sand, a spot just beyond the wrack line, and works idly at the ring on her still-swollen finger, turning it round in fruitless circles, never raising it above the knuckle. There will be more jellyfish. Later, washing up in the tight apple-light that follows dawn, a product of the early tide. When they come, she will still be here, salt-rimed from a night on the shore. She will lay herself down, await the convocation. Jellyfish beaching against her arms and legs, the crest of body on delicate body. They will cover her, glove her hands, circle her ankles. Dependant on species, it can take a jellyfish up to fifty minutes to die once out of water. In the thin lifeline of a waning tide, that time can be easily tripled. Nicola will stay with them well into the morning, their pulsing bells like so many painful hearts. Blanketed, almost head to toe, she will feel the tide recede. Her fingers will come to feel a touch gelatinous at their points, softened along their webbing. She will imagine herself sinking down, becoming something less than solid, spilling insides onto the sand.

CURTILAGE

THE BUNGALOWS' OWNERS have larded their lairs with folderols intended to inject personality, but said folderols only emphasise the blandness of the pink-brick, not very elevated elevations. This is ironic, even sad, but unsurprising since most of the folderols have been acquired from the same few shelves in the same few aisles of the local branch of B&Q.

Plants personalise the buildings more successfully, admittedly through concealment rather than enhancement: the larger the plant, and the more of them there are, the better. Trees do the job best of all, especially trees of medium-to-large size, with a low leaf-line that peppers the bungalows' blandness with broken shade, or comes close to hiding them.

I'm getting a little angry and I don't want that, so I set the word *curtilage* trundling around in my head. It's become one of my favourites over the past few months' work; I can almost hear it roll, like a prized marble or ball bearing on a polished wooden floor. The sound calms me.

Outside my skull a hot and sulky silence lolls over the neighbourhood, though a reasonably busy road runs only a couple of blocks away. The silence is invisible, of course, but I choose to picture it as a kind of vast, translucent jelly, hovering like some movie mother-ship whose clammy under-parts insinuate themselves into airbricks, letterboxes and drain-pipes, and droop between redundant chimney pots. (The wood burner craze hasn't arrived here yet, current occupants being old enough to remember what a smoky, dusty palaver all of that lugging and cleaning really is. Once they shuffle off, it will be a different story.)

Curtilage, curtilage . . .

The cul-de-sac sees little traffic; I've not been here before but it's familiar from Google Earth. See the faded Saint George's flag with the phoney wishing well just opposite! Behold the pretentious box hedging, blight-riddled! This is the sort of area whose residents secrete their vehicles inside cloned garages, and the few, parked cars are what you'd expect: practical but affordable, new-ish, and dutifully main-tained and waxed. Only one front garden is occupied. An old bloke is prodding at one of the borders with a wasp-striped, long-handled, multi-functional, new-fangled tool, all levers and springs. I have no idea what it is. He looks knackered; the plants look knackered; even the soil does. I nod and half-smile as I pass: *when in Rome*, and all that. The gardener ignores me but his dog growls and stiffens, too lazy/sun-stunned to stand. It's a Labrador. Well, of course it is. He probably got it in B&-fucking-Q, along with the concrete donkey and its begonia-festooned panniers, and that ridiculous vivid imple-ment, un-lose-able even if you've lost your bifocals or, pos-sibly, your sight.

Speakers thump out some temporarily popular drivel and a mustard-coloured Renault Mégane convertible passes, too fast. It's only three years old but there are duct tape dressings on various hood-wounds and a chunk of the rear bumper's been sheared off. Since nobody living hereabouts would consider driving under anything other than a solid (practical, affordable, dutifully waxed) roof, this has to be the estate agent. The car slews to a halt about thirty metres ahead, quite near the kerb, opposite the bungalow with the most ostentatious satellite dish and the concrete griffons camping it up on the gateposts – a flourish that manages to be both unusual and utterly predictable. The handbrake is wrenched on and the shitty music stops, leaving a reverberating silence that's still deeper than before. It's funny what the parking of a car can tell you about its driver. I know that this one hates his or her job, among other things, and I suspect that he or she is going to hate me.

I think it will be a she.

The door flies open with a screech and the predicted female emerges. She brushes her skirt down and straightens her jacket, testily. Cigarette smoke swirls from the car and I fancy I can spot tiny, abruptly extinguished crochets and quavers tumbling out with it; they drift and fade to nothing along with the fumes. The agent senses my approach and switches on a smile that hasn't been rehearsed quite enough. She's applied a generous, liverish layer of slap that's troublingly close to the paint job on her car; she has perplexing eyebrows, and fag-breath. There's a button missing from her jacket; I knew there would be. I have no idea how old she is, which probably suits her.

'Mr—?'

I concur, though she hasn't said my name. Remiss of her. I could be anyone, possibly even someone worse than the someone I am, which is possible if unlikely. She mouths her moniker, which I forget instantly; shakes my hand as perfunctorily as is possible; ducks back into the car, very arse-aware;

and then stands to offer the handful of papers she's hooked from the passenger seat. Careful to smile more sincerely than she, I refuse them and flourish the details I've printed out already. She looks affronted, but nods, and strides on worn kitten heels towards the bungalow. Abruptly she swivels and we almost collide.

'I'll let Mr T— show you round. But please bear in mind that he and Mrs T— are quite frail, so be gentle.'

Her words indicate concern, her expression the opposite. I nod, understandingly.

I mean: I do understand. I really *do*.

There are fuchsias here, rather than begonias, and shabby gnomes providing a midget guard of honour. She jabs (bitten nails, varnish at least a week old and as chipped as the gnome-paint), and the doorbell chimes 'Greensleeves'. Lace curtains shimmer and the door is opened very slowly, fully forty-nine seconds later: I count them off, in my head.

Mr T—'s clothes are unexceptional but he sports a broad, brown leather belt and striped braces: it seems he's the cautious type, and much good it seems to have done him. His handshake is firm and his palm calloused. He nods at the agent with dismissive familiarity (the bungalow has been on the market for months) but looks me up and down intently, almost rudely. This alerts me to the probability that Mr T— has eye problems, so I smile broadly, very close up and much more disarmingly than my companion.

Bingo. I should give lessons. Mr T— decides he likes the cut of my jib, and whispers to me from the doorstep, 'It's the wife, y'see. Bleedin' Alzheimer's. Wouldn't be movin' otherwise. We can't cope, no choice. Thirty-two years in this place. Love it here . . .'

I commiserate, sincerely. I tell him I'm a cash buyer, not so sincerely.

We enter reverently as if into some neglected country church. The immediate throat-catch of damp heightens that notion but only in the second until the heat hits: no country church was ever this warm. It's hotter than the street. I feel engulfed, slightly stunned, but decide to enjoy it.

We reach the first open door along the hallway, and Mrs T— nods and waves wildly. Her expression encapsulates delight and vacancy; her legs are elephantine and bandaged. She's enthroned in some complicated invalid chair, tubular and white and stark against the swirling crimson patterns of the carpet that are the only aspect of the room itself that I take in. There are crutches, certainly, and there might be pulleys, oxygen cylinders etc., but I don't stare. Mr T— tugs at my sleeve, insistent as a Mexican street boy, and as he shepherds me away the agent clucks over the old woman while texting the office and subtly wrinkling her faux-jaundiced nose.

The bungalow is a testament to poverty and sentiment. Throws, ornaments, cushions and doilies attempt to camouflage threadbare sofas and chipped veneer, no more successful in their purpose than those exterior folderols. Cute animal prints slump crookedly in cheap frames that, in turn, sit skew-whiff on floral wallpaper. There is woodchip, there is polystyrene, there is crochet; there are wedding gift relics that should be in a museum, though no museum would want them. A few sepia forebears gawp from foxed mounts with varying degrees of solemnity and/or embarrassment. I make a point of studying these respectfully but not for too long: people can get surprisingly proprietorial and touchy about their dead. More recent likenesses of absent (though, presumably, still living) offspring, awkward in the graduation clobber of obscure polytechnics, stare from bedside cabinets littered with blister packs and liniment tubes. The spattering of black mould crawling up the walls in the bathroom contrasts almost pleasantly with the polychrome anarchy of the rest of the bungalow (it's hard to get those carpet patterns in Mrs T—'s room out of my head; they were like vortices of scabbed blood). The bath and basin are pink, and the matching, pre-B&-fucking-Q bog has a cast-iron, overhead cistern and a rusting chain. The boiler, a gargantuan, floor-standing hulk, is fit only for scrap; I feel an ironic surge of fury at those uncaring, absent offspring, and calm myself by reaching into my pocket and fingering the Swann Morton retractable scalpel whose new 10A blade, the best for my purpose, is tucked away safely for now.

Curtilage, curtilage . . .

I coo, and Mr T— very nearly permits a glimmer of pleasure to break through the hard-won crust of wariness and fatigue. I can see the change; thousands wouldn't.

'Want a look outside?'

'If it's not too much trouble.'

We move along a narrow cracked path of concrete slabs, painted the same liver-hue as the carpet whorls, between the kitchen and the garage. It's roofed over with corrugated plastic sheeting whose grooves are stodgy with moss and whose ridges are Pollocked with bird-shit. I have the feeling such filth is comparatively recent and a source of embarrassment, because Mr T— keeps his gaze fixed on the ground. But his gait is admirable for one so punch-drunk from life: rolling, slightly bandy and giving off no little sense of self-worth. He's

146

reminiscent of those heavy-arsed toy clowns whose centre of gravity is so low you can't push them over. Perhaps, he was a sailor. I wouldn't have wanted to take him on in his prime, or even a decade ago. As for now . . .

I haven't seen one of those clowns for years.

Emerging into the back garden feels like bursting from a dank pool into clear air: the garden is *different*. Crimson chrysanths, pom-pom dahlias, and stringy runner beans are hardly to my taste, but the beds occupy a surprisingly large area and tell of skilful passionate industry. It's only when I look more closely that neglect reveals itself: there are unpicked vegetables and soft fruits rotting on their stalks; tools left out to rust; an under-commitment to deadheading.

Mr T— notices that I've noticed.

'Pride an' joy, used t'be. Can't manage no more.'

He clams up and barrels towards the shed; stands aside to usher me in. It's dark, cobwebbed and filled with treasures. Mr T— stays outside and mumbles something else.

'Sorry. I didn't catch that.'

'I SAID I'm goin' effin' *blind* . . .'

The old man starts off almost shouting but then his words curdle and I have to do some more sympathy, albeit from a distance. He turns away to hide tears, peering into whatever shimmering, limited vista remains for him. I perform a brisk inventory of the shed and pocket a pretty, miniature spirit level; then wait, allowing him time to compose himself. (I've always liked that phrase, implying as it does that people are somehow akin to songs, melodies, even symphonies. I see myself as something atonal and bracingly abrasive, though still highly organised. I'm not one for improvisation.)

Having allowed a decent, manly interval, I clear my throat

and say, 'Do you mind if I have another wander round inside the house? The layout's not quite fixed in my head.'

'Take your time. But I'd better . . .' He gestures resignedly towards his wife's room. 'She'll be wonderin' where I am. Mind you, after five minutes she'll be wonderin' *who* I am.'

I watch him toddle off.

A complicated folding rule and a pair of ebony-and-brass dividers disappear inside my coat; then I follow him back under the pigeon-shit canopy and into the house. The agent is mithering away; I hear Mr T— grunting in response. In the kitchen I switch off the freezer, then quietly open a cupboard and remove the lid from a full pot of honey, turning it upside down and placing it on the top shelf before I close the door. There's no need to open more jars; honey's great for the job as it has a way of finding its way everywhere, and sticks almost as beautifully as Tate & Lyle's Golden Syrup. There's none of the latter here, surprisingly. I put the plug in the sink and turn on the tap, just barely. He'll find that first and think he did it, might wonder if it's the first sign that he's following the missus.

The estate agent calls out, 'Are you OK out there?' She sounds a little desperate.

'Never better,' say I, and it's true.

'Let me know if you need any more info, won't you?'

How I hate lazy, slangy abbreviations.

Curtilage, curtilage . . .

'Of course. I won't be much longer.'

Back in the bedroom I snap the heads from two ceramic spaniels and remove all the light bulbs I can reach. I take out my scalpel, expose that elegant 10A blade, and then notice a subtle change in the light. Mrs T— is standing in the doorway. She looks enormous; a bandaged yeti slumped on a Zimmer frame. I've made the mistake of believing she was contributing to the hum of conversation that continues from her room. Silly me. I retract the blade and slip the scalpel behind my back. We look at one another.

She starts to shriek, really shriek.

'What the fuck are you doing back here? Thought we told you to stay away after last time. Croydon not good enough for you? Why don't you piss off back to your blonde slag, we don't want you—'

Curtilagecurtilagecurtilage . . .

And then Mr T— is next to her, all 'There there', and 'Come on, Mother', and 'It's not Richard, love'. He shuffles her - suddenly silent and pliable - away, and I'm alone again, touched at this obvious affection, and relieved that he didn't notice any damage. I flip back the ghastly, quilted duvets (twin beds, unsurprisingly), slice quickly down the centre of each mattress, and rearrange the covers. That won't be noticed that for ages.

The agent looks relieved to see me: dementia has its limitations. Mr T— mutters an apology and his wife, enthroned once more, smiles at me as if we've never met. Injecting a degree of ripe heartiness into my voice I tell the trio that I've seen enough of this lovely property. Two of them deliver their lines as readily as I have, the third nods and grins absently, and when all brisk niceties have been observed the agent and I see ourselves out, promising an early response.

It's milder than in the house, and the change in temperature seems to permit more ambient noise: dogs yap and a thrush pipes away cheerfully. The mother-ship has moved on, or assumed a higher altitude, allowing cooler currents and this livelier atmosphere to circulate below her clammy, drooping under-parts. The agent (still arse-aware) leads me back between the gnomes and we hit the pavement. She turns on her eroded heels, lights up and inhales suicidally, circumflex eyebrows jitterbugging.

'What did you think? Potential? It's not in the best of condition but it's a very good price and there's space for a decent conservato—'

Slowly, deliberately I make a cut-throat gesture. The agent looks confused, as well she might. I step right up to her and stare into her eyes for four seconds: I count them off in my head. She backs off, almost tripping, clutching her handbag to her belly. I shove her aside and walk away briskly.

She shouts rash obscenities from her car as she speeds past, but wisely doesn't stop.

A mile or so away, having taken the circuitous footpath-and-alley route I'd planned earlier (in case of constabulary involvement), on a quiet bridge over the town's less-than-pristine waterway I take out the SIM card from the pay-as-you-go mobile and drop it into the water. It glints and bobs, then disappears, or perhaps I just lose interest. A little further downriver I drown the phone, hurling it mid-stream: you can't be too careful and I've got plenty more at home.

Though I'm already contemplating my next outing I pause to inspect today's trophies. Coincidentally, they're all engraved with the same legend: J. RABONE & SONS. MADE IN ENGLAND. The old man's fingers have rubbed away the silver-plating on the spirit level and its bright, brass core catches the sun, very cheerfully. The dividers feel just so in my hand; the folding rule is a miracle of pivots.

I feed them to the nearest drain and jog to the station, replenished.

KISS

A COUPLE STOP in a tube station entrance, and a man nearby tightens his fingers around a detonator in his hand.

They lean together to kiss, the crowd flowing around them, a moment you can hold like a still from a film, the young woman lifting her face, silver jacket, blond hair in a ponytail, the young man bending, dreadlocks bunched at his neck in a red band.

A moment in a progression of moments, leading towards the moment their lips will meet, running on from all the moments before: the couple rising up out of the underground through the musty-smelling wind, the stale breath of old London with its shades of Bedlam and The Ripper still shifting in the tunnels with the soot-coloured mice that run between the rails, leaning together, the young man behind, the young woman leaning back, new lovers drunk on touch: while above in the glittering day, the young man with the bomb in his backpack crosses the road towards the tube station entrance, nervous, looking over his shoulder in the way he's not supposed to, been told not to, a gleam of sweat on his faintly shadowed upper lip. And the moments before that, as the young couple sat in the rattling train, the young woman's ankles crossed in her green sneakers, the young man's jutting thighs hard in tight jeans, and above in the street the lad with the backpack stood ready to alight from a bus and was jostled so he fell against the metal post. And his heart turned over, but nothing happened, and in those seconds, he breathed again, though as he stepped to the pavement he was afraid that the fuse was damaged and panicked that his mission would fail.

And the history before: the night the young couple met, lights strung in the trees in a south London garden, reggae blasting through open windows, his lithe frame silhouetted, hers pale against dark shrubs. A girl you could see as privileged, a man you could assume to be righteously, rightfully angry, and in the first few seconds, as they were introduced, that was just how they saw each other: he on his bristling guard, she potentially afraid and ashamed; and then, as he handed her a drink, each recognised in the other – she in the soft gleam of his eyes, he in the brave lift of her chin – the courage of a survivor.

While across London, over the narrow gardens and the roofs of the terraces, over the low- and high-rise council estates, the wide ebbing river and the traffic run of Euston, the young man who would carry the backpack rang the bell to an upstairs flat. Three others bent over a table scattered with batteries and wires, the boom of a nightclub, decadent sound of the non-believers, thudding up through the floor.

And the pasts further back, the stories dovetailing towards this moment.

A tall house on Highgate Hill with a laurel bush in the garden, family dinner with solicitor parents in a shining kitchen extension, the girl's younger brother and sister squabbling, her mother mildly scolding as she spooned out the pasta, then touching her husband's shoulder as she turned with the saucepan. Father looking up at her mother and smiling, as if he had eyes for no other, as if the night before, when the others were sleeping, he hadn't crept into the girl's room, hadn't hissed in her face afterwards, It's just between you and me. Though he didn't need to say it, how could she tell her mother, how could she tell anyone? A thing that wasn't supposed to happen. She stared at her father acting as though it hadn't. Perhaps it hadn't. Perhaps she had dreamt it; perhaps she was evil, filthy-minded. Perhaps she was mad. No, she wasn't dreaming; she had to face that when it happened again. But yes, perhaps she *was* mad, perhaps there was something wrong with her, for it to keep on happening. In school she kept away from the other girls, sat in the library at lunchtime, her limbs heavy and frozen, while they went off down the road to hang around the café and gossip and call to the boys. Envious, no not envious, too removed from them for envy, trapped behind a barrier, her inability to account for herself, even to herself.

But did her mother guess anyway? She would wonder that, years later. And did she blame the girl? For she reserved for the girl a strictness she never applied to her siblings, and a critical tartness of manner that made the girl feel constantly stupid and dashed. Though she didn't like to admit it to herself, she didn't want to think she was unloved. Fifteen years old, she sat on her mother's bed beside her mother as she got ready to go to a function, her mother patting her own hair in the mirror, taking up her bangles and asking, Which one? The girl was flattered to be asked and chose with care, a deep blue and a turquoise to go with the colours in her mother's kaftan, and her mother, pleased with the choice, drew them onto her wrist. An intimate moment, for which the girl was glad. And in that moment, she had the notion of telling her mother, weighed it in her mind as she'd weighed the bangles in her hands. Her mother leaned forward to adjust her mascara, and the girl watched a little crease appear at the back of her neck and was overwhelmed by a sense of her mother as vulnerable, and of the devastation that such a revelation would create. And that was when her mother, meeting her eyes in the mirror, said tartly, quite nastily, That lipstick doesn't suit you.

Then the years of anorexia, that wish to be no longer the person you see in the mirror and weighing you down, to flee her; the dropping out of university, the lack of room in your head for facts and complicated thoughts about things it was hard to make matter, the lack of point in it all. And finally, one dark night, the attempt to escape at last with a can of lager and a packet of pills.

And the long road to recovery, which she was still treading that night at the party in the south London garden, but there she was, treading it, or rather, standing still against the dark bushes as the young man with the dreadlocks turned towards her, carrying his own past of oppression.

The monkey noises and gestures, those grammar school boys going past in the morning as he turned out of the Bristol council estate, the sly and not-so-sly slurs in the playground. He stopped going, doubled back to the empty house – his lone mother gone to her hospital cleaning job – or hung around the shopping precinct. His mother summoned to the school, the anger and sadness in her eyes. The taunts didn't stop, and as he grew his anger grew too: he would flip and lash out, and in the end, he was expelled. The sleek police car drawing up alongside as he walked in the streetlight, a teenager with dreadlocks; once, on a two-mile walk, he was stopped several times. He had learned the necessity of controlling his temper, but he couldn't help a gesture of exasperation, he threw up his arms, and later his mother would find him in the police station covered in bruises.

And then the long fight for justice, and calmness, and work for a charity helping young people with such problems, and a soft summer night in a south London garden shaking hands with a new worker, the pale young woman.

And as the young man with the dreadlocks stood in court in the dock and the young woman came to in a hospital bed with a drip in her arm, the twelve-year-old boy who would eventually carry the backpack sat neatly in his uniform passing his exams, the pride of his grocer father, destined for university and the life of a doctor. But as he walked home through the winter evenings something was awry. The dark street was a gulf between squat cliffs of housing, acrid light leaking from mean squares of windows, congealed sticky rubbish, a dog slinking, guilty or sly, from a deep black alley, like the gulf between the life of his home – his anxious, conscientious parents, eager to please in this land they came to – and the life of school and the high street where the kids hung at weekends in their hi-tops, careless and entitled. He belonged in neither world. He belonged nowhere; his future, mapped out by his parents, was a mystery to him, alien. He had no real purpose of his own. Until one day after mosque, someone touched his arm and drew him aside.

And here they are now, three young lives converging, and the lives of those milling around them, the young people in jeans, the men and women carrying cases with laptops and papers, parents with a child in a pushchair, which the young man with the backpack has been trained not to see as individual people with lives, only to think of the glory of martyrdom and reward in heaven.

And here is the moment when his thumb touches the plunger, and if the fuse has become disconnected the crowd will keep flowing and the couple will complete their embrace and move on to wherever their relationship will take them, or the pulse will hit the fuse and the air around it will fly out faster than the speed of sound, and in the blast and the shock waves that follow, and the sucking vacuum created, those linear narratives will shatter, the fragments spin – a mother's resentful face in the mirror, the hatred and fear in a policeman's eyes, lights glowing in a south London garden, and the moment conceived but never fulfilled, the perfect conclusion, the kiss.

BADGERFACE

DOD'S BACK AND he's looking meaner than ever. He's come straight to the pub and even though I'm working he grabs me in a headlock and rubs his fist against my crew cut, and it hurts but I can't say anything so I just close my eyes really tight. When he's finished, he swings me round and puts his hands on my shoulders in a 'let me look at you' kind of way. His neck is short and wide and the tendons are sticking out, taut like ropes.

'Haven't got any less ugly, have you, Badge?' he says. When he's finished looking at me he lets me go and walks straight over to the bar and asks Sandra for a pint of Felinfoel. He drinks it down in one go and asks for another and I know it's going to be one of those nights.

In the six months that Dod's been gone, he's become enormous. His arms are huge, the muscles bulging from under the sleeves of his khaki t-shirt, swelling the tattoos and disfiguring them. The snake has become a python, not the elegant black mamba it was when he left, and the graceful bluebird has turned into a massive, irate eagle. There's an angel that sits on his shoulder, her arms stretching up into his sleeve, and even though I can't see it, I know that she's holding a harp above her head. She's swollen taut across his biceps, and looks more pregnant than devout. Even his thighs are straining against the material of his combat trousers. I wonder why he's come here in his work clothes, why he doesn't put on a track suit or jeans like all the other men in the village, but then I look over to where he's standing against the bar, halfway down his second pint, the flotsam and jetsam of the Ceffyl Du floating around him and I know why he's done this. The Hero's Return. He's getting pats on the back and shots of whisky bought for him, and Sandra's undone the top button of her blouse in celebration. I pick up the rest of the glasses and push my way through the throngs of well-wishers and put the pint pots down on the bar. There are still paper ghosts hanging up on the shelf behind, even though Halloween was yesterday.

'Bless him,' Sandra says in my direction, looking sad and disgusted at the same time. Dod catches my eye and winks and holds up his pint to me in a tiny salute.

When I get home, Darren's sitting on his own in the kitchen. He's chugging on a can of Stella and a Marlboro Light and I know Mam'll kill him if she finds out. I nod at him and fetch a can from the fridge. I sit down opposite and wait for him to speak. He doesn't, so I decide to get in first.

'Dod's back.'

Still he doesn't say anything. He stares at me for a while then he takes another swig of lager and pokes his fag end into the hole in the top. He crushes the can in his hand. He chucks it on the table.

'It's all right, Champ,' he says and he walks out. He's the only one who calls me Champ. Everyone else calls me Badgerface. Apart from Mam, who calls me by my proper name.

I open the top part of the window and flap my hand to clear the smoke and then I wrap his can up in a Spar bag and push it down the side of the kitchen bin. Then I sit there, drinking my beer and thinking about nothing.

I hear Dod get in sometime in the early hours. The pylons have been buzzing again, and I've been awake on and off even before the front door smashes open against the wall. Tonight the pylons are louder than usual, and I find myself wondering if this is because Dod's back. Then I tell myself that's stupid, and that's when I hear the door crash open.

There's the sound of a scuffle, and I think it's probably Dod falling over onto the pile of shoes and coats in the hall. The landing light goes on, and I know it'll be Mam. She's been fretting about today. Ever since he phoned to say he was coming back she's been jumpy, cleaning the house even more than usual, making sure there are fresh sheets on the bed and playing Shirley Bassey extra loud. She's had her roots done and her nails are all silvery-pink. Now I can hear them in the hall, and she's shushing him and he's coughing and then they're quiet for a moment. Kissing, I think.

'Baby doll.' Dod thinks he's whispering but he's too drunk to talk quietly and Mam's shushing him again. Mam's got a frilly nightie, a baby doll nightie, and that's what Dod calls her in the first week when he gets home, after he's been away on ops. It's all 'Baby Doll' in the first week when they can't keep their hands off each other, and they lock themselves in their room for hours at a time, and Dod'll come out now and again to hand me a couple of twenties and an order for the Chinese and the offy. It's Baby Doll for the first week.

For the second week it's, 'You Slag.' For that week they'll

just fight and shout and Mam will start wearing more make-up under her eyes and sit at the kitchen table in her dressing gown, staring at her fingernails and picking away at the nail polish. She'll spend more time on the phone to Auntie Gaynor, and when she puts the phone down, she'll still be crying. That's the second phase, the You Slag phase.

Then it's just pure indifference, for both of them. It's as though they don't even know that the other one is there and they exist in two isolated versions of reality, getting their own food, making their own cups of tea. They'll go out separately, him to the Ceff, her with the girls, and they won't even tell the other one where they're going. Ships that pass in the night, Darren calls them.

Dod is crying now, loud sniffles that Mam is doing her best to soothe.

I wonder if Darren can hear them from his room, or if he's fast asleep.

In the morning, I push Darren's door open and go in without knocking, but he's already gone and his bed is made, the duvet cover flat and smooth. I think about lying on it, putting my head on his pillow and making an indentation there, leaving the shape of my head on the pristine surface. I can't do it though, and instead I pick up his aftershave from the chest of drawers and spray a bit on my neck. Davidoff Cool Water. Now I smell just like Darren.

When I get to the pub for the start of my shift, it's already kicking off. It's over soon enough, mind. Sandra doesn't take any shit and she'll chuck someone out on their ear soon as look at them, even if it's Jamie who's Rabby's son and thinks he owns the place. Jamie's been going to the gym for the last few months, and I think he's been doing steroids, because he's massive and he's got this glassy look in his eyes that doesn't come from four pints of lager top.

When Jamie's left and it's all calmed down again, Sandra stands behind the bar, wiping glasses out with a cloth. She's hard as nails is Sandra. She has to be, really, to handle people like Jamie who'll smack anyone, doesn't matter if they're a man or a woman. Sandra's short and wiry, with dyed blonde hair in a tight ponytail on top of her head. Even though she's really old - late forties or even early fifties - she always wears a low-cut top, and you can see the tops of her tits hanging down inside, the skin brown and wrinkled, like potato peelings. Tommo said he got off with her once when he was off his face and she was closing up after a lock-in. He says he doesn't remember much about it but that she was really up for it and just the thought of it makes my stomach turn over.

Sandra's what you'd call a functioning alcoholic. She's not meant to drink on the job. It's illegal to be drunk and be in charge of a bar, but she's found a way round that. She'll get Alison to go to the optic right at the end and stick a couple of shots of Malibu into a glass of Coke. I don't know if Malibu has always been Sandra's drink of choice, or if she's chosen it because it's at the end of the optics, the one that's out of range of the CCTV camera, and so she can't be seen by Rabby who sits in the flat upstairs all night, just watching the footage of what's going on in his pub.

Dod comes in and goes to sit at the corner table. He catches Sandra's eye on the way through and she pours him a pint and brings it over and puts it on the table without saying a word. She gives him a half-smile, a sympathetic sort of smile. The celebrations are over. The hero has returned and now it's back to normal. I know that now he's back Dod will start to shrink. I know that the bulk he's built up while he's been in Afghanistan will start to shift; he can't keep it up when he's at home. Over the next six months he'll get smaller and smaller. He'll go back to wearing his jeans or his tracky bottoms. He'll cover up the tattoos, the snake and the bird and the angel, and he'll wander around, glass-eyed and morose, until Mam makes him phone up the PTSD counsellor and arrange some more sessions. That's how it always is.

Dod's finished his pint and he gets up and walks over to the bar. Instead of ordering another drink, though, he leans over and whispers something in Sandra's ear. She nods, biting her lip, and then she grabs a bottle of vodka from the store and lifts the flap at the end of the bar and walks through and Dod follows her over to the door in the corner. She keys in the code and Dod follows her through and the door shuts behind them.

When I turn back round to go and collect Dod's glass, I see Darren sitting in Dod's place. Darren never comes into the pub and I think that something's wrong, that something bad's happened, maybe to Mam, but Darren just smiles at me and gives me a thumbs-up and his mouth makes the shape of 'All right, Champ?'

Darren and Jamie were thick as thieves over the summer, virtually inseparable. Like Siamese twins, they were. For weeks, ever since they finished their GCSEs, they'd lock themselves away in Darren's room with the curtains shut, and it was only the sound of Grand Theft Auto crashing out from under the door that told anyone they were in there. Even Tommo and Justin Probert couldn't persuade them to go into town.

Eventually Mam said that was enough, that they needed to get out and get some fresh air and she went in and opened the curtains and turned off the Xbox. 'And start looking for a bloody job, while you're at it,' she said as they sloped off down the path. And then she sat on the sofa and cried.

Dod had only been gone for a month by then, and wouldn't be back for another five at least. Mam always found it hardest at the beginning, when he first went off on ops, because she had to readjust to being on her own again. I told her that she wasn't on her own, that she had me and Darren, and she smiled at that, and gave me a cwtch, and then her eyes went all watery, and she reached out a shaky hand and traced it down the middle of my face, all the way down my birthmark, between my eyes and over my nose and my mouth and all the way down to my chin. I knew that after another couple of weeks she'd get herself together, get used to Dod being away, but I told her that, for now, Darren and I would look after her.

I caught up with Darren and Jamie about half an hour later, and in that time they'd managed to pick up Tommo and Justin Probert and a carrier bag full of cans from the offy.

The thing about Darren and the lads is that they had a pecking order, just like Mam's chickens. Darren was always at the top, just because he was the best of them all: the cleverest, the best looking, and the most successful with the few girls in the village that were worth getting off with. Jamie came next, but only cos his dad owned the pub and he could get them served. He looks like Wayne Rooney. Then it was a toss-up between Tommo and Justin Probert. Tommo's not bad to look at but he's thick as shit and his dad drives the lorry for the sewage works, so he and his sister always smell of shit as well. I don't mind him though; he's always good for a bit of banter and usually has a good story. Justin Probert is a chopsy little twat, and he's always picking away at his acne and hacking into a tissue. Still, he's the only one of them that has a job, or near enough to a job. He's got an apprenticeship at the butcher's on Swan Road, and he always seems to have a smell of offal about him. So it's shit or guts, if you're one of Darren's mates.

They were fifty metres or so ahead of me on the path when I spotted them, but I'd recognise Darren anywhere. He was the tallest of the lot, and he had a white t-shirt on, so bright and clean that it looked luminous in the sunlight. I knew they'd be heading for the pylons and I kept my distance so they couldn't see me, or they'd tell me to go back. I ducked in and out of the hedge, sometimes crawling on my stomach across the ground, commando-style, pretending I was Dod in the desert in Afghanistan. The grass under my belly was scratchy and crisp and dry.

The lads stopped when they got to the far pylon and I knew they'd chosen that one just in case Mam came to hang the washing out and saw them sitting on the grass with their cans and fags. The far pylon was the one Darren and I had always gone to when we were kids, and I knew that if I crouched down in the tiny copse of trees just next to it I'd be completely hidden.

Tommo and Justin Probert had cracked open a couple of cans, and were chasing each other like girls, giggling and splashing lager everywhere. Darren and Jamie sat side by side on the grass, leaning back on their hands, watching them. Not looking at each other.

I wasn't sure, I couldn't see properly through the leaves,

but I thought that their fingers might have been touching in the grass. They carried on not looking at each other.

Tommo and Justin Probert started shrieking, their shirts stuck to their chests with Special Brew, completely oblivious to anyone else.

Then Jamie pulled his hand away and took out a packet of fags from the carrier bag and undid the cellophane. He pulled out the foil and tapped a cigarette out. Without asking, without offering, he turned to Darren and placed it in his mouth, and my brother's lips closed softly around it. Jamie pulled his lighter out from his back pocket. He cupped a hand round the flame and held it in front of the cigarette, waiting for Darren to take a drag. My brother put his hand over Jamie's, steadying it, and that's when I knew. I just knew.

I was out from behind the trees in a second.

'Fucking hell, Darren! Just wait till Dod finds out. He'll fucking skin you alive!' I don't know if I was angry or sad or just confused, but I ran at Darren and started hitting him, clobbering him over the face and head, throwing punches that were as weak as they were badly aimed. He pushed me away and jumped to his feet and grabbed my hands and held them down by my sides. Tommo and Justin Probert had stopped chasing each other and were watching us, frowning.

'Dod doesn't need to know, does he, Champ? Dod doesn't need to know anything.' Darren was whispering. Jamie wasn't even looking at us. He was looking away, lighting his own cigarette with shaking hands.

'Fuck, Darren, he'll find out.' I was whispering now, as well, aware of Tommo and Justin Probert heading back over to where we were standing, getting closer all the time. 'You know he'll find out. He finds out about everything in the village. Even when he's away.'

That's when Jamie jumped to his feet. He grabbed me by the collar and yanked me towards him. His teeth were mostly brown, the gums swollen and red around them, and his breath stank. I thought about him and Darren kissing and I felt sick. Jamie was filthy compared to Darren. He didn't deserve Darren. No-one did.

'He won't find out, will he, Badge? He won't find out because you're not going to tell anyone, are you?' He's quite big, is Jamie. Not really big like Dod, but short and stocky with broad shoulders and a chest like a tree trunk.

I don't remember how I got away from him, but the next thing I knew I was legging it over to the pylon. I'd climbed it before, loads of times, so I knew the exact combination of hand-over-hand movements I needed to pull myself up. I didn't look down until I was half-way up, a good twenty metres in the air, and then I saw that Jamie was still near the bottom, struggling to get a grip on the rails. Darren was standing below him, pleading with him to stop being such a dick.

Finally, Jamie seemed to relent, and slowly he climbed back down. Darren said something to him, something I couldn't hear, and then he was climbing up, one hand after the other, just like he'd shown me when we were kids.

When he got up next to me, he wiped the palm of his hand over his forehead. He wasn't as fit as he used to be. Fags and lager, I guessed, and his white t-shirt was grubby and sweat-stained. I wanted him to be the first to say something, so I waited and I leant back and looked over towards our house and there was Mam, standing on the back step, holding her dressing gown closed with one hand and clutching a cup of tea with the other, watching her chickens scratching in the dust. I wasn't sure if I could really see the dark shadows under her eyes and the wrinkles on her forehead, or if I could only see them because I knew they were there.

'Champ,' said Darren, and he'd got his breath back and he put a hand on my shoulder. We'd been up this pylon so many times that it felt natural to be there now. We belonged there, me and Darren, we were safe up there, away from everyone else. 'Champ, it's nothing. I promise. Nothing that Dod needs to know about, anyway.' I nodded, pleased that Darren wasn't cross with me.

'You won't tell Rabby, either?'

I shook my head. I didn't know much about Jamie's dad then. It was before I'd started working at the pub. I just knew that he had a reputation for being in with a bad crowd and he wasn't someone you'd mess with.

'Thanks, Champ.' We stood like that for a bit, our feet spread wide on the crossbar of the pylon, Darren with his hand on my shoulder, and I liked the feeling of it, heavy and warm and reassuring.

'Want to see something?' He was grinning now, and he took his hand off my shoulder and started rolling up the sleeve of his t-shirt. First feet, then legs and then a body and feathered wings appeared, and then a face with long hair and a halo, and above them, arms and hands holding a harp. It was the exact same design as Dod's tattoo. It was red around the edges, and looked sore and recent. He grinned at me. 'Tidy, eh? Just wait till Dod gets back. He'll love it.'

'Mam'll kill you,' I said, knowing I was stating the obvious.

'That's why I haven't told her.' Then he said 'There she is,' and I looked down to where Mam was still standing on the back step. She'd put her mug down and was waving her arms at us in a gesture that said, 'Get down from there.'

'It's all right!' Darren shouted to her. He lifted his arm up, the one with the tattoo, to wave back, and that's when he fell.

Twenty metres doesn't seem so high when you're climbing. It's over in a flash, especially when you've got Jamie coming after you. But on the way down, it's a different story. Darren seemed to fall for minutes, his white t-shirt stark against the dirty yellow grass, and Jamie and Tommo and Justin Probert just watched him, their mouths open, their hands up, clutching at their hair.

When Dod and Sandra come back down from the flat, the pub's quiet. I've collected all the empty glasses and put them in the dishwasher and Alison's refilling the optics. I'm leaning on the bar, working my way through a packet of pork scratchings, but when I see Dod I scrunch up the packet and put it in my back pocket and pretend to be straightening the bar mats.

He's making for the door, and he doesn't even look at me, but I can see his eyes and they're red, like he's been crying. I look at Sandra, and she's bent over the dishwasher. I can't see her eyes, but there's something about the way she's holding herself, her shoulders slumped, her hair coming loose from her ponytail, that tells me she's been crying as well.

As Dod draws even with me, I can see the angel tattoo on his biceps. His sleeve's been rucked up, and I can see the top of his arm, the bulge of the muscle obscene. It's so much bigger than Darren's angel. Now I can see that Dod's tattoo has changed, that it's been altered while he's been away. It's not just bigger; now the harp has gone and the angel is holding a scroll above her head, a piece of paper that curls in her hands, the edges beautifully shaded to make them look 3D. On the scroll, in perfect, fluid script, are the words, 'Darren 1999-2017.'

I close my eyes and I put my hand up to my face and trace my fingers down, between my eyes and over my nose and my mouth, as far as my chin. When I open my eyes I can see Darren, sitting at the table in the corner, and his white t-shirt is luminous in the gloom of the pub. He gives me a big, double, thumbs-up.

'It's all right, Champ. It's all right.'

ON DAY 21

NINETEEN DAYS OF rain – unprecedented, they said – and I could hardly tell it was morning. E, my youngest, was screaming. She'd had me up for four hours the previous night, so I switched her off, laid her on the bed and gently closed the door, the silence a soft blanket around me.

C and D were sitting on the floor of the living room in a junk of bright items, lost together in their intricate exchange of small powers and pleasures. The rain had kept us in, sandwiched between the flats above and below, and the weather lay so low that the window showed only the canal, slate-grey, slopping onto the towpath. I sat and started folding a heap of clothes warm from the tumble dryer. The heap shrank and the folded pile grew. I was running out of these neat, methodical tasks, so I took my time.

D threw a rampaging dinosaur at C, but it missed him and bounced off the leg of the tea table on which rested my laptop.

The machine woke with a surprised whir. It had slept through the night, and for the first time in two weeks I'd managed to leave it alone all morning. A pair of half-folded corduroys hung from my paused hands as the screen grew keen. It was rich with tiny stars and hearts and numbered dots and exclamation marks.

Notifications can't be ignored. Each one is like a bullet – I mean a bullet that would come out of a gun, not a bullet in a bulleted list, although these seem to be related in terms of urgency. You have to deal with them or they nag at you. You have to deal with them or they might smash through your body. My legs stood me up and I went over to sit at the laptop.

Some time passed. C and D started pulling at my jeans. Their pleasant babble soured to whining, and at that moment the wind spat a great hard gobful of rain at the window. A sharp breath went out of my nostrils and I reached down and switched them both off.

The switch was my secret. I'd told myself I wouldn't resort to it so much, especially with E, who was already small for her age, and such a lovely, milk-scented little thing – though so were the other two; don't get me wrong, they were the sun in my sky. But the minutes of my days were long and difficult, full of complexity and murk, and the switch was a way to get through. It was a way to sharpen the edges of life, to know where and who I was when things got fuzzy. It cleaned; it freshened. Although what helped me wasn't the switching off as such, it was the fact of the switch itself. I'd come to rely on it. And now, for the first time, I'd used the switch on all three children at once.

I stopped for a moment as the implications threatened to come clearly into my mind, but I shook them off before they could. I arranged C and D's little limbs so they wouldn't cramp. Then I returned to the laptop. It was the laptop that had shown me the possibility of this kind of ease. Its machine world was either/or, yes or no, on or off, zero or one. It was the antidote to uncertainty: that devious mould that grew everywhere if I didn't keep on top of it.

Dark had deepened the silence in the room by the time my bladder forced me up from the chair. My phone was there in the bathroom, where I'd left it last time I'd needed to come in here while staying connected to the machine world. The phone offered a sort of letterboxed version of the yes/no world of the laptop, both pleasingly contained and frustratingly miniaturised. I picked it up before sitting, and as I peed I checked its various messaging systems. There was a text from B saying he'd be home early. My husband was a departmental head – some technical department, I wasn't sure which: he said his responsibilities 'spilled over'. When they pushed him to exhaustion I'd tell him he should have boundaries, but he'd say it wasn't that simple. I didn't see why not. He worked for a company, his days a grid of meetings and targets; all of their work was in the service of crisp, black numbers. It seemed to me that it should be wonderful. B would sigh and look at me, so I'd move things along, make him a drink, rub the tough tops of his shoulders as he hunched over work. I had only ever switched him off once.

Just as I checked the time, I heard the squeal of the security gate three floors down. I flushed, washed, and ran in to switch on the two older children, and then lastly, in the bedroom, E. Her little fingers curled and grasped, and her lips plumped back up as the flow of subcutaneous activity restarted. This was the best bit about using the switch: for those first few minutes my children and I were together and fresh again, and there was a kind of crystalline peace. I picked E up and rocked her as she blinked and jerked a fist toward the sweet oval of her yawning mouth.

B turned his key in the door and I went to meet him, and that night everything was fine.

✿

On day twenty the sky lifted to dove grey, and I drove us out
to the big Asda, spinning arcs of water from the wheel-arches.
As I parked, the rain hardened again. C thought his cagoule
felt 'squishy' and refused to put it on, then refused to be put
into it. When he started shouting my fingers reached, so easily
now, for the switch. Nothing happened.

I flicked it up and down, up and down, but nothing. I took
hold of his contorting face and turned it to me, looking for
an answer from him, as if he had overcome the switch by the
force of his own will. This sudden gesture took him aback and
he did in fact stop crying. For a second, we held each other's
gaze and I was struck by the absolute strangeness of him, this
person who had come from me, and it seemed he saw the same
strangeness in me.

I lifted his sister, D, from the other side. I tried her switch.
Again, nothing happened. She squirmed away from me and
went to peer into the tiny convex mirror set within the wing
mirror, enjoying her own distorted face. E was asleep in her
car seat and I didn't want to trouble her.

I looked around the car park, hoping perhaps to see another
person in the same situation. The car park was tidily kept,
with good space for each unit of car to sit quietly to itself,
sure of its locked doors. Racing cloud reflected without sound
in the rain-beaded roofs, and for a moment I was calmed, the
noise of the children dimmed. But there was no one to help.

Who exactly was I looking for? Someone like me or
someone unlike me?

There was no one like me, I thought. All of the people I
encountered during my days seemed fine, sloshing backward

and forward with the tides of each day like happy seaweed. I, however, was up there on the surface, clinging to a broken raft, gazing into tarry liquid that would one day take me down. And that was with the switch to turn to. Now, if that had stopped working, I couldn't see how I'd be able to navigate the days at all. The laptop and my phone did much to help, but they wouldn't act directly on the children, these merchants of chaos who were forever plying their trade.

I didn't know what to do, so we entered the blue-white cavern of the supermarket – me pushing the trolley with E on the plastic seat, C and D trotting close to my legs – and I began to perform the shopping. Parallel lines of goods and lights. Staff dressed in clean white mesh aprons as if they were butchers and bakers. I soon clocked that I was the shopper in whatever scene they were playing out and the role began to feel like a good fit. Once the trolley was convincingly half-full, I felt safe enough to take an interval and I lay down on the floor between the long chest freezers. C and D ran up the aisle and down the ones either side, figure-of-eighting around the gondolas, and I was held by the cold white tiles under me and the cold white striplights above, and the pattern of the children running.

Soon, three people stood over me: a young male security guard, and two women like me. One was tapping at her smartphone. I felt a pull toward the pretty box in her hand, the universal object that could join the hands of everyone worldwide, and which, like the knife of a fugu chef, cleaned and sliced life into something that might not kill us.

The security guard felt for my pulse, which seemed unnecessary, but his warm hand on my wrist was nice. I smiled up at him. Yes, I was fine, and yes, these were my children; they were also fine. With kindness in his eyes he asked me whether I thought I could get up. Of course, I said, and climbed to my feet, straightening my clothes. The other adults drifted off, disappointed.

At the checkout, as I packed, D reached up for the handle of the trolley and started rocking back and forth, which looked like it felt good. I wished there was a trolley I could stretch up for, but of course I was grown, far too grown, and as I put my card in to pay I felt myself looming over the checkout, some giant redwood whose trunk was mostly rotted through.

When I got home I went to the laptop while the children ran about in their coats. Eventually they went into the kitchen, I registered noise, and I glanced up from the laptop as they came out carrying bowls, slopping milk and bits of cereal. They would be fine.

Time passed, and B came home. The scene made him stop on the threshold.

After he had tidied up the worst, B went out with the three children and I heard him drive off.

There was a period of heavy quiet and then he came back, carrying E.

The next thing I knew, B was pulling me to my feet, and in the bathroom he put a toothbrush in my hand with the toothpaste already on it.

Once I was in bed, he sat on top of the bedclothes and said C and D were spending the night at his mother's. I said I was tired. He told me to get some sleep, but I didn't want to go to sleep.

– But if you're tired.

– Not that kind of tired.

He sighed.

– Tell me what happened.

– I don't know.

I did know. Everything was broken because I'd overused the switch – not just by using it on all three of them at once, but by using it so often, for so long. It was the accumulation of time I'd spent detached, from all of the messy world, as if I'd been flying and flying and inadvertently strayed out of the influence of gravity, and now I didn't have the fuel to get myself back to Earth.

But to explain would have meant explaining about the switch, and I was worried that the switch might just be a metaphor, that I was simply a bad and neglectful person. It struck me that I might be losing my mind. B waited for me to say something and I waited for him to say something, but neither of us said anything and eventually he turned off the light.

I woke several times with that same feeling of losing my mind: a tangible sliding sensation in my skull, as if it were a shallow bowl filled with fluid, in a neverending process of being nudged off the edge of a table. My fingers began to ache, and I realised I was gripping the edge of the mattress.

I went to the living room, entered the machine world of the laptop.

It wasn't yet dawn when B came in, shut the lid so fast I had to snatch my fingers away, and turned without speaking. I didn't think; I lunged for his neck, my thumbs on the nape and my fingers around his throat, on his hard Adam's apple. He grabbed my wrist and pulled one hand away, but the other still groped the back of his neck for a switch. Sounds were coming from me, and a sour heat I could almost smell. I expected to be thrown, shoved backwards into the furniture, but instead he reached behind him and took hold of my hand, firmly and warmly, as if he were pulling me up from a cliff edge over which I'd slipped.

We stood for a moment, two bodies in the sudden silence.

– It's stopped raining, he said. Come on.

With E asleep in her car seat in the back, B drove us through the lightening streets and out of town, taking the twisting hill roads and turning onto the lane above the reservoir. He stopped by a gap in the stone wall from where we could look down. The water was as high as I'd ever seen it, a plane of rippled steel under the dawn sky. The engine ticked.

– It's ages since we've come out here, I said at last. There's been so much rain.

His silence hollowed my words.

I carried on.

– Remember we went up on Saddleworth, and we put the tent up behind that wall and we couldn't hear the road, and no one could see us from any direction?

– Yeah, he said after a moment. That freezing night in midsummer. You wouldn't let me make a fire.

– I know, I'm sorry. I just wanted to have the night, as it was.

That summer I was pregnant for the first time and my new state came with the sudden understanding that yes, everything in the universe *was* expanding. We lay there for hours, outside in the cold, and it stayed light, and still light, like the night would never come. Stones dug into my spine through our blanket and the chill got right to my marrow; we held hands and I watched it come dark, and then the night seemed it would never end. Such deep cold in midsummer: all the rules had been changed. The stars swam above us and I could easily have slipped off the hard ground into the billowing heart of the rest of existence, and I knew death would feel the same. I had nothing to hold on to, no certainty, and I had never been happier.

In the back seat, E stirred and shifted, then settled. With my eyes down, I told B about the shallow bowl of fluid in my skull, about flying out of the reach of gravity, the rotting redwood, the cold white of the supermarket floor. I told him about the seaweed and the raft, about the terror that textured my days, and finally I told him about the switch. Then I flung open the car door and jumped out and vomited onto the grass.

I used to live okay without the switch. We lived okay without the laptop. Then Ben brought it home, a fresh silver box swaddled in white polystyrene, and showed me the many ways in which it would improve our lives, and it did, and I gradually came to forget the time before, and who we were then.

Ben closed his door softly and stood over me, and a wind brought the clean scent of the reservoir. I looked up at him.

– I want to go back, I said.

My husband gathered me in, held my head against his chest. He whispered something, touched my hair. I have always liked his body, his man's body with its solid thighs, its uncumbersome chest, above all its neat and predictable rhythms. But in all my fleeing from the soft, the unnameable, I had forgotten there could also be this tenderness in him, and what allowing it to touch me might mean. I shook.

Evie began to wail, in her way that I understood meant nothing was wrong except she was lonely and afraid and bewildered to find herself where she was, and we would go to her, Ben or me, or both of us, in a minute. For now, the way his embrace pulled my head against him sent the texture of her cries through the bars of his ribs, resonant with the harmonics of her and him and me, and I listened as the hardly bearable music played out through that delicate instrument.

OPTICS

IN THE MIDDLE of a power cut, they sit on the floor in the dark. They have left the curtains open and the moon is high outside the window. Beth cannot remember the last time they sat so close this way. Evan holds her left hand and plays with each finger in turn, and she rests her head on his shoulder, feeling for the slight movement of his body as he breathes. The room feels still and small, as though the walls have drawn in around her.

– I've noticed something, she says. She is thinking of the tiny, needle-thin place on their daughter Rose's little finger where there is light. When she holds Rose's hand up, the light comes through the hole. It looks like a star.

– What have you noticed? Evan says.

She tells him.

– That doesn't sound possible. He says he will wake her and look.

– It's gone ten, she says. Leave her be. She'll never settle again.

He lets go of her hand but doesn't get up. He nudges her head from his shoulder. He stretches and yawns and says he might go to bed, but he doesn't get up. She wants to talk about other things, but she doesn't. The stillness has gone.

She falls asleep there on the floor and when she wakes again at four, she is alone. The power has returned and all the lights have come back on. In the kitchen, the radio she had listened to earlier has come back to life. She turns all the lights out and switches off the radio, climbs the stairs and gets into bed next to him but the sheets are cold and she cannot sleep.

In the morning, they stand Rose in the bathroom and examine her hand, which is soft and perfect and still hot from sleep. There is nothing there.

After the hole in Rose's finger disappears, another one comes, just under her jawbone. It is the size of a button. Beth can see right through to the other side of her. The edges of the hole are fuzzy. She rubs her eyes but it doesn't change. If anything, it has grown a little larger, a little brighter.

She calls her mother, who likes to make things out of paper. Birthday cards, flowers, origami swans. Before Rose was born, she made two cards for the baby, one pink, one blue, but she sent neither. Her gift to Beth after the birth was a bar of soap. It was wrapped in pleated paper and fastened with a gold sticker. When Beth looked up the brand, she found they stopped making it in 1985. She wants me to know, Beth had thought, that I haven't really been on this Earth for any time at all.

Now, as Beth talks, she can hear scissors working in the background. She imagines her mother ankle deep in clippings, fragments of paper falling all around her like snow. She remembers her mother showing her how to make paper dolls, but they always ended up separate instead of joined together.

She tells her about Rose, but her mother says there is nothing wrong with the child.

– It's all in your head, she says. – You still have a vivid imagination.

– Maybe because I'm so tired.

– She's three, her mother says. – Why is she still getting you up at all hours?

– She's my first. What do I know?

There was a time when Beth would believe in anything. When it snowed, her father would take her to look for yeti footprints in the fields. Sometimes they found them.

She takes Rose to the doctor. Rose sits on a plastic chair, her legs dangling, swinging her sandalled feet. Beth points out the places and the doctor looks, then sits back and frowns.

– They seem to come and go, Beth says.

– Do you worry a lot? the doctor says. – Some people think too much about what can go wrong with the human body.

Beth used to lie in bed counting her heartbeats. She read that a human heart makes billions of beats in a lifetime. She thought that when you reached a certain number, you would drop dead. She used to breathe deeply, trying to slow every-thing down.

– I'm not worried, she says.

The doctor gives her some cream to use three times a day.

Beth always understood physics better than biology. At school, she liked making circuits. They were predictable, logical. There used to be diagrams in the Sunday paper of things blown apart so you could see how they worked: photocopiers, faxes, cameras, televisions. Her father used to cut them out and save them for her. You could see how all the parts fitted to-gether and know exactly what was inside. But most things work differently now. There are things happening all the time that she cannot see. Things working invisibly, through the air around her, through her, as if she isn't there.

Now there is another one below Rose's right knee, bigger again, the size of a ten pence piece. When Beth puts her hand over it, the skin does not feel any different. Rose is still warm, still solid, as if there is no missing piece. But when Beth takes her hand away again, there it is. Rose thinks this is a game. She puts her hand on Beth, then lifts it away quickly and looks to see if anything has changed underneath.

Evan knows a lot of facts, such as, there's only enough gold in the world to fill two swimming pools, and there will never be any more. He knows about stars, planets, black holes. He knows how insignificant people are, how if you crammed all of time into a single day, human lives would be imperceptibly short.

He knows about the sky, about light and space, what is visible and what is not. He knows about words and how the word *lesion* derives from the Latin for *injury* and *hurt*. He writes the word *sky-sion* on a piece of paper.

– Maybe this is what they are, he says.

– You've given them a name, she says. – And I thought you didn't believe in them?

– Whatever you say.

– Do you believe me or not?

– I don't know, he says. – How can I, without seeing for myself?

– You think I'm crazy, she says.

– Well are you?

Beth goes to the doctor again to say the cream isn't really working. She gives her the piece of paper.

– Is this something? Is it a real thing?

The doctor reads the word and laughs. She folds the paper and scores it with her thumbnail while she talks, then drops it in the bin.

– It's just a word I use to describe them, Beth says. – I thought it might help.

The doctor writes a prescription for Beth.

– Giving something a name doesn't make it real, the doctor says.

Beth thinks of footprints in the snow, of paper dolls who ought to be joined at the hands, but have been severed.

The doctor suggested exercise, and Beth goes to the pool even though she is not a good swimmer. She has always been afraid of breathing at the wrong time and getting water in her lungs. She has arrived early, before they have taken the blue cover away. It looks more inviting than the water, more solid.

Two women are in the foyer. They are draping white sheets over tables. They have cardboard boxes and a plastic mannequin.

There are two swimmers in the fast lane and three in the slow. Beth swims with her face out of the water. She knows that children now don't even bother to learn the strokes where you keep your head dry. They all start their lessons by putting their faces in the water and breathing out. Everything is different now, even breathing.

When she gets back to her locker, she can hear her phone

vibrating against the locker door as it rings. She pictures Evan calling her, trying to hold on to their vanishing child, squeezing the phone between his ear and his shoulder. But by the time she has opened the locker, it has stopped. The phone says unknown caller.

In the foyer, the women have set up their tables. They are advertising a wedding fair. The mannequin is dressed in an ivory gown and there's a veil over its head, even though it has no face. One of the women tries to put a leaflet in Beth's hand as she passes. Evan says Beth should bring Rose swimming, but what if she starts to disappear in the water, and can't be found?

Beth stands in the dark in front of the bathroom mirror. She feels for the cord and pulls, and the little light flickers on. She doesn't look like herself any more. She pulls the cord and the light goes out.

In the morning, she puts Rose in front of the mirror.

– What can you see?

– Rose, she says.

– Yes, but what about this? She points at the new place just above her left elbow, where she can see all the way through.

– Arm, Rose says.

Beth visits the optician. She has worn glasses since she was fourteen. He sits her in the chair and pulls out the little card where he has written down everything he knows about her, and the numbers that describe her eyes so precisely. He takes her glasses off, gently folds the arms and places them on his desk.

She hates the strange frames he puts on her, the round

lenses he drops into the slots. They make her feel monstrous. She can never tell, can she see better with, or without? The letters on the chart seem to shift and flip. He looks into her eyes with the light. She can feel his breath on her face and smell his skin. It is uncomfortable. She wonders about her own smell. She holds her breath.

He checks for blind spots by asking her to stare into the dark and count tiny pinpricks of light as they appear and disappear. She thinks of the first time she noticed that little star on Rose's finger. The lights are brief, sometimes weak and at the very edge of what she can see.

– I wasn't sure if I was imagining them, she says when the test is finished.

He says there is nothing wrong. He picks up her glasses from the table and puts them back on her face. Everything is clear again but her head feels light.

In the morning Rose calls for her, but when Beth goes to her room, she cannot see her. Then she sees, Rose is sitting at the end of her bed, but only half there. The left side is clear, but somewhere in the middle she fades and the right side isn't there at all. Beth carries her downstairs. She can feel the missing arm holding her around her neck, the invisible leg gripping at her hips, but her heart feels as though it wants to break out of her, and it is beating too fast. She stands Rose in the kitchen and breathes slowly. She rubs the cream all over. Gradually, over the day, Rose comes back.

Beth thinks it must be her eyes. It doesn't matter what the doctor and the optician say. They can't know everything. They can't understand everything. Now, she can see the little stars, pinpricks of light, all over her own right hand. And then a place on her wrist where there is nothing. She goes to the bathroom and turns on the light over the mirror. It buzzes and flares. She cannot see herself any more. Only her right eye is visible, the edge of her brow, the top of her cheek. The rim of her glasses disappears to nothing at the bridge of her nose. She blinks hard, but nothing changes.

A GIFT OF TONGUES

HIS HANDS SWALLOW mine when he speaks. *Ich liebe dich.* And I can't reply, can't say what I want to say – I am still on Chapter 7: Politics. Unable to respond, I smile. This is how the relationship goes: we muddle along, half-understanding. Nods, smiles, and laughter fill the gaps.

The smile has communicated something. He puts a box in my hands. The gold ribbon slips its knot, coils and falls along the table, swimming into the dark below. The red crêpe crackles like dead leaves.

There is a box inside the box. The second made of glass. The light refracts as it emerges, hiding its contents in white light. Only when I cover it with my hands can I see what is inside: a long slab of meat. Pink, glistening.

'*Eine Zunge,*' he says. Chapter 3: Anatomy.

He has bought me a tongue.

It is winter in Berlin. The sun, cloud-veiled, only deepens the city's shadows. The shadows press up against the buildings, the strange music of the city pours along the streets. Sigh of bus doors, percussion of the U-Bahn. People walk, not hearing, but feeling its movement. Couples crowd the bridges of the Spree, lip-to-ear, whispering secrets the river shelters in its long exhale.

Thöre tries to strike up conversation on the S-Bahn. It is late afternoon, the cabin filled with people on their way to the Grunewald. I stand on tiptoe and speak into his ear, so that other passengers cannot hear my *kauderwelsch* German. Small hairs glance against my lips; white arms soft as peach fuzz carry my words deep into his skull.

Kauderwelsch. Gibberish. Gobbledygook.

My German is comprised of Thöre, a textbook, and the lessons that my work makes the new transplants take. Once a week, for an hour and a half and full pay, we sit in a meeting room and talk. Situational German. Please-and-thank-yous. Polite conversation for business lunches. *We look forward to working with you*. No one takes it seriously. Sometimes when we go out, the other new-starts speak entirely in English, even when ordering, not bothering with even a cursory *danke* or *bitte*. There is something exciting about this. Something rebellious. I expect someone to snap, to swear, to tell them to speak German, the way I had seen the French do in Paris. I hold my breath and wait.

No one says a thing.

I met Thöre on one such outing. The new staff, two managers, one of the company lawyers. A bar in the east, street level, light spilling out over Soviet high-rises. We sat in our corner with Bavarian wheat beers, suspended safely in a cloud of English. It was the lawyer who disturbed our seclusion, standing up to shout in German across the bar. A man came over. They hugged, kissed – once on each cheek – and he joined us, taking a seat between the lawyer and me. A couple of half-hearted waves and quiet hellos from my compatriots, and the conversation closed over his entrance. The man and the lawyer turned to each other to talk amongst themselves.

When the lawyer popped to the bathroom, the man leaned across and asked if I spoke German. His breath felt alive against my cheek, and under the reek of bar bodies, he smelled of sea salt and coriander. Emboldened by the Weissbier, I tried to remember all those meeting-room conversations. The beer made things smoother. I tried to introduce myself.

'You speak *Kauderwelsch*,' he said, in English. 'But it's cute.'

The lawyer returned and they went back to talking in German, though the man – Thöre, he said his name was, *Thöre as in Thor* – looked at me while the woman talked in his ear, smiling a deep, knowing smile.

When I stepped through the door of my apartment later that night, I pulled out the miniature German-to-English dictionary a friend had bought me as a goodbye present, and looked up what Thöre had said to me.

Kauderwelsch. Noun, neuter.

When I forget the word I want, when a phrase is beyond me, coiled slyly on the tip of my tongue, close as the tail end of a dream, *Kauderwelsch* is there, waiting in the space where the other words should be.

The train comes to a stop. Thöre leans down.

'We're here,' he says, his mouth covering, for a moment, the entirety of my ear.

He takes my hand and leads me out into the forest of the Grunewald.

'It is a very simple operation,' the doctor explains in English. 'You don't even have to be put under full anaesthetic. In fact, the results are far better if the procedure is performed in twilight sleep.'

I hold the boxed tongue in my lap. It seems drier now, under the clinic lights. Smaller. Frightened. I wonder if this is a sign that it is sick, like a dog's nose.

'And afterwards, I'll be able to speak German?' I ask.

'Faultlessly.'

Thöre takes my hand in his.

The doctor lists side-effects, reiterating after each how safe the operation is, how unlikely it is that I will suffer anything other than the pure joy of bypassing years of study.

'Strange things, tongues,' the doctor says. 'I have to say, it's really quite a wonderful gift your boyfriend has bought you. Your new tongue will open doors.'

'What about my old tongue?' I ask.

'Don't worry about that,' he replies. 'We take care of everything.'

Thöre squeezes my hand and looks into my eyes. He mouths the words: *Ich liebe dich*. Still unsure what to say, I nod.

'Excellent,' the doctor says. 'A nurse will be along in a moment to get you prepped. Just sign here.'

The pen makes a scratching sound, like an animal trying to escape.

'I can't wait,' Thöre tells me while we wait for the nurse. 'I'm finally going to be able to talk to you.'

'We talk all the time,' I say.

'You know what I mean.'

'I don't,' I insist.

'You will,' he replies.

The first present Thöre bought me was a flat white, the second a textbook. We met at a café near my work. The conversation a series of starts and stops. Almost not quites. When he talked for anything longer than a sentence, slowing down to make sure I could make him out, I let the words pass over me like water. I examined the curve of his jaw, how the stubble didn't quite reach his cheeks, the way the sunlight through the window made one eye wolf-yellow. When he asked me about myself, I responded as best I could. I knew the questions from class, but couldn't remember the right answers, only what other people had said. I told him I had a brother when I have two. That one brother is older when I am the oldest. That I am eight and twenty instead of twenty-eight. He smiled at each mistake, chin in hand.

'I bought you something,' he said

He slid an oblong of brown paper along the tabletop. I wanted to tell him that he shouldn't have, that it was nice of him, that I would repay the favour by buying him a drink. But I didn't know how. Instead I unwrapped the package, dumbly.

Inside was a textbook. A Japanese woman laughed with a blond man on the front cover. Above them, in slender green font, was written: *Die Gabe der Zungen*.

'Thank you,' I said

I flicked through the pages and saw a phrase.

'The next round is on me.'

Thöre laughed. After coffee, we took the underground in the same direction, Thöre getting off a few stops before mine. He kissed me and told me he would see me soon. After he left, I caught eyes with a woman sitting nearby. She smiled and said: *Sie sind so ein süßes Paar*. I smiled in response, unsure of what she had said. She returned the gesture and returned to her paperback. The exchange pleased me: as if I were just another German on the subway, kissing my boy-friend goodbye. It felt good.

It felt as if I were invisible.

The new tongue is stapled to the inside of my mouth. Dissolvable double-hinges, the doctor explains. Due to the need for movement, it would be impossible to bind the muscles with sutures. Instead delicate little hinges have been affixed to the join between the old flesh and the new. They glitter in the clinic lights as I move a pink hand-mirror in front of my mouth, watching my tongue lick the white walls of my teeth, brush the inside of my mouth. The mirror makes my teeth seem small, but to my tongue, these things are gargantuan: my teeth are cliff-faces, the roof of my mouth a universe wide. I put the mirror down. I shut my mouth. It feels as if I have closed my eyes.

I notice a taste. Slightly salty, like cured bacon, with a faint hint of bergamot. Tea-smoked meat. I use the new tongue to explore further; the hinges butterfly and pull at their fleshy moorings. The taste comes from all over. A taste my old tongue had forgotten. The taste of my own mouth.

'It will take some time to adjust,' the doctor says as I sign my discharge. 'Little things might take you by surprise. Just be prepared.'

'Don't worry, doctor,' I say. 'I'm already getting used to it. The only thing is the hinges. How long will they be there for?'

'A couple of weeks,' he says. 'But we'll get you in for a check-up after that, just to make sure everything's fine and the hinges have fully dissolved.'

'And my old tongue?'

'Don't worry. We've taken care of it. All you have to do now is focus on resting up and enjoying your new life.'

The tongue has made everything new. Even the air. I feel it pour over the lump of muscle in my mouth, feel it fill each delicate branch of my lungs. It is scented with the green of the Grunewald as we walk out of the clinic, and on the S-Bahn home, the stale coffee on Thöre's breath and the coriander punch of his cologne. Thöre is remarkably quiet. He sits next to me, grinning.

'What?' I ask.

'Nothing,' he says, beaming ear to ear.

'Tell me.'

'It's your accent,' he says. 'Your new one, I mean. You sound like you were born and bred in Hamburg.'

'Don't be ridiculous,' I tell him. 'Why would I speak English with a German accent?'

He laughs. His eyes reflect the trees as they pass by in the window. For a moment a house with a red roof shines there also. His expression is the same as when I make a mistake in German. Amused, affectionate. But I hadn't made a mistake. Had I?

Thöre's Berlin was different to the one I knew. The Berlin in my head, marked only by bars, restaurants, and coffee shops around my work and flat, branched out, connecting, like tendons, the smaller satellites where we met. I knew the city after a month. Not by direction, but by the memories Thöre and I made: seafood in Charlottenburg, slow walks in Mitte, parties in Neukölln. Thöre's friends. They spoke to me in German, first, then switched to English. It seemed as though everyone in Berlin spoke English, to one extent or another. Only Thöre spoke to me in German.

One night in his apartment in Kreuzberg, as I leafed through *Die Gabe der Zungen* in bed and waited for him to finish brushing his teeth, I called through to the bathroom to ask him why, when everyone else spoke to me in English, only he insisted on German. I heard him spit, heard a tap running. He came and stood in the doorway, the band of his underwear folded over slightly where he had put it back haphazardly. He looked at me as if gauging something. The answer he gave was not textbook: he stopped and started, adjusted what he wanted to say, repositioned sentences mid-flow, so that in the end all I was left with were fragments, clauses out of order.

He does not speak to me in English because he wants me to know something. Something about the truth. Or something real. Him. Something real about him. Himself, maybe. The real him.

He climbed on to the bed, moved up my legs with predatory grace, and closed the textbook in my hands as he gave me a mint-sweet kiss. Then he turned out the light. He fell asleep in seconds. I found it harder. The feeling that I had to be alert, in case I missed something, was hard to shake, even though Thöre was no longer speaking. It was impossible to relax. To help me get to sleep, I ran through the vocabulary list I had just been reading.

Augen, Nase, Herz, und Zehen. Eyes, nose, heart, and toes. *Arm* for arm, *Fuß* for foot. And *Zunge* – tongue. Chapter 3: Anatomy. *Die Anatomie.*

This is how I fell asleep: Thöre's mouth to my ear, his sleep-heavy breath keeping time. While I counted tongues, and waited to dream.

༺

I talk to people in shops, on the train, strike up conversations with strangers at work. So excited am I by my newfound ability to speak and be understood. It feels like diving: deeper and deeper into Berlin, with no need to rise and fill my lungs with English. My new tongue has gills. The half-open wounds of the hinges, now dissolved, breathe the city. Berlin tastes of ash and June and ozone.

People ask me if I am from Hamburg. I tell them that I have never left Berlin. They laugh and ask me why I have a Hamburg accent then, and when I tell them I am not German, they say I must have learned from someone who spoke *Hamburgisch*. But the woman at my office is from Frankfurt, and the only other teacher I had was Thöre.

It never felt as if I were learning German with Thöre. It was as though I were learning a language only Thöre and I spoke. From the beginning he taught me to understand him with hand gestures, repetition, and glacial speech. I spoke a language of errors, parataxis, and diminishing returns.

I knew I had made a mistake when Thöre laughed. It was a particular laughter, almost affectionate. As if my mistakes pleased him, though my pronunciation did not. Everything sounded wrong to him. The words the same but unfamiliar, pressed through the meat grinder of my mouth – I butchered the language, he said.

The only sound I made that pleased him was 'ch', as in *Ich* for I, as in *I love you. Ich liebe dich*. This he said after a month had passed. I didn't understand. To explain, he placed my hand on his chest. His hands swallowed mine. Something beat, warm and urgent, against my palm. The word came into my head in the rhythm of that beat: *das, Herz, das, Herz.* As if the two could not be separate. As if they needed each other. The first nothing without the second. Meaningless. This is what *Ich liebe dich* meant to me: something added, extraneous, something straining, and significant.

I couldn't tell Thöre this. I lacked the words. Instead I took his hand and placed it on my chest, let him feel my heart beat its own affirmation: *das, Herz, das, Herz, das, Herz.* Then I remembered something from Chapter 3.

'*Herzen,*' I said. Hearts.

He smiled. Almost as if he understood.

'I'm sorry,' he says.

I drum my fingers on the table. Rain falls against the window, muttering its response. A series of sharp taps, long sprays. Morse code on glass, there where the name of the cafe is written back to front. The words *Der Ausguck* seem almost fluent on their hand-drawn pennant.

I pick up my coffee and take a drink. Nothing. I finished earlier, but keep the cup at my mouth so I won't have to respond. While Thöre explains. How things have changed. Since the tongue.

'It's just that,' he continues. 'We've changed. I don't know.'

I gulp air like a landed fish, pretending there is still coffee in my cup.

'I thought the transplant would have made things easier. But it hasn't. It's nothing like the brochure said,' he says. 'You seem like a different person now.'

I put down the empty cup. Slowly. Attempt to work out what I am going to say. A couple appear at the window and peer in, trying to see through the breath on the glass whether there is anywhere to sit. One of them turns and says something to the other. Their words sound strange, as if the glass has inverted them too.

'If I'm not me any more, then who am I?' I ask.

'I don't know,' Thöre replies.

A bell announces the couple's entrance. They take a seat at the wall behind Thöre, both of them on the same side of the high table, watching the rain against the window while they talk. When they speak to each other, it is still gibberish to me, glass or no glass. Yet it seems familiar. What language is that?

'I'm sorry,' Thöre says. 'But I don't think we should see each other any more.'

The tongue changed everything but most of all it changed Thöre. It was as if a wall had come down. We emerged from our division, freshly gifted with speech. As if all that had come before were just whispers through brick. But it was not only a matter of language. It was all the little things bound up in it: the sighs, the many meanings of a touch, the warmth in his voice that came and went, like a square of sunlight through a window. The world was gold when it was there. But gradually, it began to turn ashen. He no longer talked to me with his chin in his hands. Now it was hands on table, eyes on fingernails. He looked as if he missed something.

Die Gabe der Zungen did not contain a chapter on relationships. I would never have been able to ask him about it, with my old tongue, would never have been able to have a serious conversation about our feelings. The new tongue had changed all that.

'Is everything all right?' I asked him.

He looked up from his fingernails. He seemed surprised to see me there.

'Of course,' he said. 'Everything's fine. Just tired.'

We said no more about it. But I felt as if I had done something wrong. He no longer laughed when I made mistakes. At first, I thought this was because I no longer made them. But soon I couldn't shake the feeling that all I was capable of was mistakes. And Thöre no longer had any patience for them.

I guess, with my new tongue, I should have known better.

I return to my old life, my old apartment, my old Berlin. But with the new tongue in my head, everything is different.

I know I have been back to my flat. I have had to wash clothes, pick up documents for work, make sure nothing is mouldering in the fridge. But when I move around it now, it feels like trespassing.

I try to reconnect with the other transplants from work, to revive the old friendships I had neglected during my time with Thöre. We go to a bar in the east. It is vaguely familiar, but the memory is dim. We settle at a table in the corner and talk in English. The language hangs in the air around us like haze, making us feel safe and invisible. As if to the Germans around us we were nothing but the faintest of shimmers on the farthest horizon.

The lawyer is there. It is the first time I have seen her since Thöre and I broke up. She is the partner of one of Thöre's friends, Elke. A slight brunette whose family ties to Bavarian aristocracy show through in the imperious way in which she ignores me. When I speak, she does not look at me. The others exchange looks. I wonder if I am saying something offensive, but no one interrupts, so I persevere. As the conversation goes on, and empty glasses crowd the table, one of them finally asks: 'When did you start speaking like that?'

'Like what?'

'Like that. Your English is weird, now. It's like you can't really speak it. And your accent. You don't sound like you any more.'

You seem like a different person now.

'Who do I sound like?'

'You sound like you're from Hamburg,' the lawyer says.

'But I'm not,' I say. 'I'm from . . .'

I sit there, dumb. The tongue in my head lolls lifeless. I try to remember but the word is not there, only *Kauderwelsch*, burning brand-hot, turning my cheeks crimson.

'I didn't mean to offend you,' the man says.

'Don't worry,' I say. 'It's yesterday's snow.'

I hear it, then. The words sound wrong; the voice is not mine. The table seems to move off into the distance. The room is spinning, or I am. Nothing is solid. I excuse myself, telling them the Weissbier has gone to my head, and dive into the night air.

The Soviet high-rises tower above me. Headlights cast long shadows along their faces as I try to find a train station. I walk. Time slips away. I do not recognise these streets; they were not part of me and Thöre. And now I am lost. In this city I thought I knew.

I hold my hand out in the road and a car stops. I climb into the taxi. As it drives to my flat, I look out the window, trying desperately to recognise just one building on the other side of the glass. But nothing looks the same. When the driver stops and asks for the fare, I ask if he's sure we're there.

'Positive,' he tells me as he takes the money. 'Hey, are you from Hamburg? My brother lives there.'

I tell him to keep the change.

I thought I would feel safer back in the apartment, doors locked, curtains drawn. But I still can't shake the feeling that the person who lives there is going to come back, that they will demand that I leave and go back to my own home. But where is that? Where am I from?

Without Thöre, I have nothing to do on the train out to the Grunewald except watch, through the window, as the city recedes. The forest slowly wins back its space. As the train approaches the stop for the clinic, I notice a building in the distance, red-roofed, surrounded by trees in neat rows. It is familiar, somehow, though I am sure I have never been there.

The doctor places my tongue in clamps, the long root of muscle drying in the air, and runs his fingers along the small bumps where the gills of the tongue have closed shut.

'Excellent,' he says. 'Barely a scar. How are you finding it, any problems?'

'No,' I say. 'It seems to be working fine. I speak German, now. No problems.'

'And faultlessly, too, I have to say. Your boyfriend must be pleased. Is he working today?'

'No,' I reply. Then: 'Yes. I mean, yes, he's working, but no, he's not my boyfriend. Not any more.'

'I'm sorry to hear that,' he says. His eyes are wet, glistening with sympathy in the clinic lights. It is strange to see the man that way. He looks like a little boy. And yet, he doesn't seem surprised.

'Does this happen a lot?' I ask.

'It is a danger,' he says. 'But most of the time, no. It depends, you know? On the people. The new tongue helps people speak, that's all. Sometimes it's a blessing, and in other cases . . .' He shrugs. 'Sometimes, post-transplant, things just fall apart. Your guess is as good as mine why. They just do.'

'Doctor,' I say. I hesitate, not wanting to offend him. I put my hands on my knees and look down at them as I speak. 'I'm sorry, doctor, but I want you to give me my old tongue back.'

He puts his hands over mine.

'I'm sorry,' he says. 'But I can't.'

'But it's mine,' I say. 'It's my tongue.'

'When you give up your tongue,' he says, 'you give it up. You can't go back to it. It's a problem of auto-immunity: you can take in a new tongue, if it's managed properly. But your body remembers the old one, and if you try to put it back in, as if it were something new, you would confuse your defences. Your body would try to destroy it.'

'What have you done with it?'

The doctor hesitates.

'I can't really tell you,' he says. 'There are issues of . . . confidentiality.'

'Doctor,' I say, 'it's my tongue. I don't think you'll be breaking confidentiality if you tell me where it is.'

'That's the thing,' the doctor says. 'It's not your tongue any more.'

'What do you mean?'

'Perhaps . . .' he says. 'Perhaps it would be better if I showed you.'

We had gone to a restaurant on Charlottenstraße for my birthday. Thöre picked German wines, regional specialities, laid all of Germany out on a table for me. The soft lights of the restaurant made everything gleam and blur.

A taxi back, and we were walking unsteadily up the stairs to Thöre's place, bodies soft and lush with wine. Thöre pressed me against the wall of the stairwell, then pressed a box into my hands, his swallowing mine. Then lip to ear, he whispered: 'One last gift.'

The box was black, its join sealed with a disc of red wax and the imprint of a 'T'. A key wrapped in red crêpe, small bow around its waist, nestled on a mound of grey silk. Next to it lay a strand of snowdrops.

'A key?' I asked. Chapter 2: The Home.

'Aye,' he said. The sound of the word, made strange by his mouth, was almost musical: as if the affirmation were carried away by it, the vowel now a note, fading, *legato*, as Thöre plucked the key from its swaddling and placed it in my hand. Little teeth of metal dug into my palm.

I turned the key in the lock. Thöre stood behind me, his hands on my shoulders, watching, seeing from just above my eye-level, his own home open to me with the swing of a door. I knew what to expect: a minimalist art print in a black frame, a concrete vase with three plastic lilies, dust on their mouths, and a glass sphere for percolating coffee. Yet for some reason, opened with a key that was my own, it seemed different. As if by some sleight of hand the room behind this door had vanished, replaced by another through subterfuge and shifting compartments.

Thöre swept me off my feet. Literally. One arm buckled the hinge of my knees, so that I fell back and into the other. The key in my hand flew up in the air.

It took me over an hour to find it again the next morning.

When I locked the door behind me on the way to work, I wondered whether the same apartment would greet me that evening, or if each turn of key would always make things feel new. A new apartment, a new Thöre. A new me.

The doctor punches a code into the wall. His hands are sheathed in latex gloves, powder blue. There is a brief sigh as the door swells open at the press of a hand. They seem so small, in those gloves. Like the hands of a child.

There is darkness before us. Then fluorescent lights shudder, flicker, race along, until off in the distance, the corridor is nothing but light. The doctor leads me down the corridor, explaining that normally this area is out of bounds, but that he wanted me to understand how it worked. We walk by glass boxes in airtight recesses. In each one, a stub of muscle glistens.

'Where do you get them?' I ask.

'Donations,' he replies. 'Donations. The tongue you have, now, for example, was donated by the family of someone who had recently passed. Originally from Hamburg, I believe.'

He stops in front of a case. The tongue inside seems impossibly small. I imagine it must have belonged to some sort of animal.

'This is your tongue,' he says.

I look at it. I look at it the way an animal looks at its reflection, recognising there something strangely familiar and at once completely other. How had I never seen it before, its swell, the lumps at the root, those bumps on its surface, like a secret written in Braille? Is the new tongue like this? Are all tongues the same? Even on the way through this room filled with them, I had only noticed their pinkness, their wetness, how fat they seemed, lying there disused.

'Unfortunately, it already has a buyer. A politician. Tongues like yours fetch a premium,' he says.

'What do you mean like mine?' I ask.

'People whose mother tongue is English,' he says. I am alarmed by the mistake. It feels dangerous. Like a trap about to spring shut.

'But it's not,' I tell him. 'English isn't my mother tongue.'

He is visibly unsettled.

'But that's what your boyfriend wrote on the application form. Mother tongue: English.'

'No,' I say, realising that in the time Thöre and I had been together he had never asked me. 'He was wrong. English isn't my mother tongue.'

'Oh,' he says, crestfallen. 'Do you have any proof?'

'What kind of proof would I have? Look, wouldn't you get in trouble if you sold him my tongue, knowing full well that, proof or not, there's still a danger that it's not worth the "premium".'

He sighs. 'I'll tell him the situation and see what he says. He might still want it. But if not, it's yours for the standard price.'

'Does this mean I can have my tongue back?' I ask.

'Yes and no,' he says cautiously. 'Like I said, we can't put the tongue back in your head. But we can give you it back, I suppose. If the buyer no longer wants it. You'd have to buy it, of course. And take care of it. It has to be kept cool and moist. When people purchase the tongues as gifts, we supply a glass box. Technically there's no reason that it couldn't be kept in one long-term.'

'Please.'

The word hangs in the air for a moment, in that room of quiet tongues. I hear the rawness in it, how desperate I must sound to him. I wonder if the tongues hear it too.

The doctor nods.

We make the necessary arrangements. I fill in paperwork, declaring that I will take responsibility for the tongue, that it will be gifted to Thöre on a date to be confirmed. The doctor signs off on the lie. After the paperwork is filed, I ask him why he is helping me.

'Let us just say that I have a certain amount of sympathy for your situation,' he says. He sticks his tongue out on its side: along its underbelly I see faint arcs, like the closed slits of gills. 'The marriage didn't last long after. Like I said, sometimes things just fall apart.'

The doctor shakes my hand at the entrance. His hand seems bigger to touch, almost gargantuan. Yet it fits perfectly into mine, as if made of a piece. I turn to leave but stop, unable to shake something.

'One thing,' I ask. 'Do you keep the tongues until they find a new owner?'

'We try,' he says. 'But some tongues aren't as popular. We keep them as long as we can, but if we can't find an owner, we have to get rid of them.'

'What do you do with them?'

'Well,' he says. 'You'll have noticed this clinic is in the Grunewald. There's a reason for that. If we can't find a new home for a tongue, they get processed into fertiliser. It's quite interesting, actually: the composition of the tongue, all the things that go into making it, produce a fertiliser that makes things grow almost twice as fast as normal. We sell it to a small paper mill nearby. Maybe you saw it on the way in, it has a red roof?'

'A paper mill?' I ask. An image flashes in my memory of a house with a red roof. It feels as if I had lived there, once.

'Yes,' he says. 'It's owned by a pretty famous publishing company. They make language textbooks. *Die Gabe der Zungen*. Maybe you've heard of them?'

That night in my apartment, I count tongues in my head, but can't sleep. Each time I close my eyes I see them: all the tongues no one wanted, falling between blades, their pink meat turned to slurry, poured on to saplings. The slim frames shake with the weight of the tongues. The leaves are slick with them. From little acorns, mighty oaks. Then with an axe, down they go. Cut and pulped, pressed, printed. And the people carry them with them as they walk, under arms, wrapped in brown paper, just as I had done – the last of someone's tongue.

I get up to fetch a glass of water. The apartment is quiet, still. Peaceful. I am growing used to its space, the hush of the cars below the window. The feeling that someone might come in at any minute has lessened.

I pour ice cubes from the freezer into a glass then fill it from the tap. Stopping for a moment, I go back and take something out of the refrigerator. Seated at the kitchen counter, the clink of the ice fills the quiet space, as I watch my warm fingerprints fade from the chilled surface of a glass box.

It lies there, under glass. My tongue. The one I can't put back in my head. It is strange to have it there, that I should be the one to keep it. It belongs to me, but at the same time, it doesn't. I can't shake the feeling that I am only keeping it safe for a time, that it is something held only until it can be passed over. Like a gift. Is this how Thöre had felt, safekeeping the tongue that now moves in my head?

A car's headlights drift through the window. Shadows dance along the walls of the apartment. Beyond the glass, Berlin glitters in the night.

He is out there, somewhere. Thöre. I will never see him again. I am sure of it. A wall has lifted itself between us, something not uncommon in this city. Our lives take place on either side of it. Any conversation would happen only through the bricks. Perhaps he has already found someone else. Perhaps he will buy them a tongue; gift it to them in a box of red crêpe, in that apartment where he had once given me a box sealed with a gold ribbon.

I still have a key. I could open that door, step between the walls, and enter. But each turn of the key, something changes. The Thöre in that room is a stranger. I do not speak the language he speaks. Though we share a tongue, now.

Under glass, a long slab of muscle. Pink, glistening. *Eine Zunge*. A gift, kept for the time being. One day, I will give it to someone. I will say the words: *Ich liebe dich*. And they will not know what to say. But, perhaps, they will respond. Somehow. In another language. One of slightest touches, of tender embraces – of hands, and lips, and tongues. One day. *Eines Tages*.

KIERAN DEVANEY

SITCOM

HELLO, RICHARD SAID, today I'd like to talk to you
about an idea for a sitcom I've been developing. It's about a
serial killer. He gets caught after several killings and is given
various consecutive life sentences, adding up to two hundred
and fifty years of imprisonment. This is all back story though,
and will be revealed in the first couple of episodes of the
sitcom, in flashback. When we first see the main character,
he is being taken into prison. He goes into jail and he's got
these two hundred and fifty years to serve, so you think, he's
never going to make it. And this is a tough prison he's in too,
maximum security. It's a punishment that's intended to last
the remainder of his life. But this guy, the main character, he's
in there, in prison, and let's say he's forty when he goes in,
right? So he's forty years old, and he lives in the prison for
fifty years, until he's ninety. Still no chance of a parole hearing,
no chance of any change to the sentence. He admits what he
did by the way, there's no doubt over his guilt. As I say, that's
all back story. We first see the guy when he's in prison, at age
forty, and he lives for fifty years there, which is more than
his entire lifetime before he went in. And we see that he gets
a few years taken off for good behaviour, but he also has the
odd run-in with the prison warders and so on, so his sentence

209

gets extended at other times too, but roughly it balances out. And so we see him at age ninety, being denied the possibility of parole by some official, and he, the protagonist, says to this official that he can deny him parole, it doesn't matter because he's going to survive for the entirety of his sentence, and when he gets out of prison, not only will this official be dead, but his children will be dead, and their children will be dead, and their children will be dead, and so on. So he's this man of ninety, already one of the oldest prisoners in the world, and he comes out with this.

Another decade passes, and he's a hundred years old. He's served sixty years of a two-hundred-and-fifty-year sentence. There's some talk in the press of him being released – how much longer can he possibly live? they say, but there are equally strong voices that continue to condemn him for his crimes, and in the end he's not released. Another decade or so passes, and he becomes the oldest person alive, older than any other human on the planet, and in prison. And the thing is, he looks quite good on it, he could easily pass for eighty. So it's at this time, around the time he becomes the oldest person alive, that two quite different public reactions take place. One is that there's a call for the death penalty to be used in this case and the other, perhaps more interesting, is that a few people start to take seriously his claim – which by the way he has made public in the few press interviews he has been permitted to give – that he is going to survive the sentence and be released. Both reactions come from a similar point of view. They both acknowledge that something is going on here, but they approach it from different directions. The death penalty isn't employed, however, and the protagonist begins to receive letters from people who feel that they can gain something from interaction with him, despite the fact that he's spent most of his life in prison. He begins to gain a following and, in some people's eyes the very fact of his longevity exonerates him from the crimes he has committed. He continues to live and, at a certain point, he becomes the oldest person to have ever lived, alive or dead. He's a little frail, but still, his doctors say, in good health. He reaches his one-hundred-and-fortieth birthday, and soon he gets to the one-hundred-year anniversary of his incarceration. He has been something of a thorn in the side of successive governments, but this date brings a renewed call for his release (along with a renewed call for his death from some quarters). How can you, people say, keep people locked up for all that time? The families of the victims are all dead, almost nobody in the world was alive when the original crimes were committed, nobody remembers them, but the government stands firm. The mere fact of his living so long does not, they say, mitigate against what he did, and any sentence given must be respected. One official, speaking publicly on the matter, is even drawn to say that if he was to live and serve the entirety of his sentence, he would be released as any prisoner would: the first such official acknowledgement of a feeling that has been percolating for decades. And then, a few months shy of one hundred and fifty years old, he is taken ill. The doctors say that he has cancer, and inoperable. He's given weeks to live. There is a great deal of reaction to this – some people greet it with elation, he is merely human, and mortal, and others are devastated for precisely the same reason.

Again, both reactions are just iterations of a deeper belief, or anxiety about the possibility of someone living for so long and not dying, and this deeper belief is itself embedded within a fear of death, a great anxiety about mortality. So he is moved to the hospital wing of the prison and watched over by guards and doctors. Of course, he has no family left, no friends, and he is not permitted any outside visitors.

He is hours away from death. A guard is stationed outside his door and he is left to die, alone in his room; newspaper editors make space for his obituary, television stations place reporters outside the prison where they are met by protesters both for and against him. The night passes and in the morning the doctors open the door to the room to find the bed empty, the prisoner sitting in the corner. He raises his head to them, and shakily gets to his feet. He rubs his eyes. Every minute that passes he is a minute older, for another minute he's the oldest man that has ever lived. The doctors run tests and find that the cancer is in remission, he is healthy again. There is uproar. Outside the prison the two sets of protesters clash.

The government of the day is forced to make a statement which is careful not to suggest that they are unhappy he hasn't died, but which assuages the increasingly virulent calls for him to be put to death. Support for him continues to grow, and the news of his survival leads to this support becoming more intense – certain strands become more cultic, and there are rumours that he is being worshipped as a living deity. This comes to a head when a middle-aged man attempts to copy the sequence of murders in an attempt to extend the length of his life. He is caught midway through the sequence and is jailed. Again, there is public outcry. Time continues to pass, the copycat killer dies in prison; the protagonist reaches two hundred years old. He has served one hundred and sixty years of a two-hundred-and-fifty-year sentence. A short time after that, a guard attempts to murder him. He is stabbed several times but survives. The guard goes to jail and dies fifteen years later.

The pressure on successive governments to do something about his case mounts and then falls away. He is remembered and then forgotten. Time passes constantly. On the occasion of his two-hundred-and-thirtieth birthday he is permitted to give an interview to a newspaper. He reiterates his claim that he will survive the sentence, but says that he is constantly tired, and sleeps as much as he can. The series of photographs that accompany the article are made up of close-ups of his face. The captions declare his expression inscrutable, but if you really look at them, it is possible to read the face as an index, a spore. Here is a man who had spent nearly two hundred years doing nothing except being a prisoner. The article estimates the cost, to the state, of his incarceration. It details the various different institutions he has been housed in, the major world historical events that have occurred during his time in prison, the prisoners he has known as friends that were now among the numberless dead that had lived and died during his imprisonment.

It is also around this time that a flurry of academic books are published. There are medical studies in which doctors claim that testing and examination revealed no special qualities about the man, it is simply that those things which kill people had not happened to him. Every moment he lives, the odds against him living a moment more grow longer and longer, but he does not die. He is named as being in the top ten longest-living animals on the planet. Philosophers debate the meaning of a life which spans several centuries but which has no access to the world. Membership of his cult grows, and their actions became more sophisticated.

Lawyers, politicians, lobbyists, CEOs and other powerful people number among his supporters, and they begin to exert more and more pressure. He himself, when asked about his followers, is characteristically gnomic, only saying that he hopes they will not be disappointed in him. The central component of their campaign concerns the immense scientific and social significance of a life that had been lived for so long, and the great human tragedy that it had been mostly lived in captivity. Several academic historians are among their ranks, and they consult archives and records to discredit the victims that the protagonist had killed, showing them to be malicious people, unworthy of such a punishment in their name.

All this leads to a long, drawn-out review, which lasts several years, and tries to adapt existing legislation to the current circumstances. All those decades ago, it is asked, when this sentence was handed down, it was done so in a spirit which assumed that the prisoner would not live to be anywhere close to release, surely therefore it is merely a symbolic figure, the two hundred and fifty years, and not to be taken literally. Therefore, should the prisoner not be released? Has he not suffered enough for his crimes? Has he not made amends? The report recommends his release, though it admits that such a release, which rewards the prisoner for something essentially out of his control – his longevity – does some damage to the power of the rule of law. The government of the day consider the recommendations of the report and choose not to uphold them. He remains in prison, and ages.

He lives to be two hundred and fifty. Many of those involved in writing the report, producing the articles about him, campaigning on his behalf, are dead. His supporters continue to grow in number, and the occasion is marked by yet more articles, books, papers, and speculation. Many of those alive now hope to be alive when his sentence ends, forty years hence, though that does not stop the protests and the campaigning for early release from continuing, though successive governments show no sign of acquiescing, out of fear of seeming weak, of giving in to the myth.

Time continues to pass. He is two hundred and seventy, then two hundred and eighty. Merely a decade of the sentence remains. Again he is taken ill, again he recovers. Another interview is granted. How does it feel, being so old? he is asked. Do you ever think you'll see the outside world? Do you worry about adapting to life as a free man? His answers, though they possess a quiet grace, give little insight. But to see him talk, to be in his presence, that really feels like something, the journalist writes. He writes that he cannot decide if the prisoner is lucky or unlucky. Though it appears very prominently and is widely read, the article is a disappointment, as all previous ones have been. If everybody lived this long, one commentator writes, our prison system would not allow this. One question, however, that the journalist asks does pique the interest of all readers. Just at the close of the interview, the prisoner barely awake in his chair, gaunt, saintly, is asked, Would you kill again, if you were released? Oh yes, yes, he replies quietly.

Hysteria mounts as the day of release approaches. The estimated cost of the increased security around the prison and the procedure for release are commented upon with a great deal of derision from all sides, but, it is argued, this is what is necessary to prevent a riot. The sitcom ends on the last day. There are two huge camps of protestors – those for and those against, those who have come to see their deity and those who have come to spurn, to gawp and to declaim – they are kept separate, long lines of law enforcement between them. Every major news organisation, and hundreds of minor ones, have media presence outside the prison. It feels as if the preceding two hundred and fifty years were always like this, that these events are instantiations of a mindset that extends beyond individual thinking. People have been thinking and talking about this man for more than two centuries – he is the locus for debate and argumentation that unites minds across time. Many of those assembled are there just to catch a glimpse of something – a piece of sleeve, a hand, that will feel historic. It feels as though the preceding two hundred and fifty years were leading up to this moment. Amid all the speculation about what happens next, what he will do with himself, whether his release will show him to be just an old man with some unique, unidentifiable biological quirk, or whether he will ascend and take his place among the pantheon, amid all that, there is the chatter of people jostling for space, selling food, the grey air, those working and those using their leisure time to do this, families, kids.

The sitcom ends like this: There is a hush at the front of the crowd, they think they've seen something, and it spreads backwards. People check their phones for updates. The feeling dies down and goes away, people start to chat again, but then it returns, this time more palpably. Dozens of officials start to emerge from the door of the prison. There is cheering, crying.

Singing breaks out among some of the more dedicated cultists, and they beat out rhythms on improvised percussion. The crowd moves forwards. There are skirmishes, arrests. The line of officials stand outside the door for several minutes. Everyone feels as though what is going to happen ought to have happened, the singing continues, people become restless. There is more activity at the doors, some men go in, others come out. They don't look at the crowd, they are behind fences, behind lines of police. Their job is simply to get an object from one place to another. In the weeks leading up to the day, there has been much speculation about how the release will be managed. Those campaigning on his behalf argued that he should be permitted to walk out of the doors alone, see the crowds, some of whom have camped for days, even if he was then taken away in a van. This, despite a last-minute legal battle, was not allowed; he would be released in a van and taken to an undisclosed location. The sky stays grey, it is mid-morning. The earth is churned by moving feet; afterwards the whole area will be bereft of grass, empty, brown. Another five minutes passes, and another. Bodies shift around. People make sarcastic comments, they joke. Short sentences are uttered, everywhere the news reports nothing happening. Nothing happens again and again. In time, there is activity at the door, the officials move to one side, they form a line and ensure it's precise. Nobody knows if it's theatre they're seeing, or boredom. The larger doors open, some people are quiet, some raucous. The television coverage reaches a pitch. Welcome is sung. People spit at the ground, people swear, or cheer. The opening remains empty for a minute or so. The van drives out, as far as the first gate, which opens, and to the second gate, which also opens. There is a lot of noise around. Dogs bark over the singing, there are banners, crying. The van gets out of the gate and drives towards the people. A line of police cordon it off, things are thrown, and shouted. The van has no windows, or markings. And as the sitcom draws to a close, we don't see the man inside it, but we see that it is a simulacrum of the entire imprisonment. He is here, among the people, though distant from them, invisible to them, yet still having an effect on them, whether it be positive or negative. The van winds through the people, who rush towards it, are held back. A bottle of energy drink hits the side, thuds off it and onto the ground where it is seized. Kicks are aimed at the van, declarations of love, of forgiveness, are yelled at the van. The driver is behind black, bulletproof glass. The television reports that he is out. It gets all over everywhere, everyone hears about it. Inside the belly of the van is the prisoner, the world's oldest man, two hundred and ninety years old, being driven to an undisclosed location, where he will be freed.

NEW DAWN FADES

THE FIRST TIME you check the online map for the post-code that you think about all the time, it's soothing. It lulls you in a way you could never have anticipated. You're drunk, and it's late, and the next day you will check your phone for messages you should not have sent. The phone is a malevolent object that ruins your life. The laptop can be also, if you are not careful. But writing an email on it in this state feels less impulsive, so you're unlikely to do it. You put the phone somewhere safe, the top of the fridge maybe, the laundry pile. You type in the postcode on your laptop. You look at nothing, because there is nothing really to see: no street view, no satellite view, just greyed-out boxes. You look at it for a very long time.

There are other spots in the world that you do not feel compelled to look at, and which you will never go back to. You do not think of these places. They are a dark patchwork on the world, as if the lights have gone out. The specifics of these places are dank and featureless. They are a suffocating dark. You think about how big this area would be were it stitched together like a quilt. A country. A small country. Do not think it.

You search for somebody's name on the nights when things

become worse. One name becomes a procession of names, typed into the box. The history of your browser cleared, as though they could spy on you. Small ghosts called up. Why do you keep calling them up? On the dish rack at the other side of the room, a single plate and a single fork are drying. The tap has a drip that you no longer register, spending so much time with it, but anyone else would. When J comes round he comments on it but you do not care.

The names reveal pictures. You have seen all the pictures already, there are no new surprises here. You are forever amazed by how close you can feel to a person from such a distance and isn't that the miracle after all, the molecules and static which conjure them but do not conjure them – and then when you are drunkest, when the nights are at the worst, you search for yourself, which always gives you the unreality feeling, because it is not your name any more, it hasn't been for a while, but you will always turn around when somebody says *Lucy*, and it will always be with that same queasy mixture of dread and of hope.

You have turned the computer off before J comes round, but when you go to get a glass of water you are alarmed to discover that it is back on somehow. The map back on the screen. This is a dangerous oversight, you tell yourself. Anyone could have seen. Not that it would matter. But it is strange that you remember turning it off. The remembrance of another evening, automatic behaviour skipping a turn. You are drunk as usual, it's true. You turn it off and then you hold your glass with both hands as you drink your water, staring at the black screen.

Yes, you think of yourself as a teenager, walking along the harbour wall. The bench you liked to sit on near the folly, the smoke from the refinery bleeding out against the sky. You liked to watch the tankers serene in the water, the sense of arriving and leaving and arriving and leaving. You liked to buy a half-litre of vodka from the tired-looking supermarket just back from the seafront, apple juice or cloudy lemonade to mix it with, a mouthful of alcohol and then a mouthful of the mixer and sometimes you spat it right out in an arc, usually landing on the grass but sometimes reaching the water, you thought, though you never saw it hit. It doesn't matter. You can picture the water breaking regardless, your undeniable impact on a landscape where you felt insignificant, always. Less than a circle in the water. Less than a dream, like another kind of ghost called up. It is soothing to think about the things you like or have liked over your lifetime. To list small animals and the sensation of clean laundry and different foods. This is its own sort of topography, your own landscape of safety. It is soothing to think of the ways you can be and remain safe. You can look but you can't touch. You can look.

The routine settles. You get home from the office where you spend your days writing mind-numbing press releases on subjects that you do not care about, and you take a beer from the salad compartment, where no salad lives or is likely to live, and you open it carefully – cold sound of its opening a relief that makes you want to sob, almost, but you don't – and then you settle in in front of your computer. You might look at other things first. The news, your emails. There is something that needs responding to with urgency. You have been putting it off. You put it off again. You read a story about the melting ice caps. About starving polar bears drifting into an unknown world. You are so sad for these bears, a sadness out of proportion, a sadness that makes you close the tab.

What you do is, you open up the map and at first all you see is a non-localised grid. The green, the blue, the creased lines of roads and rivers and borders. Then you type in the postcode. It's memorised, of course. You'll be able to recite it like a litany, some kind of prayer, even decades after. But you don't know this yet. The postcode zooms you in. Sometimes you do not type the postcode but just the town, or the town next to it, so that you can scroll closer to it at your own speed. Inch by inch, the cursor moving slowly. The anticipation of it. Sallow light washing over your face. You click in and close as you can get to it. You stare at basically nothing until your eyes become tired, the beer finished.

One morning when you go downstairs, the computer is on somehow. Again, you must have been so drunk. The map is up, and zoomed-in. You go to turn it off, but you find yourself looking at it instead. Moving the cursor around it, like you're trying to reveal something hidden, but there is nothing to be found.

Yes, you think of yourself sometimes when you were in your early twenties in another city, a city you do not often go to but one that you could, if you wanted – if you prepared psychically in advance, if you made the arrangements – the pinwheeling dark energy of a thousand parties, of houses with damp mattresses on the floor and parks fruiting with the greenery of early spring, of walking for a long time through the streets. It seemed to belong to you. There is nostalgia and a faint dread when you think about this city, but nothing too drastic.

And how good it felt to get the bus for an hour, two hours, outside of the city limits. And how good it felt to go to the museums and sit in front of your favourite picture, sculptures, and wait for the art to dazzle you, to be undone, to be insignificant in the only good way.

You are being haunted by yourself, you think half-seriously, considering the mystery of the screen. You are your own worst ghost. OK. You take the computer to a place in town that runs a full diagnostic, and they tell you there is nothing wrong with it. They recommend covering the webcam as a precaution, which you do with a patterned child's plaster that you find at the bottom of your make-up bag, and it reassures you a little, which is enough.

You go to a new city on a trip, a neutral city. A change of scene, no computer, though it makes you anxious. Alone you stand on bridges and watch the water as it floods under, and while you do think about jumping in, you don't. In restaurants you eat cured meats served on wooden boards. In the last restaurant, dinner, a bottle of grass-fresh white wine. The city goes to sleep early each evening. Every morning for the three days you wake up there: pearlescent light over water. Yes, you know that in a city such as this you can feel pure and good and hopeful again, though you cannot stay. Really, it's not for you, as much as you might want it to be.

When you arrive back at your home, dark and uninviting, the first thing you check are the rooms upstairs for intruders, the windows for signs of entry. You pause at the entrance to your living room. The screen is glowing, though you checked and checked and checked again that it was off before you left. The sickly light draws you forward. You sit down and even though you are tired from the flight, hungry and thirsty, you type in the postcode again, almost crying because you have gone some days without it, because you want to look so badly, because you are afraid of so much and to be able to look this one thing in the eye is something, something, though you can no longer tell whether it is comfort or self-flagellation or both.

J comes over to talk about the holiday. He is the only person who really comes to your house. His hair has grown too long, almost reaching his shoulders. He fixes the tap this time and talks to you as he does it. You tell him about the cured meat and the serenity of the wide streets, the rivers. You do not tell him about the computer flickering on. In return for the act of handiwork you cut his hair in the bathroom by the light of a faltering bulb, a towel around his shoulders, flushing the hair down the toilet. You go to bed together. In the tepid moonlight from the open curtain you stare at his face but he sleeps the way adults rarely sleep, which is to say he sleeps like something has been switched off in him. You envy this idea, the radical simplicity of his body's workings.

In that moonlight you think that if you keep going back to the pure and good city you will ruin it, the way you ruin everything else. There will be some kind of incident. You will throw up or be violent in the street, or you will shout at someone or sleep with someone or lose your head. You will throw yourself in the river after all. A place will disappoint you like a person will. No more pearlescent lustre. No more pastel water. You will always be there in the place. The place will always be there with you. You understand it goes both ways. You understand this, in the morning when J has gone, when you are looking at the map again. You have hoped that a new city, a broadening of your topographies, will have fixed this in you. Spreading you and your feelings around like butter on toast, diluting the intensity of your territories. It has not fixed anything in you.

This is how it goes. A quick escalation, a decline that

spirals in on itself. You start to look first thing, waking up to the screen already on – normal already – and it makes you late for work. You are not able to stop this, and in the second week your boss has a word, and you promise to try and improve, but you do not. You can't stop looking. On the bus into work, still late, you call up the address on your phone. It is so unremarkable. You can hardly remember what the house looks like, though you know if you were inside you would be able to recognise every room even if blindfolded. You are distracted when J comes round, so he comes round less. You barely notice. The pull of the address is like a stricture, a squeezing sense of panic. After one weekend you are two hours late to the office and you are fired on the spot.

You search for the names more often too. There is no new information. These people could be dead, for all you know. But still there is power in a name. A mother calling for her runaway child in the supermarket; you want to fall to the floor. You leave your basket. You go into another shop and you buy the apple juice and vodka of your teens as though anchoring yourself to something, some integral idea of personhood, but you had that old name then too. Nevertheless, you drink the vodka. You become very drunk and you call up the map again. You start to look at the timetables of trains, of hotels, and when you wake up in the morning you have not called anyone or sent a shameful message, but you have booked train tickets, a journey for the next day.

You close your eyes very tightly and lie on the sofa all day trying to delay the decision. The only time you move from your position is when someone comes to the door and bangs loudly. They will see your movement through the hall if you go upstairs and hide, so instead you crouch down by the side of the fridge where nobody can see you, not even through the window of the kitchen. It is the postman or J, you know this, the only two people who have reason to visit you. And yet, and yet, and yet. You stay crouched down with legs folded, electric blood, until it is properly dark. The beam from next door's garden light pools into yours but does not reach you. The stars are not out. You move onto your hands and knees. You decide, yes, you will go. Somewhere there is hope in it.

And you remember, that night when you are sleepless again, about the time you thought you were dead. When you had not spoken to anyone for several days, and you were in one of the cities you do not think about, and you were alone, and you had your old name. You had not yet thought about shucking off that name and all that was stuck to it. You were dead and you were a ghost, and when you flickered to somewhere beyond sleep and waking you saw yourself back up there, back up at the folly watching the boats come in, as if you had never left. And yet, still, when you came round, the world did not feel off-limits to you. The opposite. As soon as you were well enough you packed your bags. The streets were quiet and sluiced with rainwater. Any cars were too loud in the tender silence. It was all new to you, the hated city, emerging from the thick air of your room.

It could be that easy if you let it, you think to yourself. There is no reason it should not be. You pack your bags again. The computer will not turn off at all now, even when you put the laptop lid down and then push it up again, so you leave it. It is fixed on the map, the screen brightness turned all the way up. You leave it as it is, and you finally understand.

CONTRIBUTORS' BIOGRAPHIES

JULIA ARMFIELD lives and works in London. She is a fiction writer and occasional playwright with a Master's in Victorian Art and Literature from Royal Holloway University. Her work has been published in *Lighthouse*, *Analog Magazine* and *Neon Magazine*. She was commended in the Moth Short Story Prize 2017, long-listed for the Deborah Rogers Prize 2018 and was the winner of The White Review Short Story Prize 2018. Her debut collection, *salt slow*, was published by Picador in May 2019.

ELIZABETH BAINES' stories have appeared in numerous journals and anthologies, and Salt have published two collections, *Balancing on the Edge of the World* and *Used to Be*. Salt have also published her novel, *Too Many Magpies*, and reissued her earlier novel, *The Birth Machine*. She has been a prizewinning playwright for Radio 4 and has written, produced and performed her own plays for fringe theatre. Her latest novel, *The Story Keeper*, will be published by Salt in 2020.

NAOMI BOOTH was born and raised in West Yorkshire. Her novella, *The Lost Art of Sinking* (Penned in the Margins), was selected for New Writing North's Read Regional campaign 2017 and won the Saboteur Award for Best Novella. Her debut novel, *Sealed* (Dead Ink Books), is a work of eco-horror. It was short-listed for the Not the Booker Award 2018 and Naomi was named a Fresh Voice: Fifty Writers to Read Now by the *Guardian*. 'Cluster' was long-listed for the Sunday Times Short Story Award 2018 and the Galley Beggar Short Story Prize 2018. Her new novel, *Exit Management*, will be published by Dead Ink Books in 2020. She lives in York and lectures on Creative Writing and Literature.

RUBY COWLING was born in Bradford and lives in London. Her short fiction has won awards including The White Review Short Story Prize and the London Short Story Prize, and has been short-listed in competitions with *Glimmer Train*, *Aesthetica*, *Short Fiction* and *Wasafiri*. Publication credits include *Lighthouse*, *The Lonely Crowd*, the Galley Beggar Press Singles Club and numerous print anthologies. Her collection *This Paradise* was published by Boiler House Press in 2019.

KIERAN DEVANEY lives in Birmingham. His novel *Deaf at Spiral Park* was published by Salt in 2013.

VICKY GRUT's short stories have appeared in new writing anthologies published by Picador, Granta, Duckworths, Serpent's Tail and Bloomsbury. Her non-fiction essay 'Into the Valley' was mentioned in *Best American Essays*, 2013. Her short story collection, *Live Show, Drink Included*, was published by Holland Park Press in 2018. She is currently working on a creative non-fiction book that follows her Swedish grandmother from Paris and Stockholm in the 1920s, to Bangkok in the 1930s and Stalin's Moscow in the winter of 1940.

NIGEL HUMPHREYS is an Anglo-Welsh poet living in Aberystwyth. Having worked as a retailer, a computer programmer and a postmaster, he retired in 2000. He is the author of four collections of poetry, among them *The Hawk's Mewl* and *The Love Song of Daphnis and Chloe*, with a fifth to be published in 2019. Also forthcoming, from Zagava, is a collection of ghost stories. He is a member of the Welsh Academy and Literature Wales.

SALLY JUBB received the Andrea Badenoch Award (Northern Writers' Awards) in 2015, for a selection of short stories. Since then, her work has appeared in various anthologies, including the *Bristol Short Story Prize* and *Bath Flash Fiction* as well as *Brittle Star* and *The London Magazine*. She won the Colm Toibin Short Story Prize in 2017, and Brittle Star Short Story Award in 2018. She is currently working towards an MFA in Creative Writing at Birkbeck College, London. She wishes to thank New Writing North.

JOHN LANCHESTER is the author of five novels, most recently *The Wall*, and three works of non-fiction.

SOPHIE MACKINTOSH was born in South Wales in 1988 and is currently based in London. Her fiction, essays and poetry have been published by *Granta*, *The White Review*, *The New York Times* and *The Stinging Fly*, among others. Her short story 'Grace' was the winner of the 2016 White Review Short Story Prize, and her story 'The Running Ones' won the Virago/Stylist Short Story competition in 2016. Her debut novel *The Water Cure* was published by Hamish Hamilton in the UK in 2018 and by Doubleday in the US in 2019 to critical acclaim and was long-listed for the Man Booker Prize. Her second novel *Blue Ticket* will be published in 2020.

LUCIE MCKNIGHT HARDY grew up in West Wales and is a Welsh speaker. Her work has featured or is forthcoming in various places online and in print, including *The Lonely Crowd*, *The Shadow Booth*, *The Ghastling*, and as a limited edition chapbook from Nightjar Press. Her debut novel, *Water Shall Refuse Them*, was short-listed for the Mslexia Novel Competition 2017, long-listed for the Caledonia Novel Award 2018 and is published by Dead Ink Books.

PAUL MCQUADE is a writer and translator originally from Glasgow. He is the author of *Hometown Tales: Glasgow* (Orion, 2018), with Kirsty Logan, and the short story collection, *Between Tongues* (Cōnfingō, forthcoming). His work has been short-listed for the White Review and Bridport prizes and he is the recipient of the Sceptre Prize for New Writing and the Austrian Cultural Forum Writing Prize.

VESNA MAIN was born in Zagreb, Croatia. She is a graduate of comparative literature and holds a PhD from the Shakespeare Institute, Birmingham. A lecturer at universities in Nigeria and the UK, she also worked at the BBC and as a college teacher. Book-length publications include: a novel, *A Woman with No Clothes On* (Delancey, 2008), a collection of short stories, *Temptation: A User's Guide* (Salt, 2018), and a novel in dialogue, *Good Day?* (Salt, 2019). Her autofiction, *Only A Lodger . . . And Hardly That*, is out now from Seagull Books. She lives in London.

ROBERT MASON, formerly an illustrator, started writing in 2010. *Other People's Dogs* (Caseroom) was published in 2013, and Reflex Fiction have published his work online and in print. He has been long- or short-listed for the Fish and Galley Beggar short story prizes, the Manchester Fiction Prize, and the Observer/Anthony Burgess Arts Journalism Prize. Currently he is writing a novel set in Kent at the end of the hippy era, *Grim Down South*, and a biography of his body, *Wound Man*.

ANN QUIN was a British writer born in Brighton in 1936. Prior to her death in 1973, she published four novels: *Berg* (1964), *Three* (1966), *Passages* (1969) and *Tripticks* (1972). During her writing career she lived between Brighton, London and the US. She was prominent among a group of British experimental writers of the 1960s, which also included BS Johnson and Christine Brooke-Rose.

STEPHEN SHARP is a 61-year-old writer who has suffered from schizophrenia for over 30 years. His work has appeared in *Ambit*. His last job was as a volunteer for Oxfam.

SAM THOMPSON is the author of the novels *Communion Town* and *Jott*. He was born in London and now lives in Belfast. His website is samthompsonwriter.com.

MELISSA WAN was born 1991 and moved to the UK at the age of eight. She went on to study sociology and urban theory in Manchester, where she now lives. She began writing for the stage but turned to prose after reading Walter Benjamin. She was awarded the inaugural crowdfunded BAME Writers'

Scholarship to study Creative Writing at UEA, where she is currently working on her first collection of stories.

REN WATSON is a scientist and writer. Her work has appeared in various places in print and online, including *Tears in the Fence, Brittle Star, The Fiction Desk* and *Under the Radar.* Short-listed in the Brighton Prize in 2017, she lives in Manchester.

ADAM WELCH is a writer and editor based in south-east London, currently working in the fashion industry. His fiction has been published in *Ambit* and long-listed for the London Short Story Prize 2018. He is a 2019–20 Jerwood/Arvon Mentee. He has a website at adamwelchwriter.com.

ACKNOWLEDGEMENTS

The editor wishes to thank Jennifer Hodgson and Kishani Widyaratna.

'Smack', copyright © Julia Armfield 2018, was first published in *Lighthouse* issue 16 and is reprinted by permission of the author.

'Kiss', copyright © Elizabeth Baines 2018, was first published online in *The Mechanics Institute Review* and is reprinted by permission of the author.

'Cluster', copyright © Naomi Booth 2018, was first published online at Galley Beggar Press and is reprinted by permission of the author.

'On Day 21', copyright © Ruby Cowling 2018, was first published online in *Wasafiri* and is reprinted by permission of the author.

'Sitcom', copyright © Kieran Devaney 2018, was first published online in *Fanzine* and is reprinted by permission of the author.

'On the Way to the Church', copyright © Vicky Grut 2018, was first published in *The Harvard Review* issue 52 and is reprinted by permission of the author.

'Curtilage', copyright © Robert Mason 2018, was first published online at Galley Beggar Press and is reprinted by permission of the author.

'Nude and Seascape', copyright © Ann Quin 2018, was first published in *The Unmapped Country: Stories and Fragments* (And Other Stories), edited and introduced by Jennifer Hodgson, and is reprinted by permission of the publisher and the author's estate.

'Cuts', copyright © Stephen Sharp 2018, was first published in *Ambit* issue 231 and is reprinted by permission of the author.

'The Heights of Sleep', copyright © Sam Thompson 2018, was first published online in *The Mechanics Institute Review* and is reprinted by permission of the author.

'The Husband and the Wife Go to the Seaside', copyright © Melissa Wan 2018, was first published in *Seaside Special: Postcards From the Edge* (Bluemoose Books), edited by Jenn Ashworth, and is reprinted by permission of the author.

'Optics', copyright © Ren Watson 2018, was first published in *Brittle Star* issue 42, as 'Sky-sions', and is reprinted by permission of the author.

'Toxic', copyright © Adam Welch 2018, was first published in *Ambit* issue 232 and is reprinted by permission of the author.

BEST BRITISH SHORT STORIES

Best British Short Stories 2011
(978-1-907773-12-9)

Best British Short Stories 2012
(978-1-907773-18-1)

Best British Short Stories 2013
(978-1-907773-47-1)

Best British Short Stories 2014
(978-1-907773-67-9)

Best British Short Stories 2015
(978-1-78463-027-0)

Best British Short Stories 2016
(978-1-78463-063-8)

Best British Short Stories 2017
(978-1-78463-112-3)

Best British Short Stories 2018
(978-1-78463-136-9)

RECENT BOOKS FROM SALT

NEIL CAMPBELL
Zero Hours (978-1-78463-148-2)

SAMUEL FISHER
The Chameleon (978-1-78463-124-6)

VESNA MAIN
Temptation: A User's Guide (978-1-78463-128-4)

STEFAN MOHAMED
Falling Leaves (978-1-78463-118-5)

ALISON MOORE
Missing (978-1-78463-140-6)

S. J. NAUDÉ
The Third Reel (978-1-78463-150-5)

HANNAH VINCENT
The Weaning (978-1-78463-120-8)

PHIL WHITAKER
You (978-1-78463-144-4)

NEW FICTION FROM SALT

ELEANOR ANSTRUTHER
A Perfect Explanation (978-1-78463-164-2)

NEIL CAMPBELL
Lanyards (978-1-78463-170-3)

MARK CAREW
Magnus (978-1-78463-204-5)

ANDREW COWAN
Your Fault (978-1-78463-180-2)

AMANTHI HARRIS
Beautiful Place (978-1-78463-193-2)

S. A. HARRIS
Haverscroft (978-1-78463-200-7)

CHRISTINA JAMES
Chasing Hares (978-1-78463-189-5)

NEW FICTION FROM SALT

VESNA MAIN
Good Day? (978-1-78463-191-8)

SIMON OKOTIE
After Absalon (978-1-78463-166-6)

TREVOR MARK THOMAS
The Bothy (978-1-78463-160-4)

TIM VINE
The Electric Dwarf (978-1-78463-172-7)

MICHAEL WALTERS
The Complex (978-1-78463-162-8)

GUY WARE
The Faculty of Indifference (978-1-78463-176-5)

MEIKE ZIERVOGEL
Flotsam (978-1-78463-178-9)

This book has been typeset by
SALT PUBLISHING LIMITED
using Neacademia, a font designed by Sergei Egorov
for the Rosetta Type Foundry in the Czech Republic.
It is manufactured using Creamy 70gsm, a Forest
Stewardship Council™ certified paper from Stora Enso's
Anjala Mill in Finland. It was printed and bound by
Clays Limited in Bungay, Suffolk, Great Britain.

LONDON
GREAT BRITAIN
MMXIX